Bowen

Annie Seaton

A Bec Whitfield Mystery:1

Bowen River

This is a work of fiction. Characters, institutions and organisations mentioned in this novel are either the product of the author's imagination or, if real, used fictitiously without any intent to describe actual conduct.

Copyright © Annie Seaton 2024

ISBN 978-1-923048-60-7

The moral right of the author to be identified as the author of this work has been asserted.

Bowen River

Annie Seaton lives near the beach on the mid-north coast of New South Wales. Her career and studies spanned the education sector, including working as an academic research librarian, a high-school principal and a university tutor until she took early retirement and fulfilled her lifelong dream of a full-time writing career.

Larapinta, the fifth book in the Porter Sisters series, won the Romance Writers' Association of Australia Ruby Award for long contemporary novel in 2023. *Kakadu Dawn,* the sixth and final book in the Porter Sisters series, was a finalist in the Australian Romance Readers Awards for 2023. *Whitsunday Dawn,* her first book with Harper Collins Australia, was a finalist in the 2018 ARRA Awards and was voted Book of the Year in the AUSROM Readers' Choice awards. *Kakadu Sunset,* Annie's first traditionally published book with Pan Macmillan Australia was shortlisted by the Romance Writers' Association of Australia Ruby Award, in the long book category in 2015.

Each winter, Annie and her husband leave the beach to roam the remote areas of Australia for story ideas and research. She is passionate about preserving the beauty of the Australian landscape and respecting the traditional ownership of the land. For those readers who cannot experience this journey personally, Annie seeks to portray the natural beauty of the Australian environment—its spiritual locations, stunning landscapes and unique wildlife.

Readers can contact Annie through her website, annieseaton.net, or find her on Facebook and Instagram.

By Annie Seaton

Daughters of the Darling
From Across the Sea
Over the River
By the Billabong
Books 4-5 to follow in 2025

Home to the Outback *(2025)*
Loving Lucy
Adoring Angie
Just Jemima
Inviting Isabella

Pentecost Island Series
Pippa
Eliza
Nell
Tamsin
Evie
Cherry
Odessa
Sienna
Tess
Isla

A Bec Whitfield Mystery
Bowen River
Shadows on the Shore (June 2025)

Duckinwilla Days
Coming Home
Secrets and Surprises
Books 3-7 to follow in 2025

The House on the Hill series
Beach House
Beach Music
Beach Walk
Beach Dreams

Sunshine Coast Series
Waiting for Ana
The Trouble with Jack
Healing His Heart

Second Chance Bay Series
Her Outback Playboy
Her Outback Protector
Her Outback Haven
Her Outback Paradise
The McDougalls of Second Chance Bay

Bowen River

Standalone Books
Whitsunday Dawn
Undara
Osprey Reef
East of Alice
Bowen River
Four Seasons Short and Sweet
Deadly Secrets
Adventures in Time
Silver Valley Witch
The Emerald Necklace
An Aussie Christmas Duo

Richards Brothers Series
The Trouble with Paradise
Marry in Haste
Outback Sunrise

Bindarra Creek
Worth the Wait
Full Circle
Secrets of River Cottage
Bindarra Creek Duo
A Place to Belong

Love Across Time Series
Come Back to Me
Follow Me
Finding Home
The Threads that Bind
Love Across Time 1-4 Boxed Set

The Augathella Girls
Outback Roads
Outback Sky
Outback Escape
Outback Wind
Outback Dawn
Outback Moonlight
Outback Dust
Outback Hope

Augathella Short and Sweets
An Augathella Surprise
An Augathella Baby
An Augathella Spring
An Augathella Christmas
An Augathella Wedding
An Augathella Easter
An Augathella Masquerade Ball

Bowen River

Dedication

This book is dedicated to Vic Winterford, who passed in October 2024. Vic, father of my dear friend Sue, was an amazing man who lived life to the fullest until he passed in his ninety-ninth year.

Bowen River

Chapter 1

Bowen River
Friday morning, March 14.

The crow's feathers gleam blue-black in the early morning sun as it sits silently, a sentinel in the low branches of the native willow halfway between the creek and the road. It will soon be time for the vehicles to pass, creating dust that will hang over the dirt road for most of the day. The crow is content to roost and observe the seed pods scattered along the creek bank. The autumn mist hovering low over the water evaporates as the heat of the day quickly builds.

Bowen River is fed by a spring, and even in the driest of months, this backwater in the creek between the old *Strathallyn Station* homestead and Mt Douglas is a small oasis in a scrubby landscape. The billabong, edged with tall, river red gums, has shady groves on the downstream side, well away from the road. Surrounded by native willows, the occasional Burdekin plum, and clumps of the shiny green blades of settler's flax, the creek has long provided a haven for wildlife. Little has spoiled the tranquillity of this quiet backwater in the years since cattle grazing began over a century ago.

Bowen River

Until recently.

In years long gone, the white settlers driving mobs of cattle to Bowen Downs discovered this picturesque glade. As the early network of rural roads developed, stone causeways were built in three locations along the creek. These heritage-listed causeways ensured that the old roads continued to be used by intrepid travellers and those looking to disappear into the wilderness.

Now, the noise of passing trucks and the constant dust destroy the peace of the oasis, and most creatures have moved further down the creek away from the road.

But the crow remains, watching and learning, determined to protect its territory. As the sun climbs higher, a sudden squawk from above breaks the morning silence as his mate is disturbed. She rises and swoops along the creek away from the road.

Small stones fly into the settler's flax as the wheels of an approaching vehicle crunch on the gravel. The work trucks and company four-wheel drive vehicles will come later; it is unusual for a vehicle to pass this early in the day. The eyes of the crow follow the boxy white vehicle as it accelerates up the hill and passes beneath his roost. A woman stares at him through the high window, her skin white in the morning light.

He knows they will return later. The road is impassable three bends after the shiny paddock.

Bowen River

Leanne

A single crow perched low in the willow stares back at her, its beady eyes fixed on the ute. A shiver runs down her back, and she looks ahead. She's hated crows ever since she was a child. Her grandfather, Robert, once told her that when someone dies, a crow carries their soul to the land of the dead, and she has never forgotten.

'Relax, Leanne.' The driver glances at her as the car slows slightly.

'I don't have time for this.'

'Be receptive.' His voice irritates her, as always.

'Nothing you can show me is going to change my mind.' She turns her head away and stares out the car window again. 'I only came because the kids are on an excursion today, and I drove them to school early. I don't want to see what's happening out there, but I'll humour you. For the last time.'

'I appreciate your time. I *will* change your mind, Leanne.'

'You won't.' She folds her arms as he changes down a gear, and the vehicle labours up the steep hill. 'How much further is it?' As always, the view to the south from the crest soothes her. The tension in her chest eases, but she refuses to look north where the first array of photovoltaic panels scars the landscape.

'It's just past the Suttor Causeway.'

'What? No way! There's no development out there. I thought you were taking me to the solar panels. That causeway's too far to go, and the road's shit anyway. It doesn't even go that far now. The road was washed away at the second causeway last summer. Turn the car around.'

'You have to reconsider. What I am going to show you will make it worthwhile.'

'I don't *have* to do anything.' Her voice is firm. 'Take me back now.'

'It's a surprise, and I know a way. I want to show you a property.' His voice is persistent, and anger rises in her gut. 'You have to get over this pig-headedness. It's renewable energy. Solar farms are the way of—'

Her interruption is swift and hard. 'Solar *farms* are a pretty way of describing something that will destroy our environment, community, and agriculture. Our *lives*. The well-being of our community will be disrupted by this construction and the ongoing impact of these installations over the next how many years? They are *not* farm*s*; that's just a pretty name for them. They're solar electricity-generating plants and it's not happening on or near my land. Turn around. Now.'

'Don't be like that, Leanne. Forget about the development for a while. Consider your options.' The calm determination in his voice irks her. 'When you see this block, you'll fall in love with it straight away. It has a river frontage of four hundred metres, and it's prime agricultural land. You can grow whatever you want to grow there. You can run more cattle. I know the company is prepared to increase the compensation offer.'

'I don't know of any properties like that out this way, and I'm not interested anyway. The company can go take a flying leap. We are not moving. My land has been in our family for over a hundred years.'

The driver huffs a sigh and accelerates slightly as they descend into the valley. The wheels spin, and a wallaby bounds across the road ahead. The seat belt bites into her shoulder as he brakes suddenly and pulls to the side of the road.

'What are you doing? There's not enough room to turn around here. You'll have to go to the next causeway.'

'We have to walk from here to see the river frontage. Hop out.'

'No!'

She turns to face him, and his expression is strange and intense. For the first time, something like fear runs down her back. 'Take me home now.'

'We've come this far. It's not far to walk.'

'I'm not getting out of the car.'

He turns the ignition off, removes the keys and climbs out.

She tries to lock her door as he walks around to the passenger side, but he uses the remote to unlock it and wrenches the door open. Reaching in, he grabs her arm, and she plants her feet firmly against the firewall, but he is too strong for her.

'What the hell are you doing?' Her voice is almost a scream, and her skin burns when he squeezes her upper arm.

He doesn't speak as he drags her out of the car and pushes her into the low scrub at the edge of the road. One of her sandals falls into the dust as he grabs her hair with his other hand.

'Let go of me! For God's sake, get back in the car and take me home.' Her voice trembles, and fear now crawls through her body like ice.

He doesn't respond. Her words vanish into the oppressive silence. 'All right,' she stammers, her tone shaking. 'Show me this place, and then we'll go home. Just wait—my sandal. I need to get my sandal on.'

He ignores her, shoving her roughly down the hill towards the river. She trips, landing face-first on the unforgiving ground. She struggles to push herself up, but the slope is too steep. She tumbles backwards, and the sharp, brittle grass scrapes at her skin.

Above her, his footsteps crunch steadily closer. As she hits the bottom of the hill, her phone slips from the back pocket of her jeans, landing just out of reach. She tries to grab it, but there's no time. Blood drips from her chin as she forces herself to her feet and bolts towards the river, her heart thundering in her chest.

His heavy breathing fills the air, each ragged exhale following her. She stumbles forward, her steps faltering, desperation driving her. But she isn't fast enough.

A hand snags her hair again, yanking her backwards with brutal force. She lets out a strangled whimper as terror surges through her. Turning, her wide eyes catch the glint of the gun in his hand. It swings towards her in a blur, and a scream escapes her lips.

Panicked, she tries to step back, but the ground betrays her. Her foot rolls into a hidden depression, and the sickening crack of her ankle shatters the air. Pain explodes up her leg, so intense it steals her breath. She gasps, unable to keep her balance, and collapses as the world tilts around her.

Before she can cry out, the gun slams into her temple with a dull, sickening thud. A wave of darkness engulfs her, swallowing the pain, the fear, and everything around her.

***

The road has been quieter today, but dust still lingers in the fading light. The crow loses interest in the sporadic traffic as the afternoon lengthens into the evening. He caws for his mate to return as the rest of the flock settles in the branches above. The convoy of vehicles and the one truck that has passed today loaded with metal poles make their way back to the human settlement. The sun is low when the boxy ute roars up the hill. The crow lifts his wings and swoops across the front of the car, which has disturbed his rest.

The woman with the white skin is no longer there. He glides across the water, goes back to his tree and sleeps.

Chapter 2

Bowen River - Five days later.
Bec Whitfield

My father always said I'd come home one day.

Two years, I told myself. Two years, and I could go back to the city. Or the coast. Anywhere other than this town I swore I would never return to.

I gripped the steering wheel tightly as the signpost ahead indicated Bowen River was only thirty-five kilometres away. My twenty-year-old Landcruiser shuddered as it hit a corrugation when we turned onto the Bowen River Road. Anticipation fought with dread in my stomach. At the moment, dread was winning by a mile.

'Holy friggin' hell.' The stale smell of a beery breath from last night wafted over to me. 'Where are we?'

Gray had been asleep when we turned off the Bruce Highway at Bowen, but now, with the potholed road, sleep was impossible.

'Jesus, babe, you told me it was in the bush, but this is the end of the earth.'

I wished I'd been stronger. When my transfer came through a month ago, my second thought—after an immediate reaction of how unlucky I was that my transfer was to Bowen River—was that this was an opportunity for Gray and me to go our separate ways. I assumed he wouldn't come and it would be an easy split. I was stunned when he said he wanted to move north with me, but then I realised he had nowhere else to go. I'd tried hard to dissuade him, but he'd argued that we could make a new start away from the city. When the transfer had come through, I had been about to tell Gray it was time for him to move out.

At least he acknowledged that something was needed, but I didn't want to make a new start. I'd ignored his behaviour for way too long. I might be a tough cop, but as far as relationships went, I was a coward.

I could thank my father for that. It had always been easier to ignore than react.

Gray looked away from me, his brow furrowed as he saw the scrubby bush and dead grass. 'A dirt road, for God's sake.'

'It's roadworks.' I swung the wheel to the right to miss another big dip, keeping my eyes firmly on the road ahead. Maybe the landscape alone would change his mind about staying.

I could only hope.

'Mum mentioned there's a solar farm being built on the other side of town, and the company's putting money into improving the road. A sweetener for the community.' I kept my voice light. I'd never told Gray I'd grown up in Bowen River. And knowing him, he never would have considered I'd once lived there, even though he now knew my parents lived here.

'Jeez, take it a bit bloody slower then.'

'I'm travelling to the conditions. If you want to do better, feel free to drive.' My temper slipped, and strangely, it eased my tension.

'You know I'm a city driver.'

'I know you're a city boy. And you would be a city driver if you had a car of your own.'

'Jesus Christ!' He grabbed for the dashboard as the front left wheel dipped again.

The closer we got to Bowen River, the more I realised how stupid I'd been. I'd not been back once since I left for university twelve years ago, a naïve teenager. When Mum and Dad wanted to see me, they came to Brisbane. And that was a very rare occurrence. I'm sure Mum wanted to, but if Dad said no, then that was the way it was. I only lasted a year at uni, and much to Dad's disgust— "dens of iniquity" were mentioned in several phone conversations—I applied and was offered a place in the Recruit Training Program of the Queensland Police Service just after the Christmas of my second year away.

I had no desire to return to the small township where I'd grown up.

Ever.

The stultifying conformity of living in a remote rural town where my father was the local Presbyterian minister and the memories of growing up in a draughty manse that was over a hundred years old firmed my refusal each time Mum begged me to come home for Christmas, or Easter, or my birthday every year. In Brisbane, turn of the century workers' cottages were in high demand, valued for their historical charm and character. In Bowen River, the old Presbyterian manse held neither. Draughty and austere, the only thing held by that structure were my memories of an unhappy childhood.

I guess if I'm honest, there were some happy times there. I loved school, and I applied myself to learning. I had some good friends, and I was allowed to go out and ride my bike along the track to Bowen River and occasionally play at some of my friends' houses, but my father vetted all interactions and outings. I abandoned all those friendships when I moved to the city, and I lost touch with home. I completely blocked those seventeen years in Bowen River and began to live the life I wanted.

A life of freedom.

So, the universe, or God, or whoever you believe in, had the last laugh when my long-awaited transfer came through, and I was posted to Bowen River Police Station as senior constable. Three hundred and thirty-six police stations in the whole of Queensland, and I would have chosen three hundred and thirty-five of them over the small town I grew up in. But the temptation of the long-awaited transfer north won out. I had a plan and was following a path to apply for a detective position eventually. Once I succeeded, I could complete the detective training program. My boss in Brisbane told me that, with my recent experience in the Child Protection and Investigation Unit and rural experience, I would have a good chance of breaking into the detective ranks.

So, in short, I applied for a transfer, was transferred to Bowen River, and accepted the position. Now, I was on my way home.

Not the "home" my father referred to each time they visited the city. His coming home referred to his beliefs and my return to the "flock".

'One day, Rebecca, you will return to Jesus, and he will welcome you home. Luke told us, "God's grace welcomes even those who seem irretrievably lost but who repent".'

The landscape was as barren as I remembered. Low scrubby trees provided an occasional flash of green against the dry yellow grass encroaching on the grey bitumen of the road. No houses, no vehicles, and no wildlife.

No life.

Nothing's changed. What have I done?

My lips clamped together, and I forced myself not to grind my teeth.

Straightening my shoulders, I opened my mouth and inhaled deeply before I spoke again. 'I told you Bowen River was in the bush. It's three hundred kilometres to Townsville, the nearest city, and I doubt very much whether you'll be able to stroll down from the police house to get your double-shot macchiato every morning. I warned you, Gray, you're not going to like it up here. I told you not to come.'

'I'll be fine. I'll keep busy working remotely. And we can buy a coffee machine.'

My thoughts were dark. *On my credit card. And live off my pay. And not have to contribute rent.*

Nothing was said like, 'I love you, babe, and I want to be with you.'

'Gray?'

As he turned to me, he put his hand on my knee. 'Calm down, babe. What's up?'

'Remember what you promised when we left the pub in Mackay last night?'

His face screwed up in confusion, and he shook his head slowly. 'Sorry, I was tired and I had a couple of beers too many.

My head's still throbbing like a bastard.'

'Open the glovebox and get a mint out. You still smell like those couple of beers too many.'

He shot me a nasty glance. 'What did I promise?'

'You promised you'd watch your language at my parents' place.'

He sniggered, and dread coiled thickly in my gut.

Did I say I was a coward?

'Okay. I'll do my best.'

I glanced across at him and caught the eye roll. 'Best is not good enough. My parents have standards, and I want you to promise you won't swear in their house. It's only for one night.'

'For fuck's sake, Bec! How old are you? You're a grown-up. Your olds have to accept you the way you are, *and* your partner. If it's that bad there, we'll call in, say hello and go stay in a motel.'

'There's only one, and it's full. We're only staying with them until the police house is ready tomorrow. Or at least I hope it's tomorrow. They said they'd sort it by today when I rang.'

'Okay then, we'll stay at a pub tonight. No matter how far we are into the boondocks, there has to be a pub with rooms.'

'There is one pub with rooms, and it's full too.'

Trust me, I'd tried. I didn't want to sleep at my parents' house either, but there were no alternatives.

'Full? Tourists out here? Can't see that happening.' The expression on his face spoke volumes about his first impression of the Bowen River region.

'No. Workers from some construction site. Mum said they've put a heap of dongas at the caravan park, too. It won't be hard. Just be nice and polite, watch your language and it'll be fine. I know Mum and Dad are looking forward to meeting you.'

Well, Mum would be. Dad never looked forward to anything.

I lifted one hand from the wheel and put my hand on top of Gray's. 'And Gray, one more thing. We'll be in separate rooms. That's a given.' I forced my voice to sound casual. My gut was churning, and we were still half an hour out.

'Fuck. What do they think you are? A virgin? Not the party girl, Bec Whitfield, I'd heard about before we even met. Are you for real?'

'Gray, please. It's just swearing, not even a bloody, and no taking the Lord's name in vain. No Gods or Jesus. Probably not even a jeez.'

'You're not sounding like you, babe. The Lord's name? Jeez! So why can't we move straight to the police house tonight?'

'I told you yesterday. It's not ready. My predecessor only left yesterday, and it has to be cleaned and sprayed today.'

'And what happens if I'm my usual uncouth self?'

I flinched at his sarcastic tone. 'My parents will be disappointed.'

'And you? What about you, Bec? What will you be?'

'I'll be disappointed too, but I'll be showing respect to my parents. If you can't do that for me for one night, maybe you should have listened and stayed in Brisbane.' When I'd given up my rented apartment to move north, Gray was left without anywhere to stay, and I knew he didn't have enough saved for a bond and a month's rent.

'Don't be like that, babe.' He squeezed my hand, but I lifted it away and took the steering wheel with both hands again. 'Okay. You can trust me.'

I knew that was the last thing I could do. Gray had let me down so many times over the past few months. I might have left my religious upbringing behind, but my values were still rock solid. Very different from his take on the world. His understanding of honesty was loose, and so far, I'd had no proof that he worked outside the law, but I sometimes wondered.

And that made my job as a cop even harder.

'Mum.' I blinked back unexpected tears as I shut the car door and hurried over to the steps where my mother waited. It had been more than four years since they'd last visited me in

Brisbane, and she'd aged since then. Her face was pale, and new wrinkles drew her lips in, even with her happy smile.

'Oh, Becky. It's so good to see you.'

One rogue tear rolled slowly down my cheek as I was enfolded in a rare, tight hug against unfamiliar rose-smelling softness. Physical affection had not been a part of my growing up.

'You too, Mum.' I hugged her briefly, uncomfortable, and then pulled back, brushing my hand across my cheek.

'I was so happy when you rang and told us you were coming home.' Mum turned as the wooden screen door banged shut.

Dad stood at the top of the steps. The dark, unpainted timber of the house filled my vision, providing a macabre backdrop for my father.

The dread curled again. This was the only home I'd known as a child. My parents had moved here five years before I was born. The North Queensland Presbytery closed the church when I was sixteen. Dad retired from the ministry, and they were offered the old manse at a nominal rent. They'd been there ever since.

'Hello, Rebecca. It's good to see you come home finally. I told your mother I would only believe you were coming when you arrived.' My father walked slowly down the steps, gripping the handrail with one hand. 'And now you have.'

'Ah, ye of little faith,' I said, unable to help myself. 'It's good to see you too, Dad.' I held my hand out to Gray, and when he took it, I squeezed a little tighter than necessary as a warning. 'Mum, Dad. This is Gray. Gray, my parents, Jim and Peggy Whitfield.'

I flicked a nervous glance to my left as Gray dropped my hand and stepped forward.

Chapter 3

Strathallyn Station - Winter, 1925.
Elspeth

Elspeth Valentine lay on the grassy bank beside the horseshoe-shaped billabong in the bend of the Bowen River, her head resting on the fleece blanket. Father would kill her if he knew she'd taken his Blue out for a ride, but there was no chance of him finding out. He'd driven into Bowen to pick Mother up from the train and they wouldn't be home until late afternoon. Ronald Burnham, who looked after the stud, had gone to Townsville to look at some new horse stock so no one would know that she had taken Blue, Father's prize stallion, out for the afternoon. Billy, the stable hand, wouldn't breathe a word of what she had done; she could always trust him.

Mother had insisted they purchased a Model T Ford from the Canada Motor Company in Townsville last year; she'd visited her sister, Elspeth's Aunty Kathleen, in Rockhampton as often as she could talk Father into driving her to the train at Bowen. He hated driving, much preferring to be in the saddle. Before Father had bought the vehicle, it was quite common for him to ride to Bowen and Ayr for race meetings and return on the same day. He was an excellent bushman and was well-respected in the local equine community. He'd developed *Strathallyn Station* into one of the best thoroughbred studs in the region. Their station had evolved from virgin bushland to a large station with modern buildings for the workers, well-kept gardens and fine stockyards and dips.

This year, he had been credited with more wins than any other owner in the state and at the last three meetings of the North Queensland Amateur Turf Club, he had been awarded the high honour of the Bracelet. He was vice president of the Bowen River Turf Club and an active member of several committees that contributed to public and pastoral matters in the region.

Since he'd become involved with the local war council, her father had handed over much of the running of the stud to the manager, Mr Burnham, and a horse trainer looked after his race horses. Elspeth knew that there was no future for her at *Strathallyn*. She would be free to pursue her dreams.

Elspeth adored her father; she'd inherited his love of horses, but Mother was a different matter entirely. She didn't understand Elspeth at all, and while she was away, it was wonderful being alone in the homestead.

Well, almost alone. At least Mrs Revesby, the housekeeper, and Mary, the housemaid, left her in peace. Each weekend, they went to their homes in the tiny village of Bowen River, and it was wonderful to have her freedom. Today, being Saturday, she had done her chores early and now had the whole day ahead. A day to please herself and not be concerned with "being a lady" as Mother constantly harped.

Blue whickered as he moved closer to the water. He turned his head as though to check she was all right. Elspeth lay back on the soft grass, staying completely still as a small wallaby ignored Blue and hopped down past him to the water. She watched the small creature as it drank and nibbled at the lush grass, and when he moved around the bend in the creek, she lay back and watched the occasional cloud move slowly across the clear blue sky. This backwater of Bowen River was one of the most beautiful places in the world, out of the places that she had seen anyway. Her pictures of those places she dreamed about—Scottish castles, the canals of Venice, the Swiss Alps, and the spires of Prague—were all in her head, described by Miss Caroline Edmonds, her history teacher at All Hallows in Brisbane.

Elspeth's limbs were weightless as contentment seeped through her, and she dreamed of the trip to her grandmother's cottage in Scotland that Father had promised for her twenty-first birthday. Gran's suggestion of a visit was in the letter that had arrived last month, wishing her a happy nineteenth birthday. Now that the Great War was long over, it was safe for her to travel alone. She would forget Mother's vocal opposition and her steely determination for Elspeth to marry well locally. The most recent argument had come a week ago.

'It's time you were thinking of settling down close to home, Elspeth,' Mother said at breakfast the morning she was leaving for Aunt Kathleen's. 'You're never going to meet a suitable husband over there.'

'I thought that would be the place to meet a most *suitable* husband if that was what I wanted, Mother,' she retorted.

'No, you need to be at home.'

'But Father met you in London, and you came back here with him.'

'And that's exactly why I know you should stay here. I don't want you to have to settle over there. Far away from your family and all that's familiar.'

'There is family over there. Gran is in Scotland, and Aunt Cecy and Uncle Reginald are in Devon. Besides, I don't want to settle *anywhere* for a long time. I want to see the world. I'm *going* to see the world.'

That brought a frown to Mother's perfectly made-up face.

'And besides,' Elspeth persisted because she knew how to trouble Mother. 'Where am I going to meet a husband here at Bowen River, even if I wanted one?'

'We'll take you to Townsville to the races next season. There'll be many young doctors and solicitors there who will be looking for a genteel young woman to take for a wife.'

To take for a wife!

Elspeth couldn't resist a dig. '*And* many horse trainers who will be looking for an excellent horsewoman. That would suit me much better.'

'You are not going to—'

'Come on, girls. I could hear you arguing down the hall.' Father walked into the room with last week's newspaper tucked under his arm. The mail truck would come to Bowen River this morning. It was an event that only happened once every ten days, and everyone looked forward to hearing the current news. There would be a week of reading awaiting them when he came home from taking Mother to the train today. She hoped that the mail he collected would include the month's issues of *The Horse and Rider.*

'You don't have to get married until you're ready, Bethie,' her father said with a sidelong glance at Mother. 'When you meet the right one, you'll know immediately.' He walked over to the table where Mother sat, holding her fine china cup delicately between her fingers. She smiled when he dropped a kiss on her cheek, and Elspeth thought how pretty her mother was. 'Won't she, my sweet Amelia? Just like you did.'

'Get away with you, Jack! Don't encourage her!'

'Our daughter loves her horses just like I do, and I'm sure

she'll meet somebody suitable that we'll all be happy with. And most importantly, someone with whom *she'll* be happy to spend her life.'

Mother drew a deep breath and pushed her pale hands against the highly polished dining room table until she stood straight. 'Our daughter will not marry into the horse industry. And that is my last word on the subject.'

That conversation had stayed with Elspeth and made her even more determined to leave home for Scotland as soon as she could.

Miss Edmonds had told them of her travels and taught them the history of medieval England, the Crusades, the Renaissance, European art, and so much more. Their teacher described the castles, the cathedrals, and the landscape, and Elspeth was fascinated. So much more interesting than her life in the bush at *Strathallyn,* and so far removed from the isolation of where they lived. The small village of Bowen River was twenty miles away, and Bowen was much further.

She hung off Miss Edmonds' every word, and her desire to experience those places herself was born and grew with every lesson. History quickly became her best subject, and she topped the class in their final exams.

One day soon, she would travel there, exploring and learning about the past.

As she lay in the dappled shade on the soft grass, her eyelids grew heavy, and Elspeth let her daydreams take her to the future she craved. She dreamed of kings and queens, castles and spires. In the warm afternoon sunshine, her eyes closed slowly, and she slept deeply.

##

Elspeth woke with a start when Blue whinnied loudly. Three crows sitting on the branch above him cawed loudly. He began to prance, agitated by the sudden noise. She sat up quickly, not knowing for a moment where she was, and then she remembered she'd ridden Blue to the billabong.

Falling asleep in the daytime was so unlike her.

'Oh, damnation.' She scrambled to her feet, brushed the grass from her jodhpurs, and then grabbed the rug from the grass. She threw it over Blue; his back was still warm from the afternoon sun. 'Come on, Blue Boy. We have to get home fast. If Father and Mother get home before us, we'll be in big trouble. He'll be so cross he'll take Mother's side next time.'

The shadows were lengthening, and Elspeth looked up to the cloudless sky. The sun had dropped behind the trees; the afternoon was much later than she'd first thought.

Grabbing the reins, she swung up onto the blanket on Blue's back, put her head down, and rode like the wind across the paddocks and through the rolling foothills that flanked the western side of *Strathallyn*. As she rode along the fence line of the back paddock, she could see dust rising to the east. Hopefully, it was a couple of the stock riders checking for cattle.

Oh, double damnation! It was the Ford. They would arrive at the homestead before she would.

Elspeth thought quickly. If she took the shortcut past the back of the dam, she'd have to clear three fences, but that way, she would get home before them.

Young Billy, the stable hand, could water Blue and cool him down for her. She didn't even have time to walk him the last mile; Elspeth knew she was being foolhardy; the last thing she needed was for Father's prize racehorse to get overheated and risk muscle damage. With any luck, Father would go into the house with Mother before he came down to the stables. She could have a quick wash, get changed, and be sitting reading when they arrived.

'Come on, boy, not far now.' She crouched low and cut through the stand of eucalypts to avoid rising in the open paddocks. Low branches brushed her face, and she crouched lower until they broke into the paddock. Blue cleared the three fences with ease, and she whooped with delight as the world sped past. She slowed him to a trot as they came into the yards and looked around for Billy. A puff of dust rose when her boots hit the ground as she slid off and pulled the blanket from Blue's back.

'Billy! Billy, where are you?' she called loudly.

Looping the reins over the gate post, Elspeth smoothed her hand over the stallion's flank; it was full, so she knew he wasn't dehydrated. She took off at a run around the back of the stables. Maybe Billy was inside. Knowing that Father was away, he was most likely asleep in the hay. He was even slack when Father was here, and she knew her father was losing patience with him. But he was a soft touch. Billy was a local lad; his father had returned from the war with damaged lungs and couldn't work, so the station had employed his two oldest boys. Colin left after a couple of weeks, but Billy stayed. No matter what he did—or didn't do—her father kept him on.

'Billy?'

All was still and quiet; there was no sign of the young stable hand.

'Oh, drat!' Elspeth cursed as she ran around the side of the stables; perhaps he was in the training paddock. But if he had been, he would have seen her ride in.

If she didn't find him soon, Elspeth knew she was going to have to look after Blue herself; she was wasting time looking for Billy. She couldn't leave Blue without sponging him down; she'd do it quickly and then get back to the house. It would be all right if Father knew she'd been riding. As long as he didn't know she'd taken Blue out.

As she ran around the corner, her breath pushed out hard as she ran full tilt into a rock-solid chest. Firm hands gripped her arms, and for a moment, her heart sank as she thought her father was already here.

'A fine ride, madam. You ride like the wind.' The voice was deep and unfamiliar.

She tried to take a step back, but the man kept hold of her. Elspeth wrenched away from his grasp and tilted her head back. She looked up at a face she'd never seen before.

'Who are you? What are you doing in our stables?' She was tempted to call for help, but by the look of things, there was no one around to hear her.

He didn't answer and stared back at her, his eyes dark and hooded. His skin was pale, and there were deep grooves on either side of his mouth. A streak of dirt ran down one cheek, and a frisson of uncertainty sent a shiver down Elspeth's back.

Finally, he spoke. 'That's a fine horse you were riding.'

'I asked who you are.'

'My name's Delaney. Thomas Delaney. And you are?'

She drew herself to her full height, which, unfortunately, was not much over five feet. 'What are you doing here?'

Blue whinnied, and she turned. For the first time since she'd dismounted, she noticed a strange horse on the other side of the gate. At least the stranger wasn't a swaggie if he was on a horse. After the war, there had been a lot of men coming to the house on foot asking for food, but the numbers had lessened over the past couple of years.

'I'm assuming you are Miss Elspeth Valentine, and if that is the case, it is your father I am here to see.'

'For what purpose?' Her tone was haughty, and she wondered how he knew her name and threw a glance at Blue and then over the gate. The dust was getting closer now, and at any moment, she would hear the car's motor.

'I believe that is your father's business.'

'Very well.' She backed away. 'I have to tend to my horse. My father will be home shortly.' She gestured to the road. 'You'll see his motor coming soon.'

He nodded. 'I'll wait here.'

'And Mr Delaney?'

'Yes, Miss Valentine?'

'I would be very grateful if you didn't mention to my father that I have been riding.'

As his mouth spread in a wide grin and his eyes lightened, Thomas Delaney shed ten years from his face, and Elspeth realised he wasn't anywhere near her father's age as she had first thought. Laughter lines appeared around his eyes, and a lock of jet-black hair fell over his forehead as he leaned towards her and whispered.

'Perhaps I can tend to your horse for you, and then you will owe me,' he said, and she knew there was no malice in his words.

Chapter 4

Bowen River State School - Wednesday morning.

'Jen? Sorry to disturb you. Have you got a minute?' Sheree Lovatt tapped on the door of the deputy principal's office and waited for Jen McMahon to lift her head from the paperwork she was reading.

'Of course. Come on in. What's up?'

Sheree sat down when Jen gestured to the chair opposite her. 'I know you're busy with the timetable but I think I need to do a notification. Actually, not *think*. We do need to make a notification.'

Jen's brow wrinkled in a frown. 'Who?'

'Two. Jonas and Mandy Delaney. I have a feeling that they might be back with Randall.'

'That's their father?' Jen had moved to Bowen River School from the coast when she'd taken a promotion a year ago and she was still coming to grips with the broader school community.

Sheree nodded. 'He had intermittent custody rights last year, and the poor kids were often hungry and dirty. We did a few notifications then and had several interviews with Mum. Dad always refused to come into the school. I'm pretty sure Leanne—their mum—put her foot down, and he left town. There was never any formal custody arrangement or, unfortunately, any intervention by child safety as far as we knew.'

Jen nodded. 'And what have you noticed now?'

'I caught Jonas at my desk this morning, opening my drawer, and when I walked in, he flushed and looked guilty. When I asked him what he was doing, he said he was looking for a pencil. He might have been because he hasn't had his books or pencils at school all week. He's one of the brightest in my class, but he's off task. He was fine last week, and he had a great time on the excursion to the mine on Friday. Then I noticed Mandy in the playground when I arrived this morning, and she was sitting on the bench under the trees by herself. Patricia told me this morning that the kids in the kinder class have been complaining about her smell. They both look dirty again, and I suspect they haven't been bringing lunch to school.'

'Doesn't sound good. I'll make the notification this morning. Can you get them both before the bell goes and see if they need something to eat? Pauline's in the tuckshop already. Keep it low-key.'

'I will. Also, you need to know that earlier in the week, I didn't give any thought to it being a child protection issue. I thought at first Jonas was just off task, so I've called Leanne a few times to talk to her, but her phone went straight to voicemail, and that's really unusual. She likes to know what's going on with the kids all the time, and even last week, when she got a new number, she rang me straight away to change our records. I've left a couple of messages, but she hasn't gotten back to me. How do you want me to deal with it when she calls back?'

'Leave it with me. I'll let Cathy know to put her straight through to me when she calls. I'll see if I can get the children to see Karen through the day, too. I'll send a few kids to her on the pretext of a dental check or something.'

'Is Karen in our school today? I thought it was her day at the high school.'

Jen looked at the school nurse's timetable on the board beside her desk. 'You're right. I'll give her a call and see if she'll come across town.'

Sheree stood. 'I'd better get to my classroom. Thanks, Jen. It's frustrating. All these changing rules and procedures for notifications, and then even when we notify, nothing happens. We're too far from anywhere.'

'Yes, I know what you mean,' Jen said. 'It was certainly different in the city, although I did have a case once when I was in one of the rural schools at the back of the Sunshine Coast. I notified them, and child protection officers came up the mountain within an hour.'

'Must have been a reason for it,' Sheree said. 'I guess they often have more information than we do.'

'They did what they needed to do. Of course, I can't say any more about it, but it restored my faith in the system a little bit, but that's been sorely tested since I've been up here in the north.'

'Like everything. Understaffed and not enough funding. Same at the hospital and in the police service. Mark and I often have this conversation over dinner.'

'It is.' Jen put down her pen and rested her elbows on the desk. 'It's the kids who are important, so it's up to us to make sure they're safe if we don't get a response.'

'Thanks for your time, Jen.' Sheree walked out to the playground and looked across to the corner. Amanda Delaney was still sitting in the shade by herself.

Sheree walked over and crouched down beside her. 'Hi, Mandy, you're not playing with the others today?'

The little girl shook her head.

'You're not feeling sick, are you?'

Mandy shook her head again. 'I'm hungry.'

'Did you have some breakfast today?'

A silent headshake, and her bottom lip wobbled.

'Let's go down to the tuckshop and see if we can get some Vegemite toast. How would you like that?'

'Yes, please.'

As they walked down to the tuckshop underneath the classroom block, Mandy reached for Sheree's hand. 'Can we get some toast for Jonas too, Mrs Lovatt?'

'Didn't Jonas have any breakfast either?' Sheree asked, choosing her words carefully.

The little girl's head moved from side to side.

'Come on, we'll go find him. We've only got a few minutes before the bell goes.'

Sheree looked around for Jonas as they walked down to the tuckshop together, but there was no sign of him. She'd talk to Pauline, the tuckshop manager, and have a quiet word with Jonas and send him down when class went in.

'Would you like a drink of milk too?' Pauline asked Mandy as she went to the fridge.

'Have you got strawberry? Please?'

Pauline and Sheree exchanged a glance.

'I have.'

The bell went as Mandy finished eating.

'How about we wash your face and hands before you go to your classroom?' Sheree asked.

'Okay, but Mrs Lovatt? Maybe don't tell Jonas I had breakfast at school.' Mandy's eyes were wide. 'Maybe he can have some, but don't tell him I did. I'm not supposed to—' The little girl pursed her lips together and looked away.

'Not supposed to what, Mandy?' Sheree kept her voice soft and gentle even as her concern deepened.

The little girl shook her head. 'Nuffing.'

'All right.' Sheree wondered what Mandy had been going to say as she took a wet wipe from the dispenser on the bench and moved closer to her. Her hair was lank and dirty, and as she wiped the little girl's face and hands, Sheree could smell urine as though she'd wet the bed and not had a bath.

Her heart sank. She loved teaching, but at times like this, it was very hard.

Poor kids. Some people didn't deserve to have children. She wondered what Leanne was doing, letting Randall have the kids again. That was the only explanation. He'd been gone for a year or more, and they'd been doing really well.

Leanne was a good person and a hard worker, and she cared for her children, but she'd made a bad choice for a partner. Sheree was thankful that Mark was a wonderful husband, and their two kids had settled into uni in Cairns.

Leanne held down a couple of jobs, working at the caravan park on the west side of town and two mornings a week at IGA, and still volunteered for tuckshop on the days when Pauline was short. Still, Sheree knew that most of her time was taken up fighting the proposed solar farm development on Valentine's Road.

'Off you go to class, Mandy.' With a sigh, Sheree headed off to her classroom. She'd keep a close eye on Jonas today and make sure he had something to eat at little lunch.

Chapter 5

Bowen River - Wednesday - 11.30 a.m.
Bec

'Mr and Mrs Whitfield, it's a pleasure to meet you. Bec's told me so much about you.' Gray's voice was almost smarmy, but at least he was being polite.

'*Reverend* Whitfield.' The tone in my father's voice told me Gray had already been judged and found wanting. I could fully understand that. The problem was that I would be the one blamed for whatever was found lacking in him.

Mum raised her eyebrows when Gray leaned over and kissed her cheek, but ever the peacekeeper, she clapped her hands lightly and shooed us inside as though we were her chickens, which I assumed were still in the backyard.

Nothing had changed. I'd swear the weeds growing along the front of the house were the same ones as the day I'd left.

'The jug's boiled, and I've made some sandwiches and scones,' Mum said. 'And there's homemade jam from Dad's plums.'

'I'll help you, Mum.' I flicked a glance at Gray. 'Can you bring the bags in from the car, please?'

'At your service, ma'am.'

I glared at him, and I knew this wasn't going to have a good ending. For the hundredth time since we'd left Brisbane, I regretted not being firm and telling him I didn't want him to come. Telling him we were over.

Bloody coward that I am.

It was bad enough that I was here in the old house with my parents. Not only that, but even after I was in the police house and started work on Monday, I knew they would be privy to everything I did. The new senior constable in a town where everyone knew everyone else's business.

I followed Mum into the house, and Dad stayed at the bottom of the steps, watching Gray open the back doors of my Landcruiser.

'Where's your car?' I asked. It was usually parked in the driveway.

'Dad put it in to the garage to get something done to it.' Mum shrugged. 'I walk to most places, so it doesn't matter to me.' When we reached the kitchen at the back of the house, she turned to me with a frown. 'You know I've put you into separate rooms.'

'That's fine. I knew that would be the case. It's your home, and I'll respect your wishes.' I looked around, surprised. The kitchen had been painted a pale green, and yellow checked curtains hung over the window at the sink. 'This looks nice,

Mum.'

She nodded. 'I wanted it to be nice when you came home. I painted your bedroom too, and I found a pretty pink chenille quilt at the op shop.'

I couldn't help myself; I walked over and hugged her. Maybe being away and mixing with friends who knew how to show their feelings had healed me more than I'd realised. 'Thank you, you shouldn't have. We're only here for one night.'

Guilt sat in my throat like a stone when Mum stiffened in my arms, and tears welled in her eyes. Maybe I'd had a rotten childhood, but it couldn't have been much fun for her either, living in this small town and this old house for almost forty years. Day in and day out, with few friends and having to put up with my father. She deserved sainthood.

'It was very thoughtful of you.' I stepped back, and Mum crossed to the sink and flicked the switch on the jug. I moved past the black combustion stove to the chair on the other side of the table, years of habit still ingrained in me. The table was already set, the same mismatched china and the mauve net cloth she'd always used covered a plate I assumed held the scones. A damp tea towel covered the sandwiches.

'Looks like you're organised.'

'I'll make the pot of tea. You go and show Gray where your rooms are.' Mum hesitated and frowned. 'I hope he drinks tea.

We don't have any coffee.'

'He'll be fine. He'll probably just have a cold drink. Do you have cold water in the fridge?'

Mum nodded, and as I left the kitchen, she was headed for the same green Kelvinator that had been there for as long as I could remember.

The wooden screen door at the front of the house creaked, and I hurried down the hall. Dust motes rose from the threadbare carpet as my shoes disturbed the thin fibres. It made me think of one of the first books I'd read at university, where the Earth was described as a mote of dust suspended in a sunbeam. That single phrase had been the catalyst for a new perspective for me, along with William Blake's poetry. I was seventeen years old and beginning to question the beliefs that had been the cornerstone of the Christian household I'd lived in. I'd spent at least eight hours every week of my life up until then in the church: morning service, evening service, teaching Sunday School, attending youth groups, not to mention the Bible readings and prayers at home after dinner every night.

Was it any wonder that as soon as I left home and entered what I perceived as the real world, I'd begin to question the doctrine I had been immured in all my life?

Was it any wonder that I broke out, left university, and didn't come home? Gray's comment in the car about party girl Bec

Whitfield, with the reputation that preceded me, hadn't been far off the mark, and my second year away from home had been one of experimentation.

My stomach began to churn as the prospect of the night ahead loomed. What the hell had I been thinking about when I accepted the transfer to Bowen River? I hadn't anticipated coming home would be so hard. I'd only thought of it from the job side of things; I'd given little thought to moving back near my parents and dealing with my father.

And I had at least two years ahead of me here.

'Bec?'

I jumped as Gray tried to open the screen door, a scowl on his face.

'Sorry. I was miles away.'

'I wish we bloody were,' he muttered. 'What is this place? Did you really live here before?'

Anger began a slow, steady burn, but I pushed it away as I opened the door for him. 'Be nice, Gray. Mum's gone to a lot of trouble. She's even painted some of the house because we were coming.'

'Needs more than a coat of paint,' he said as he shoved through the doorway, dropping my overnight case at my feet. 'Should be demolished.'

'Where's your bags?'

He rolled his eyes. 'I'm not staying here. No beer, and I'm sure we'll have to say our prayers before we go to bed.' His chuckle offended me. 'Where's the dunny? Outside?'

By the time I'd shown him where the bathroom was—at least the toilet was inside these days—and we went back to the kitchen, Dad had come in the back door and was sitting at the head of the table.

Mum stood beside Dad's chair, waiting for us to sit down. 'Gray, would you like a cup of tea or a cold drink with your sandwiches?'

'All good, thanks, Peg.' I cringed when he held my eye and waited for what was coming. 'I'll go out to the Cruiser and grab a beer out of the Waeco.' I knew he was doing it on purpose. 'I can still taste the dust from that shit of a road.'

Before I could speak, Dad's chair scraped back on the worn lino, and he stood, towering over the table.

'I'll ask you to drink it outside, please. We don't condone alcohol in our house. And please watch your language.'

Gray shrugged and sauntered to the door. 'Whatever.' He paused before he went outside, staring at my father. 'But last time I looked, Rev, "shit" wasn't a swear word.'

The wooden screen door slammed behind him, but my shoulders stayed tense. I had a whole night to get through. There was no conversation as Mum poured my tea and silently passed the plate of sandwiches. I took a curried egg sandwich and forced myself to chew. It tasted like cardboard, and I forced it down.

Dad gripped his mug and stared ahead as we sat in silence.

I was torn. Even though Dad's attitude was wrong, it was their house, and they were entitled to respect. We were the interlopers, but still, I wasn't going to apologise for Gray's behaviour.

I knew everything Dad objected to. I knew it all: alcohol, sex outside of marriage, drugs, smoking, gambling. I'd tried them all when I moved to the city.

I drained my teacup and stood. 'Thank you, Mum. That was lovely.'

'Why don't I put some sandwiches on a plate, and you can take them out to Gray,' she said, reaching for one of the plates.

Dad scowled.

'He's okay. Just a bit out of sorts from the long drive. I'll take him into town and show him around. Check out the police station, and look at the police house.'

Mum grasped my words as though they were a lifeline to normality. 'Will you be in the police house on the hill?'

'No such luck,' I said. 'The sergeant gets that one. We'll be in the old fibro one in Scott Street.'

'Living in sin,' Dad muttered.

I had to get out of there before my temper spilled over.

'We'll be back later.' Before I could leave, the front screen door creaked open, and Gray strode down the hall. He stood in the kitchen doorway, his scowl matching Dad's.

Mum and I exchanged a look.

'I was just coming out to the car,' I said. 'We're going into town.'

'Good. I need to buy a carton. I could've sworn I packed one in the back of the Cruiser. I pulled everything out, but there was no beer. And there are no coldies in the Waeco either.'

Yes, he had packed one, even though I'd asked him not to; I took it out before we left Brisbane. I left it in the garage for whoever moved into the apartment. He hadn't gone looking for it yet because we'd stayed two nights in pubs: the first night in Gladstone and the second one in Mackay.

'I'll drop you at the pub,' I said shortly.

Mum and Dad followed us to the door.

'I'm cooking some pickled pork,' Mum said. 'Will you be back for tea?'

I shook my head. 'Don't worry, Mum. We'll eat in town.'

Her face crumpled, and she went back inside. Dad stood at the door watching as I drove out feeling like a bitch.

I'd seen that look before. Self-righteous judgement, and I had been found wanting.

The silence in the Landcruiser was filled with tension as we headed into town.

'So, what the fuck was all that?' Gray said, his arms folded as he glared at me.

'Didn't I ask you not to swear at my parents' house?'

'We're not in the fucking house now. For fuck's sake, Bec, what the hell is going on with you? Where's my girl gone? Where's my cop? My tough cop who can swear with the best of them. And where's my beer?'

'I asked you one simple thing, Gray. It's all about respect, but I guess you don't know a lot about that.'

'Oh, so it's all my fault, is it?'

'One simple thing, I asked you. And what did it take you? Five minutes there, and you were goading him. I saw the way you looked at me. It's only for one night. I told you my parents were different. Couldn't you have shown a little bit of respect? It's their house, and that's how they live. Surely you can put up with it for one night.'

'No, I'm not going back there. You can, but I'll find somewhere else to sleep. Now show me this town. I'm already having second thoughts.' He sneered as we drove down the main street. 'And you're going to be a cop here? What are you going to do? Help little old ladies across the street? Is there a bus out of this dive?'

'A bus to where?'

'What's the nearest big town?'

The cowardice that had plagued me for the past two weeks disappeared in one flash. 'That's a great idea. Go back to Brisbane, Gray. Forget the bus. I'll drive you to Bowen, and you can catch the Greyhound tonight. I don't want you here either. You knew I didn't want you to come with me. We're done.'

We'd been at this point many times before, but I'd always backed down. This time, I meant it. Maybe I was seeing Gray from a different perspective today.

'Fuckin' oath, we are.'

I accelerated down Main Street and pulled up in front of the police station. 'Wait here. I'm going to let the sergeant know I'm in town. Then I'll take you back to Bowen.'

He looked out the passenger window. 'Where's the pub?'

I gestured to the Central Hotel about fifty metres down the street. 'There.'

'Come and get me when you're done.' He got out and slammed the door.

I glanced at my phone as I walked through the gate of the police station and up the three steps towards the main door. It was just after one, and I hoped the station wasn't closed for lunch. A white Outlander was parked at the side of the building, and then I noticed a silver Kia Stinger behind it, the same vehicle I used when I was on highway patrol in North Brisbane.

The police station looked the same as it had when I'd walked past it on the way home from high school in year twelve. Even though the town was small, when I was in school, there was a P-12 school there to cater for the town kids and those living on outlying properties.

The new police station and the separate primary school had been built the year before I left, and if anyone had told me back then that I'd be working here one day, I would have laughed. Even at sixteen, I knew I'd be getting out of this place.

As I approached the front door of the station, I pushed away the lingering angst of the afternoon and my anger at Gray. Despite being in Bowen River, the challenge of taking up the position of senior constable in a small station excited me. And with no Gray to take up my time and emotional energy. I quickly worked out the trip in my head. Ten minutes here, an hour back to Bowen, get Gray sorted—no, stuff him, I'd just drop him off at the travel centre in town—and then an hour back here. He could find his own way back to Brisbane.

The door was open. A young guy in uniform stood behind the counter, and he looked up with a smile as I walked in.

First plus for the station.

'Hello, what can I do for you?' He didn't look old enough to be out of school. I glanced at the black rank insignia on his shoulder. At my guess, he was a probationary constable.

'Hi. I'm Senior Constable Bec Whitfield from Brisbane. I'm starting work here on Monday. I just hit town.'

'Hi, Bec. Good to have you here. We weren't expecting you this week. I'm Probationary Constable Aaron Scott. I'll give the sarge a holler.'

'Thanks.'

I looked around while I waited. Bowen River Police Station was a more modern station than the ones I'd worked at in Brisbane. I nodded with satisfaction, noting how tidy and organised the front office was. The walls were clean, and the lino floor held no scuffs. A wooden leaflet holder on the wall adjacent to the counter held recent literature on seniors' safety and personal safety, and the posters on the board were all current, not faded or curled with age; they were arranged neatly with even spaces between each edge. That said a lot about the management of the station to me. It also was an indication of the type of town Bowen River was, with the leaflets and posters all in English, not catering to a multicultural environment like the city stations I'd worked in. The chairs in the public waiting area were unmarked, and a large pot plant sat on the table between them.

Maybe Gray was right, and the work here wouldn't be as challenging as I was used to. But it was a stepping stone on my journey to becoming a detective.

Despite the doubts that crept in, it looked like a pleasant

place to work, and I would do it. Two years at least, unless a promotion opportunity came up.

Aaron reappeared, followed by a broad-shouldered man with short-cropped grey hair. He came around the counter and held out his hand. 'Sergeant Mark Lovatt. Good to have you here, Senior Constable Whitfield.'

'It's good to be here.' I smiled. 'And please, call me Bec.'

'Let's get straight to business, Bec,' the sergeant said. 'We're short-staffed this week. Now that you're in town is there any chance you'd be able to come on duty sooner? We have a couple of situations brewing, and it would be great if you could start sooner.'

'Situations?' I said with a frown. Maybe not such a simple place.

'Yes. A suspected missing person case we need to follow up on quickly, and there's been a lot of trouble down at the corner pub in the last week or so. One extra person at the station would make a big difference, and without sounding sexist, being female will help with one of the interviews we've got ahead. There are two small children we need to interview, and if we can't locate their parents, we'll have to find a temporary placement for them. At the moment, we've got no certified carers in town.'

'Of course I can. I've just got to take a quick trip to Bowen now, but I'll be back in a couple of hours. I could come in around four and start this afternoon.'

'Terrific. We've got a lot to do. I'll leave Aaron in the station, and I'll handle the pub.'

'Who's missing?'

'A local woman by the name of Leanne Delaney. At this stage, we're not sure how long she's been missing or if she even is.'

'Leanne Delaney? Around thirty years old?' I asked.

'That's right.' He looked at me intently.

'If it's the Leanne Delaney I'm thinking of, I went to high school with her. You may not be aware I grew up in Bowen River.'

'No, I wasn't.' His eyes held interest and approval. 'So, you'll have some local knowledge. Good. Her employer is concerned that she hasn't turned up at work, and she can't get her on her mobile.'

'Where does she work?'

'At the local caravan park and the IGA.'

'What about her husband?'

'Not married. An ex-partner who's in and out of jail.'

'Okay. I'll get into my uniform and come in as soon as I get back from Bowen.' I pulled my car keys out of my back jeans pocket. I was keen to get back quickly. 'It's good to be here, Sergeant.'

'Have you booked accommodation in town?' The sergeant reached up to the key rack on the wall behind the desk and lifted down a set of keys. 'If you have, you won't need it. The cleaners and the pest guy from Bowen got the house done this morning, so it's ready for you to move in now if you want.'

'We're—' I shook my head— 'I mean, I'm staying with my parents tonight. They still live in Bowen River.' I took the keys he held out. 'Is it still the old house in Scott Street?'

'That's the one. It's been done up.'

'Okay. I'll see you when I get back. Thank you.'

'Good to have you on board,' he said, and Aaron lifted his hand in a friendly wave as I left.

There was no way I was going to tell Gray the house was ready. My mind was in work mode already.

Leanne Delaney. I remembered her well.

Chapter 6

Bowen River - Wednesday 12.30 p.m.
Bec

I opened the back of the Landcruiser to a mess. I'd packed our gear neatly before we left Brisbane, and the back was full to the top of the windows. Gray had remembered a pressing task somewhere and arrived home about half an hour before the time I'd told him we were hitting the road. He'd left a couple of bags out for me to load in the car and his laptop. Typical. His dependence on me had grown considerably since he moved into my apartment eight months ago, but that was over now. I'd put them in last so he'd be able to get to them easily, along with my laptop and overnight bag, but since he'd looked for the carton of beer I had taken out, the back of the car was a mess.

I eventually found and lifted out his heavy kit bag and his small suitcase. When I found his laptop, I put all his bags on the back seat; it would be easier to get his gear from there when I dropped him off, and then I'd go straight to the station.

Shit. My uniform was at the house in my case. I hesitated, biting my lip, trying to decide what to do. I'd have to go back to the house to get changed when I got back.

The grass crackled beneath my sneakers as I walked back to

the driver's side. Yellow and dry, it looked dead. Even when it rained at the coast, the moisture always seemed to miss Bowen River.

As I drove down the main street, I checked out the shops and buildings. I'd spent a lot of time at the library when I was in high school; it was the one place I was allowed to go. It was still in the same building, on the corner near the park and opposite the hardware store across the road. The bakery was boarded up, and I guessed that the supermarket that had opened up the month I'd left had eventually put them out of business. I turned right, heading towards the manse. As I passed the bus depot, a guy walked out and crossed the driveway, heading for a ute parked on the road. A grin lifted my lips as I pulled up beside the parked ute and opened the window.

'Gidday, stranger,' I called.

He looked up, and as soon as recognition crossed his face, he sauntered over to my car.

'Well, look what the wind's blown in. Becky Whitfield, what are you doing in town? I haven't seen you for years.'

'Hey, Tommy, you haven't changed a bit, mate.' Tommy Evans and I had been great mates in high school.

He rested his hand on the edge of the open window. 'Oh yes, I have. I'm older and wiser than that pimply youth you used to fancy. I answer to Tom now.'

'Ha. You wished, back in the day. But older and wiser wouldn't be a bad thing. And I'm Bec these days,' I said with a grin. Maybe being back here would have some positives apart from the job.

'So, what are you doing with yourself these days?' he asked.

'I've come back to town to work.'

'At the school? You went to uni to do teaching, didn't you?'

'Nah.' I shook my head. 'I only lasted at uni for a year. I joined the police force. I'm the new senior constable in town.'

'Wow! That's great, Bec. We'll have to catch up. You might remember Lacey, my wife. Lacey Donaldson? She was a couple of years behind us at school. We've got two kids too.'

'That'd be great. I do remember her; she was in my netball team. You can fill me in on who else is still around.'

'What about you?' he asked. 'Married? Kids? The school could do with some more kids.'

'Nope. A single career woman.' I was now anyway, and I could start moving on once I got Gray out of town. 'Do you work here at the bus company?'

'I *own* the bus company these days. My dad passed away a couple of years ago.'

'I'm sorry to hear that. Your dad was a good man.' His father had been a deacon in the church, but he hadn't forced his kids to go to Sunday school or church. 'Anyway, I've got to rush. I'll see you around, Tom.'

'For sure. Welcome home.'

The town was quiet as I locked the car and walked across the footpath to the pub. I'd never been inside before—that was a given being a daughter of the local minister—but the mix of spilt beer and stale cigarette smoke, absorbed over years by the timber and the threadbare carpet in the days before smoking was banned, was the same as any old pub I'd been in.

Gray was holding court at the end of a green laminate bar with a couple of young guys. He turned and had the grace to look sheepish for a moment before he flashed that trademark grin—the one I'd once found appealing until I discovered the insincerity behind it.

'Hey, babe, come on over and meet the guys. They work out at the solar farm. I'm settling into town already. Harry and Craig, this is my Bec.'

I'm sure he was settling in. Give Gray Cameron a beer and a form guide, and he would fit in anywhere.

I nodded at the two men. 'We have to leave now.'

'What do you want to drink?' He ignored my request.

'I don't want a drink. We have to leave now.'

'Oh, later, babe. We're just waiting for the next race.' He gestured up to the bank of screens in the next room, each one at a different race meeting.

'Outside, Gray. I want to speak to you.'

He rolled his eyes. 'Gotta do as I'm told, guys. I'll be back soon. I hope that tip was a good one, Harry.'

He tried to put his arm around me as I walked out the door, but I shrugged it off. 'Sounds like I can get a job at that new solar plant you were talking about. If my online stuff doesn't work up here, that is. I didn't notice a post office.'

'Get in the car, Gray.'

'No, it's their shout, and I want to watch that race.'

'Get in the bloody car.'

'Ah, my Bec's back. Am I allowed to swear now, too?'

I wrenched open the passenger door. 'Get in.'

He grabbed my arm as I went to walk around to the driver's side.

'Let go of me.' I looked up at him. An angry sneer had replaced the easy-go-lucky expression. He must have seen I meant business because he let go.

'Okay. I'll get in, and we'll talk.'

'There's nothing to talk about. I'm taking you to Bowen to catch the bus.'

'Come on, Bec. Don't be stupid.' His beery breath was on my face, and I took a step back. 'I'm sorry. I did the wrong thing back at your olds' place. How about I go back and apologise?'

'I'm taking you to Bowen. Now. You can get back to

Brisbane however you want. There's a bus or a train.'

'Fuck off. You think I came all that way with you to this pissy little town to turn around and go straight back?'

How had I ever thought I could spend my life with him?

My voice was cold. 'Let's have some truth here. You came all that way because you had nowhere to live once I gave up *my* apartment, and your free ride was about to end. Well, it's ended, Gray. So, get in the car, and I'll drive you back to Bowen. Or go and hang with your new mates, but if you decide to stay, you're on your own.'

'Come on, babe. Don't be like that.'

'What's it going to be, Gray? I'm not changing my mind. We're done.'

'I'm staying.'

'Fine.' I kept my voice even as frustration took hold. I should never have brought him with me. It was going to be hard enough working in town with Dad here, let alone Gray. 'You're on your own. Completely.'

Gray turned to go back into the pub and then stopped. 'If I'm going to find somewhere to bunk down, you'll have to give me some cash to tide me over. I'm a bit short.'

I didn't speak as I reached into the car and got my purse. I peeled off three fifty-dollar notes and shoved them at him. 'That's it. Your bags are on the back seat.'

I stood there with my arms folded while he lifted them out of the car.

'And you were wrong, Bec. There is a room at the pub. I've already asked.' He strode off and stopped again. 'We'll talk tomorrow when you've gotten over the shits. Have a lovely night with your parents.'

I stared after him until he disappeared into the pub, and then I went back to the car.

Damn. If Mum and Dad were out, I wouldn't be able to get my uniform.

With a bit of luck, they should still be at the house; I'd just run in and get changed. I hoped they were home; they locked the place up like Fort Knox when they went out. Always had. I'd always wondered what they were worried about losing, but as I grew up, I put it down to Dad's need for privacy. He'd hate me being back in town in a public role.

They'd be home. I couldn't imagine anywhere else they'd be.

Dad was sitting on the single plastic chair on the porch when I got out of the car.

'Where is he?' he said.

I nodded as I walked up the front steps carrying my boots. 'He's gone.'

'I'm sorry about that, Rebecca, but I'm pleased to see you

still have a little sense.'

The drive from the pub was only two streets, too short to regain my equilibrium, so when Dad had a go, I lost my temper.

'You're sorry that he's left?' I ignored the jibe about my intellect.

'No, I'm very sorry about your choice of partner.'

'You can stop being sorry because it's over. I'm sorry that I brought him into your home and that his behaviour was disrespectful.'

I didn't say "inappropriate" because apart from being an absolute arse, Gray hadn't really done anything that bad. A couple of swear words and a mention of alcohol. In a way, it was cathartic for me because it brought back all the memories of the household I'd grown up in. I didn't have to put up with it now, and I swore I wasn't going to let my father bring me down. I had a job to focus on. I had to stay there tonight: Mum had done all that work in the house.

Mum walked through the front door, a tea towel over her shoulder. 'Have you come back for dinner after all? Where's Gray? We still eat at five.'

'We won't be here for dinner, Mum. But you can leave me some on the stove if that's not too much trouble.' It wouldn't hurt me to sleep here for one night, seeing Mum had gone to so much trouble.

Mum frowned. 'For you? Or for both of you?'

'No, just mine. I went to the police station, and I'm starting the afternoon shift now. I just came back to get into my uniform.'

'Why?' Mum looked confused.

'They need me there tonight. There's a lot of work to be done.'

Dad's voice came from behind me. 'You might get a shock, Rebecca. Coming here, thinking it would be an easy job. We have more crime here now.'

I hadn't thought anything of the sort, but he wasn't going to get a rise out of me. It wasn't appropriate for me to mention Leanne Delaney until I knew what was going on.

'What sort of crime?' I asked casually.

'Petty thieving. Car stealing, breaking and entering. Matthew said, "My house shall be called a house of prayer, but you make it a den of robbers". Our town is not the same town it was.' He lifted his eyes and looked across the top of my head. 'In fact, your mother and I are thinking of moving to the coast.'

Mum's mouth dropped open. 'Are we?'

'If it's God's will, that's what will happen.'

I moved towards the hall, hoping that was true. If Dad wasn't in town, my job would be a lot easier, but I was sure he was just trying to get a rise out of me again. 'I have to go and get changed.'

Once Dad got started on the scriptures, he could go all night.

'Are you starting early because of the missing girl?' Mum asked.

'Missing girl?' I said, staring at her.

'Yes, Wilma next door heard the news at IGA and told me after you left. Poor Leanne.'

Dad's plastic chair clattered on the porch behind him as he jumped to his feet. 'No, not *poor* Leanne. She was just another sinner in this godless town.'

'*Was?*' I swung around to face him, my eyes wide and my mouth open. 'How dare you speak like that. I thought you were supposed to be a Christian. If that's the sort of attitude you have, I'm glad I *pissed* off out of here as soon as I could.'

Mum looked horror-stricken, and I touched her hand lightly as I walked past.

'If you're still up when I get home, I'll have a cup of tea with you, Mum. But don't wait up specially. I could be very late.'

'I'll give you a front door key so you can get in,' Mum said, her voice quiet as she threw a nervous glance towards my father.

'Just leave the door unlocked. I'll let myself in.'

'No, we will not leave the door unlocked. It's all started since those solar workers moved to the hotel and the caravan park.' Dad's voice was tight. 'Now they can look for a murderer amongst them.' He closed his eyes. "You shall not murder, and whoever murders will be liable to judgment".'

'As far as I know, it is only a missing person's case at this stage. Have you heard more?' It was obviously around town, so whatever I found out could only help.

'No, Wilma only told me about her not turning up at work,' Mum said with another quick glance at Dad. 'That's how the police found out about it.' She turned to my father. 'Who told you, Jim?'

'You did when you came home from that woman next door.' Mum looked confused, and Dad turned on his heel and walked down the hallway. 'I can smell the vegetables burning.'

I went to my old bedroom to get changed. It was different with the painted walls and new bedspread on the single bed, but that still wasn't enough to stop my tension from growing as I stepped inside.

The memories of the times I lay on that bed, bored and miserable, flooded back. Somehow, putting my uniform and boots on made me feel better. I'd been rude to Dad and sworn, but damn him, I wasn't going to bow to him. I wasn't sixteen anymore.

'Oh, my goodness, look at you, Becky. You look so grown-up in your uniform.' Mum put a hand to her mouth as I walked into the kitchen.

'If I'm not grown up at thirty, Mum—or almost thirty—I

never will be.'

'Don't say that, love. It's tempting fate.' She looked nervously over her shoulder. 'Poor Leanne was your age, wasn't she?'

Why was everyone talking about her as though she was dead?

'Don't worry, Mum.'

'I'll try not to, but I will lock the door.' She reached into her apron pocket and whispered as she handed me a single key. 'Here's the spare key. Please don't lose it.'

By that, I guessed Dad didn't know she was giving it to me. I leaned over and kissed her cheek. 'Thank you, don't wait up late, okay?'

It was something that we'd never done when I was home. There was never any physical affection between them.

Mum's eyes glinted with tears. 'It's wonderful to have you home, sweetheart.'

Chapter 7

Bowen River - Wednesday 2.00 p.m.
Bec.

With Gray deciding to stay in town, I had some extra time, so I detoured via Scott Street on the way back to the station and pulled up outside the police house.

I closed my eyes. I was not going to think about him or give in to the anger that simmered because he'd decided to stay in town. It was my fault for bringing him here. He'd be thinking that I would get over what he saw as a minor spat, and I'd welcome him back with open arms in the next day or two.

This time, he was in for a rude shock. Being back in town and in Dad's presence had firmed my determination. The reason I had taken up with Gray and stayed with him for longer than my past failed relationships had become painfully obvious to me today. I'd been kidding myself in Brisbane, but now I knew I'd stayed with him because I wanted to be needed by someone.

It was just a shame that it had been Gray because I knew he didn't need *me*. He never had. He only wanted what I could provide him with: a roof over his head, a comfortable existence, an internet connection, and regular sex was the icing on top.

Pairing up with Gray and then having him move in had put

an end to my constant search for someone who cared about me. The few relationships I'd had before him hadn't lasted, and I'd been let down. I'd tried too hard, and any guy with a casual attitude towards permanency ran a mile.

Eventually, we decided it made more sense for him to move into my place. It had taken a while for me to wake up to the fact that it wasn't me he needed. What he'd needed was a home base. His IT work dealing in product delivery—I never knew where the parcels came from or went to—involved many trips to the post office. It all happened from my apartment in Cleveland. For someone who worked with people, I knew very little about what he did. I'd been involved with my work at the Bayside station. It had been a tough workplace, dealing with several rough areas, and I'd worked long hours and didn't have the energy to find out about his work.

Thinking about the wasted year was making me angry, and I needed to clear my head to start work. I had calmed down since I'd left Gray at the pub, but the thought of him being in town didn't sit comfortably with me. He had a nasty streak, and I knew if he got a few more beers in him, he was likely to do—or say—anything.

Well, he could try it on, but knowing him, he'd soon get sick of the small town and leave. I knew he had a friend in Cairns, so if he caused any problems, I'd suggest that maybe he could go there. I'd pay his airfare; it would be worth it to get him away from me. He could freeload off someone else for a change.

I turned my attention to the house. The sergeant said it had been renovated, but from the outside, it looked pretty much the same as before. There wasn't much of a garden, only a couple of shrubs with wilting flowers set on either side of the front gate, but the edges were neat, and the lawn was mowed. A yard that wouldn't take a lot of looking after.

I walked down the path and opened the front door with the keys he'd given me. The clean, sweet smell of cleaning products greeted me. The walls had been painted in a soft grey, and large white tiles ran down the hallway floor. I glanced into each furnished bedroom and took a quick look at the kitchen and bathroom. I grinned when I saw a coffeemaker on the kitchen bench. If Gray had been moving in, I *wouldn't* have had to buy one.

I locked the door and walked to my car feeling content; it wouldn't take me long to unpack my clothes and linen and the few personal things I'd brought with me. I'd never had much in any of the apartments I'd lived in, as each time I was transferred, I moved close to the station where I worked.

The best thing about this house was that I could leave my car there; it was close enough to the station for me to walk to work. I considered leaving the Landcruiser there now but remembered that Mum was expecting me back tonight. I parked at the side of the station beside the Outlander and went inside.

The sergeant was near the counter, and there was no sign of Aaron.

'You're back early,' Mark said.

'I didn't have to make the trip after all.' For a moment, I wondered if I should tell the sergeant about my personal circumstances, and then I reminded myself of my experiences at Bayside. Sharing too much gave people an opportunity to take advantage of you. It was no one else's business, and I'd make sure Gray didn't impact my work.

'It's good that you're here early.' He nodded and unlocked the door on the right-hand side of the counter. 'Come on through to the back. I just want to thank you again for starting early. There have been a few developments since you left. We need to move on this straight away.'

He preceded me down the hallway, pointing out his office, the interview room, the lunch room, and the male and female washrooms. When we reached the end of the hall, Mark led me into a workroom that ran the width of the whole building. Four computers sat on desks along the side wall, and another sat on an adjacent desk with the biggest screen I'd seen in a station.

He must have noticed me looking. 'Fifty inches, and it's been great to use. The layout of the room meant we couldn't use a data projector.' He gestured to the windows along the back wall. 'That suited us because, with only three to four staff, we don't need one.'

I grinned. 'And that means no death by PowerPoint either, Sergeant.'

Mark smiled back. 'Don't be too hasty. You have to sit through an induction to the station with me yet. And call me Mark, no need for formality here.'

A boss with a sense of humour. That was a plus.

His smile faded away. 'We're going to throw you in headfirst, Bec. We need to get working on this case now. We'll do the induction next week.'

I nodded. 'Anything I need to know in the meantime, I'll ask you or Aaron.'

'Take a seat, and I'll fill you in. Coffee while we work?'

'That'd be great, thanks. I had a cup of tea and some lunch at my parents' place a couple of hours ago. When I saw the coffeemaker at the police house it got my craving going.'

'So, you checked out the house. All okay?'

'Really good.'

'Your parents still live in Bowen River?'

'Yes, they do.'

He frowned. 'Whitfield? Jim and Peggy?'

'Yes.' My contentment deflated a little.

He nodded and didn't comment further as he turned towards the kitchen. 'How do you take your coffee? It's only instant.'

'Black, please.'

Another thing in Mark's favour—making coffee for the staff. Not using his seniority to be waited on. That was a rare thing in the force.

But I wouldn't use that to create a relationship. The one thing I'd gradually learned since joining the police force was not to tell my life story to everyone. I was here to work, do the best job I could, work my way up and not form close social relationships at the station. My experience at Bayside had reinforced that. Nothing major had caused me any grief, but the cut-throat competition for recognition and promotion meant that the workplace was not a collegial one, and you had to watch your back. I'd bide my time here, although being such a small town, I guessed there would have to be social contact with my colleagues.

When Mark carried in a tray with three coffee mugs and biscuits, Aaron followed him into the workroom. He took the mug handed to him.

'Thanks, Sarge.'

'I asked Aaron to come in too. We have a bell on the front desk if anyone needs us.'

I took my coffee and nodded my thanks.

'We can go through the reports we already have in,' Mark said as he stood beside a blank whiteboard. He reached for a biscuit, dunked it in his coffee, and picked up the whiteboard marker. 'We became aware of Leanne Delaney's missing when several people expressed concerns about her whereabouts. She's a single mother and lives thirty-five kilometres west of town on a family property. She has two children. As far as I can ascertain from her current employer, her ex-partner last left about a year ago. He comes and goes. Her two employers have reported her current absence from work. Each has stated an unexplained absence is out of character. The school bus driver also called an hour ago and expressed his concern. I only had a quick phone chat with Tom because he had to leave for this afternoon's school run. Bec, I'd like you to go and see him when he gets back.'

'The local bus company?' I asked.

'Yes, the driver's name is Tom Evans. He runs the company and he does the run that goes out to the outlying stations to the west. Morning and afternoon.'

'Yes, I know Tom. He's a local from way back, too.'

'How long since you moved away?' Mark looked at me curiously.

'I've been gone twelve years. Since high school.'

'Okay. Your knowledge of the district may help, although

it's changed a lot even in the six years I've been here. The coal mine and the solar farm developments have seen an influx of workers. The new workforce has changed the nature of the town.'

'Yes, I believe it has,' I agreed.

'You said earlier that you knew Leanne Delaney.'

'Yes, we were friends for most of my school life, but I haven't spoken to her since I left town.'

'She's twenty-nine, and her children, Jonas and Amanda, are nine and six.'

'And do we know the story of her husband?' I queried. 'Who is he? A local?'

Aaron's eyes were wide and his expression was one of self-importance as he followed the conversation. I guessed it must be the first real investigation he'd been involved in.

'As far as I know, it was a de facto relationship. Randall Simms worked locally until he moved away. He left town around a year ago, but he didn't live at the property for a year or so before that. That information is from the local state school. But I must add that he was known to us. Minor stuff, drunk and disorderly. Some suspected drug dealing, but never proven while he was here. There was some gossip of him being inside, but I haven't confirmed that yet. I'll get you to chase that up, Bec.'

I nodded and wrote his name into my notebook. 'The

school's involvement?' I asked.

'My wife is a teacher there, and she knows the kids and their situation. Suffice it to say a child safety notification has been made, irrespective of what we establish.'

'Have they talked to the children?'

'No, they didn't want to push them at this stage.'

I raised my eyebrows. I knew the drill. If a notification has been made, there is some cause for concern about the children. 'Okay, fair enough.' I drank some of my coffee—not bad for instant I noted with approval—and put my cup down and looked at the whiteboard as Mark began to draw a timeline. The coffee hit my bloodstream, and I focused as he divided the board into three columns: work, school and bus.

'This is the sequence in which the information came in,' he said as he wrote the time of Tom's call at the top of the third column. 'Tom's bus picks the kids up at the gate on Valentine's Road every morning around eight. Valentine's Road is off the Suttor Creek Causeway Road, and he said the two kids had been waiting by themselves for the last few days. He thinks it was since Monday, but he doesn't know if Leanne was there last Friday because he had a casual driver and Tom had a day off to go to the dentist. Leanne usually waits with the kids, and the same in the afternoon. He said she waits for the bus to drop them off, and they walk back to the house with her. He said she's usually there when he drops them off, but he hasn't seen her this week.'

'And can we contact the other driver to ask about last Friday?'

'Yes, I'll get you to get the details from Tom when you talk to him and follow up.' Mark paused and turned to Aaron. 'Actually, Aaron, to save us some time, I'll get you to go over to the bus depot office now and get the contact details for that driver from the office.'

Aaron nodded. 'I'll walk over. Won't be long.'

'And check what time Tom comes in from the afternoon bus run, please.'

I leaned forward as Aaron left. 'If she lives out at the Valentine place, it's about three hundred metres from the house to the road. As far as I remember anyway, perception of distance is a bit different when you're a kid.'

'I've never been out to the house, so I can't comment.' Mark moved to the school column. 'Just after Tom called, my wife dropped in to see me during her lunch break and raised the school's concern about not being able to contact Leanne. They'd tried to call and also tried her two workplaces with no luck. Apparently, there have been some issues with the kids this week, and they suspect Simms is back on the scene. They don't have any contact details for him.'

'I'll look for him on Q-Prime as soon as we're done here.'

'Yes. I haven't had a chance yet. We've been busy since you left, and I've been talking to both of her employers, who rang with concerns. I think the word might be spreading around town. Leanne hasn't turned up for work this week at either the caravan park or IGA.'

I pulled a face. 'My mother mentioned it when I called before. Looks like we need to get out to Leanne's place and establish if she *is* missing, and then talk to the kids.'

'Yes, and after what happened at Tara recently, you and I will go, Senior Constable. Aaron can man the station. If we can't confirm her whereabouts by tonight, I'll ring the detectives at Bowen and get them on board.'

The sergeant moved to the work column and wrote 2.05 p.m. at the top. 'Jean Purdue is the owner of the caravan park, and she rang after Tom's call.'

'Mrs Purdue must be a fair age now.'

'Eighty-one and still running the park. Apparently, she and her husband started it up back in the seventies. Leanne works the office a few mornings and does the cleaning. I suggested she may have decided to go away, but Jean disagreed. She said Leanne is very reliable and communicates any change of plans. The manager at IGA called about fifteen minutes later. Same story. Very reliable. No show is very much out of character.'

'Who do you want me to talk to first?' I asked. I knew what I'd do, but I didn't call the shots here. I'd go straight out to the house.

A door closed at the front, and Aaron called out. 'It's only me. The bus depot was closed.'

'Okay.' The sergeant put the whiteboard marker down and looked at his watch. 'It's three-thirty now. Aaron, you can take over out the front. Bec and I will go out to Valentine's Road around four. We'll be back in time for me to go down to be at the pub when the workers come off shift. Bec, I've got a couple of calls to make. I'll issue you with your firearm now, and then you can go over to the caravan park and have a chat with Jean before we head out.'

The probationary constable beamed, and I sensed this was the first time he'd manned the front desk alone in the station.

'Come on, senior constable, we'll get you sorted,' Mark said.

Chapter 8

Bowen River - Wednesday 3.30 p.m.
Bec

The sun beat down on my head when I went outside. I'd forgotten how hot it could get out here in autumn. I'd gone soft, used to the lower humidity and the sea breezes of the coast. I walked past my Toyota and headed for the Stinger at the side of the building. The door handle was burning hot. Familiarity took over as I slipped into the driver's seat of the highway patrol vehicle. The smell of the leather and the sight of the dashboard equipped with radio, scanners and the large screen in the centre brought my self-confidence rushing back. I placed my hand on the palm reader of the Stinger's flat dashboard and brushed my fingers over the buttons that accessed the radio and siren.

No matter how much I had let Gray use me, and no matter how much my father thought I was a waste of space, as a police officer, I was in my element. I was a good cop, and I had every intention of doing my best at Bowen River. My focus now was on Leanne Delaney until we established she was okay. I fervently hoped we would confirm that this afternoon, but the situation was concerning.

'Don't assume,' I told myself. Facts. Evidence.

Bowen River

I took a deep breath, and the purring of the twin-turbo V6 settled me even more when I started the engine. A contented smile played on my lips as I crossed town and headed towards the Bowen River Tourist Park. The caravan park was on the west side of town. I turned left off Main Street and headed up the hill.

Leanne and I had ridden our pushbikes up this hill when she had been allowed to come over to the manse. Occasionally, when we were in our first year at high school, her father would drive her into town on a Saturday afternoon and drop her off with her bike. The first time she'd been allowed to visit, she'd been amazed that we didn't have a television in the lounge room. The next time she visited, she'd insisted on bringing her bike.

Leanne had been a good friend, and once she'd gotten used to our house, she didn't judge me. Her parents and her elderly grandfather had been kind to me on the couple of occasions I was allowed to go out to their property, but our close friendship had been brief because Dad had disapproved of our friendship. Leanne's parents had not been "salt of the Earth", or whatever the biblical phrase was he'd used at the time. My father had quite a collection of biblical quotations at his disposal as a reason for why I couldn't do certain things. As I got older and started to listen to his sermons in church, I began to realise that most of his sermons were a stringing together of a lot of those sayings and verses, and the message he was purportedly sharing held no substance.

Leanne's family were Catholic, and that was enough to put a blight on their souls, according to Dad. They probably went to the pub too, or had the occasional beer, so they weren't a suitable family for me to spend time with. I'm sure he thought being a Catholic was contagious, so I was kept sheltered, and our friendship gradually petered out. But Leanne had always been kind to me and didn't laugh at me like a lot of the kids did until I learned to stand up for myself.

I gave a bitter laugh as I pulled up outside the caravan park. Dad had tried his best, but I had eventually found my own way. I patted the biometric palm reader on the gearshift; the police car knew more about me than my father ever had.

I locked the car and walked through an opening in the shoulder-height hedge that hadn't been there when I was growing up. A couple of bright blue butterflies danced over the greenery and settled on the top of the leaves near the gap. A row of cabins now blocked the view of the bush to the west. The same ramp led to the office, and I slid open the screen door and stepped inside.

As my eyes grew accustomed to the dark interior, I realised it was Jean Purdue sitting behind the counter, tapping into a computer.

She certainly didn't look eighty-one. I stood back and

observed her until she finished what she was doing.

'Thank you,' she said when she finally looked up. 'I'm pleased to see that you've taken notice of my phone call.' Her voice was gravelly from years of smoking.

'Good afternoon, Mrs Purdue. I'm Senior Constable Bec Whitfield.'

Her eyes narrowed. 'Bec Whitfield? Same one who grew up in the old manse?'

Is everyone going to judge me because of where I came from?

I swallowed and nodded. 'That's me. Haven't lived here for a long time, though.'

'I remember you when you were a kid,' she said. 'Doesn't seem that long ago.'

'Probably fifteen years ago since Leanne and I used to come in here and buy ice creams.'

'I remember it well. You used to go down to the river with her and lie on the grass underneath the weeping willows. Welcome home.'

'Thank you. You've got a very good memory, Mrs Purdue.'

'I do, and that's why I'm so concerned about Leanne. She's never done anything like this before. She's worked for me since she left high school. She was here when she was pregnant with both her kids, and she was totally reliable even when that useless bastard treated her badly.'

That got my attention.

'Is there somewhere private we can sit and have a chat?' I asked.

'Yes.' She stood, came around the counter and walked across to the door. She locked the sliding door and turned around the sign that gave a mobile number for when the office was unattended.

'I'm not expecting any more tourists to arrive today, and the boys in the dongas won't be back for their dinner until 5:30.'

'The park's changed.'

'Yes, the mine brought the dongas in, but I get the rental. We built the extra cabins when we heard what was happening with the solar farms. That company came in and built the cookhouse. I hire the cook. The boys from the mine and the construction workers from the solar farms all eat there, even though the pub doesn't like it. It's certainly kept our caravan park afloat.' She shook her head. 'I keep saying "our", but Johnny passed away about ten years ago.'

'I'm sorry to hear that,' I said as I followed the elderly woman into a small kitchen area.

'Would you like a cup of tea?'

'No, thank you. I've got a few more calls to make this afternoon so it would be good if I could ask you a few questions now.' I pulled the notebook and pen from my shirt pocket. 'Can you tell me when you first began to be concerned about Leanne not coming to work?'

'Yesterday afternoon. She works for me on Tuesday, Wednesday and Thursday afternoons. When she didn't arrive yesterday, I tried to call her because I thought one of the kids might be sick. She's usually pretty good when the kids aren't well. She'll give me a call the night before if she can and that gives me a chance to get someone else in. I'm getting a bit long in the tooth to be doing it all myself these days.'

'I think you're doing pretty well,' I said.

Her smile was sad. 'Anyway, Leanne didn't turn up, and when I couldn't get her on the phone, I rang the school to see if the kids were there, and they were, so I thought she must have told me she had something on, and I'd forgotten.' She stared into the office, and eventually, I prompted her.

'And then?'

'When she didn't turn up today, and I still couldn't get her on the phone, I began to worry. It's just not Leanne. I wouldn't put anything past that ex of hers, especially now that it looks like she might get paid out for her property.'

'Paid out for her property? Who by?'

'Strathallyn Solar are buying up a lot of properties around there to develop more solar farms. There's a division in the town.

Same as the mine, some of us support it because it's brought a lot of money to the town. Workers who rent, and eat and drink, and would you believe even tourists who come to see it? God knows what they find attractive about a row of shiny solar panels in a paddock. But, like I said, it brings money to businesses, and it keeps us afloat. The town was slowly dying before they came and things have improved. But Leanne is dead against it. Both the solar farms and the coal mine and what they do to the landscape. She lost her fight against the mine when it was first proposed, but since the solar farms are taking more and more land around the town, she's become very vocal about the damage she says they cause. When they made the first approach, she refused to let them on her property.'

'So, she wouldn't be popular with those in town who see the development as good for Bowen River?' I said with a frown.

'You can say that again. She's made some enemies, that's for sure. She got herself into a bit of trouble at the pub a couple of weeks back.'

'Does she go to the pub much?'

'Don't get me wrong, she didn't go there to socialise. She went there to drum up support for her group and came up against some aggressive workers one night.'

'Does Sergeant Lovatt know about this?'

'No, she played it down. Since Leanne's parents passed,

she's become very private.'

I nodded. 'Tell me some more about her ex-partner. And did she have any other boyfriends?'

'In a word? Randall Simms is a low-life. I don't know how she ever got tangled up with him. It was around the time that both her parents passed within a few months of each other. She'd lost her grandfather not long before that, and she was really close to him. I think she was lonely, and Simms came on the scene. A really good-looking bloke with the values of a jellyfish. Sergeant Lovatt knows all about him. And no, no others that I'm aware of, but like I said, Leanne is a very private person.'

'Okay, thank you. Has she mentioned Simms being around lately?'

'No. Look, I could be overreacting, and she may have had somewhere to go, and the school said the kids are there, so maybe I'm worrying unnecessarily.' Jean Purdue held my eyes, and I could see the concern in hers. 'But it's just not like her. I'm going with my gut feeling. It's never let me down before.'

I wasn't going to tell her that she wasn't the only one with concerns. 'As soon as we make contact with her, we'll let you know.'

'Thank you.'

'One last question. What's her mood been like over the last few weeks? Has she seemed worried about anything?'

'Oh God, yes. She's totally focused on hanging onto her land. It's all she talks about, and she's got herself all worked up. But if you're thinking suicide, don't even go there. She's a good woman and a damn good mother to those kids considering what she's been through.' My question must have annoyed her as her tone became defensive. 'If I'd been able to get out there, I would have driven out there to check myself, and I wouldn't have bothered the police. But I had no one to man the office, and we're full this week.'

'I'm pleased you contacted us. I think I've got enough information here, so we'll go out to her place and get back to you as soon as we establish what's going on. Thanks so much for your concern, Mrs Purdue.'

'Thanks, love. I'm sorry I got a bit snippy with you. It's good to have a local back in town. You were always a good kid, and I admired how you always smiled despite living in that house.'

I knew she didn't mean the old building I'd grown up in. My father hadn't been well-liked in town, and I'm sure that was one of the reasons the church attendance had dropped off, and the Presbytery had closed the local church.

'Thank you,' I said. 'It's good to be working in Bowen River.'

I headed back to the car, ready to take the trip out to Valentine's Road.

Chapter 9

Strathallyn Station, 1925.
Elspeth

When she heard the Model T Ford turn into the circular driveway at the front of their homestead, Elspeth stood, brushed down her clean dress, patted her hair to make sure it was neat, and then she went to the kitchen to put the kettle on the hob.

Thanks to Mr Delaney, she even had time to take out the cake that she'd made before her ride. It had turned out perfectly which was most unusual for her. Her cooking was rarely successful—much to Mother's disapproval—it must be the new gas stove that Father had installed for Mrs Revesby last month. Elspeth's hands shook as she sliced the apple cake and arranged some slices daintily on one of Mother's fine china serving plates. She would be the lady of the manor this afternoon, on her best behaviour, praying that Mr Delaney would keep her secret.

Elspeth knew exactly who he was now. She had entirely forgotten about the new horse trainer who was arriving this week. There had been several new workers on the station over the past year. Her father was very much involved in the new Soldier Settlers' Scheme and was often on the train, going down to Sydney or Melbourne and away for weeks as the federal government tried to nut out a new scheme that was going to provide opportunities and gratitude to the people who had defended their country in the Great War.

Over the past few months, two stock riders had settled on land at the back of the station. Father had divided one of the back blocks of the station into four one-thousand-acre blocks, and two of those had been allocated to the two stock riders. Perhaps Mr Delaney was going to take up one of the others.

Elspeth wondered how successful the land grants would be because the blocks that had been portioned off were away from the river. Granted, there were a couple of dams down there, but as soon as the rain stopped, those dams dried up very quickly in the northern heat. She had also heard him speak to Mother about the soldiers having no experience on the land.

But she trusted her father. He knew what he was doing, and his heart was well and truly in the right place. He was very proud that he had been able to hire a returned soldier as his lead horse trainer. He had spoken highly of Mr Delaney, and Elspeth had not taken much notice.

Her heart beat faster than usual. A pleasant shiver ran down her back as that strong face came to her thoughts. Nor could she forget the feel of Mr Delaney's hands on her arms. Even though he had gripped her firmly, in hindsight, he had been gentle with her and unfailingly polite.

But she was now in his debt. And she wondered how he would expect her to honour that debt.

When she ran to the house, Mr Delaney led Blue around to the stables. After hurrying up the front steps and taking them two at a time in a most unladylike manner, she looked along the road from the high verandah at the front of the homestead and let out a sigh of great relief. The car was still a good two miles away. She flew down the hall, filled a jug with cold water, tore off her riding clothes and pushed them out of sight beneath her bed. She placed a cool flannel on her face to take the rosiness from her cheeks. Her hair had been full of grass and twigs, and she managed to pull them out and drop them through her open window before she put on her best dress.

Heat filled her face as she thought of Mr Delaney looking at her. She must have looked like a tomboy.

Five minutes later, she was in the kitchen setting out the afternoon tea. Mother would frown when she saw there were no dainty sandwiches, but that displeasure was a hundred times better than her father's ire would be if he found out she had been out on Blue.

Elspeth walked out onto the veranda and stood demurely with her hand on the top stair post as he helped Mother out of the front of the car.

Her mother looked up at her with a smile. 'Hello, sweetheart.

It's good to be home. You look lovely.'

'It's good to have you home too, Mother. How's Auntie Kathleen?'

Her mother walked up the steps, and Elspeth smothered a grin, thinking about how she had raced up them not fifteen minutes before.

'She's good. The new baby is much better behaved than Neville was. I don't think I'll have to go back for a while.' She reached the top step, leaned over and kissed Elspeth's cheek.

Mother frowned. 'You're not catching a chill, are you? You're very warm.'

'No . . . yes, I'm well. I mean, no, I'm not ill. I was pouring the boiling water into the teapot when I heard you arrive.' Elspeth stumbled over her reply.

She linked her arm with her mother's, and they walked down the hall together as Father unpacked the bags from the car.

'What have you been doing with yourself all week? I hope you haven't been out in the heat.'

'I finished my embroidery. That doily with the English garden. Now I'd like you to teach me how to tat a lace edge on it. I baked you an apple cake this morning, and it is actually edible! I was just reading the paper when I heard the car coming, and I put the kettle on to boil. I knew you'd love a cup of tea. It's a long drive from Bowen, and it is very hot today. Oh, and I went for a ride this morning.'

Guilt had started to prickle her neck. She might as well tell a little bit of the truth.

'Can I smell cake?' Her father's footsteps paused in the hall for a moment as he put Mother's bags in their room, and then he appeared in the kitchen doorway. 'Oh, good stuff. Apple cake.'

'Your favourite, I know.' Elspeth smiled. 'Oh, Dad, I was down at the stables earlier. There's a man there waiting to see you. Delaney, he said his name was.'

'He's a day early,' Father said. 'I'll just go down and see him before I have a cuppa.'

'What about your cup of tea and cake?' Elspeth tried to delay him in case Blue was still being sponged down. 'I've already made the tea.'

'No. It was rude that I wasn't here when he arrived. I won't be long.' He looked across at her mother as Elspeth tried to think of another delaying ruse. 'Would it be appropriate if I brought Mr Delaney up for a cup of tea, dear? When I met him in Ayr, he seemed to be quite a gentleman.'

'That would be a kind welcome for him, Jack. Elspeth, I'll unpack my case and have a bit of a wash before I have mine, too. We can make a fresh pot, and we'll move to the dining room.'

'No, the kitchen will be fine, Amelia. I'll be back shortly.'

Elspeth's heart thudded as she stood on the veranda and

watched her father walk across to the stables. They were quite close to the homestead. 'Wait. I'll come down to the stables with you,' she called after him.

'No, help your mother unpack. I'll be back with Mr Delaney in a few minutes.'

'I hope he's washed the dirt off his face,' she muttered under her breath.

As he was almost to the stables, Thomas Delaney walked around the side of the building with Billy at his heels. She watched as her father shook hands with him.

Elspeth groaned. Father stood talking to the newcomer and pointed across the paddock, and Billy scampered off.

So far, so good. Father didn't look cross.

Yet.

Elspeth jumped as her mother spoke beside her. 'Come on, we'll freshen up the pot. Here they come.' She gestured for Elspeth to follow her. Mother was halfway down the hall, and Elspeth stopped in the doorway and craned her neck, looking down the driveway.

Her father was smiling as they walked towards the house.

'Thank you for making the cake, sweetheart. Did you have any trouble using the new oven without Mrs Revesby?' Mother stopped and turned when Elspeth didn't answer. 'What are you looking at?'

'Nothing.' Elspeth hurried down the hall.

'I'm quite hungry. It's such a slow trip on the train from Rockhampton to Bowen, but I had a couple of newspapers to read, and the scenery was quite nice. I took notice of the distance this time, and I figured out where our property is at Marlborough. We'll have to go down there and look at the homestead one day. I believe it is a fine house. Perhaps when you marry, you and your husband could look after that property.'

Elspeth certainly wasn't going to cause any dissension this afternoon. 'Perhaps,' she said as footsteps sounded on the front stairs, and her heart lodged in her throat.

##

A rough railing topped the fence at the end of the racecourse that Father had built a mile away from the house. The long, low building behind her provided accommodation for the manager, the horse trainer and the stable hands, but Elspeth kept away from it as she walked across to the track. She'd managed to stay out of trouble in the five days since Mother had arrived home. Mr Delaney had been true to his word, and Billy hadn't mentioned her riding Blue. The afternoon tea in the kitchen had been pleasant enough. Mother stayed in her good dress and greeted Mr Delaney warmly.

'Welcome to *Strathallyn Station*, Mr Delaney.'

'Thank you, Mrs Valentine. You have a beautiful

homestead. I love these high Queensland houses.' His voice was deep and had a slight lilt, and Elspeth wondered where he was from.

Once they'd drunk their tea, exchanged social pleasantries, and commented on the excellent cake, Mother had excused them. 'Come, Elspeth, we'll leave your father and Mr Delaney to talk. Come for a walk around the garden with me. I want to see if my seedlings have survived this heat.'

Elspeth had jumped up, collected Mother's and her cup and plate, and carried them to the sink. When she turned, Mr Delaney was staring at her. He glanced at her father, but he was telling Mother about the wallabies that had eaten the new shoots from her plants. Mr Delaney looked straight back at her, his eyes full of laughter. She held his gaze, and her cheeks heated when he winked at her. The hide of him!

But Elspeth couldn't stop thinking about Thomas Delaney. She'd had no good reason to go to the stable for the past five days, and on several occasions, she'd found herself on the veranda looking to see if she could see him. She'd been rewarded with a glimpse one morning when he'd ridden Blue past the house and had been disappointed when he hadn't noticed her.

Father's latest horseflesh acquisition arrived on a truck late yesterday. He'd talked of nothing other than his new horse for the last week.

'He was foaled in 1912, out of Miss Babbie. She was a brown mare by St Sirius, a son of the legendary St Gregory, and her maternal pedigree can be traced back to Lady Babir. The mare was served by Miston, who's won several English Derbys. Babir Boy came over in the *SS Persic* along with ten other thoroughbreds. I've had my eye on him for six months.'

Elspeth held back her giggle as Mother's eyes glazed over. Once upon a time, she would have admonished her father for talking about the breeding in front of Elspeth, but Mother had finally accepted that her daughter was as interested in horses as her father.

But perhaps not in as much detail as he was, Elspeth thought.

Father handed the stallion over to Mr Delaney as he had to attend a board meeting at Bowen Hospital today. Mother had decided to go to town with him to shop, and Elspeth relished her day of freedom.

But I will stay away from Blue. She'd take Bandy, her mare, out for a ride to the billabong. She climbed the rail, crossed her arms on the rough timber, and watched as the new horse thundered past with Mr Delaney on his back.

He was *good*. Elspeth knew her horses well, and that one was a fine animal, but even more so, she appreciated the way the new trainer was riding him. Crouched low on the neck of the animal, his hair whipped up in the wind, she could see his grin as they raced past. They circled the track twice more, and Elspeth wasn't surprised when Mr Delaney cantered across to where she stood, resting her arms on the rail.

There was no doubt Thomas Delaney was a very handsome man. His raven-black hair fell across his face. His skin was fairer than usual for a man who worked outside. He looked as though he hadn't ever worked in the sun at all. Perhaps he'd worked at a racecourse in the city and spent most of his time inside the stables. Or perhaps he'd come from a southern state?

The one time she'd asked Father about him—or more about his experience than the man—he had been preoccupied and not been forthcoming with any information. She hadn't wanted to seem too curious, so she let it go.

She jumped as a warm nose nuzzled her hands. Babir Boy had walked quietly up to her, and she hadn't noticed.

'Good morning, Miss Valentine.' That *voice*.

'Good morning, Mr Delaney. He is a fine specimen. My father was very disappointed he had to go to Bowen today.' Elspeth ignored the warm shiver that had run down her back.

She waited as the stallion sniffed at her pockets, and she turned them out. 'Sorry boy, I haven't got anything with me today, and I don't know if I'd be allowed to give you a treat anyway.'

'He can have a reward. He was perfect to ride.'

'I don't have anything. Some of the horse trainers that Father had before wouldn't let me bring treats down to the field, so I've got out of the habit. None of them stay long out here, so I guess you won't either.'

Mr Delaney slid off the horse and looped the reins over the fence post. In one lithe movement, he put one hand on top of the railing and before Elspeth realised what he was doing, he'd climbed over and was standing beside her.

His demeanour was confident, but the confidence didn't seem to stay with him. His head was held high, but as she watched closely, his shoulders bowed, and then he dropped his head. He took a deep breath but didn't speak again as he looked at the ground.

Perhaps she'd overstepped the mark by making assumptions about him.

She hesitated, wondering whether to stay and talk to him or whether to go back to the house. He lifted his head and looked at her, a strange expression on his face.

Her experience with young men—although he was certainly not a *young* man—had been limited. There were very few around *Strathallyn Station*, and when the country dances were held in the hall at Bowen River, Mother had always said that it was beneath them to attend.

A slow smile crossed Mr Delaney's lips as he looked at her,

and she realised for the first time who he reminded her of. When Miss Edmonds had taught them about the Romantic Poets, she had told them how she imagined what the poets would look like. 'Raven black hair, fair skin, and lips made for reciting poetry, ladies. Anyone who writes poetry like the Romantics must look like that,' she'd said. Elspeth had been very disappointed when she found a photo of William Wordsworth in the school library at All Hallows. He didn't look romantic at all.

She looked up at Mr Delaney, wondering if those lips had ever recited poetry.

'So, Miss Valentine, I was hoping that perhaps you would ride with me today and show me around the station. Would that be acceptable to you? Or would you prefer your own company?'

Elspeth couldn't help herself. She smiled and recited:

'O Solitude! if I must with thee dwell,

Let it not be among the jumbled heap

Of murky buildings; climb with me the steep, —'

A warm voice joined hers and she met his eyes as he recited the next lines of Keats' *Solitude* with her.

'Nature's observatory—whence the dell,

Its flowery slopes, its river's crystal swell.'

'Oh, my goodness,' she said. 'You know Keats' poetry?'

Elspeth widened her eyes.

'Know and love,' Mr Delaney said. 'Does that mean that you

will spend the day with me, even though our autumn is not quite Keats' "*season of mists and mellow fruitfulness*"?'

'Autumn is my favourite season.' This time, she grinned at him. 'Shall I pack a picnic lunch and take you to the most beautiful place on *Strathallyn*?'

Chapter 10

Bowen River - Wednesday 4.30 p.m.
Bec

Sergeant Lovatt looked up as I walked back into the station. 'I sent Aaron down to grab a burger. I've asked him to keep the station open until we get back. I know the word is around town. How did you go?'

'Interesting.' I hung the keys of the Stinger on the board. 'I can see that Leanne may have made some enemies in a few places. The company, the workers, and the community who support the economy of the solar farms and maybe the mine. Also, Mrs Purdue had nothing good to say about Simms, her ex, and she wasn't aware of any new partner on the scene.'

'Leanne has been a strong opponent of solar farms in the region, and the local support has varied. She's done her research and provided some very good arguments.' Mark nodded as Aaron came in, the aroma of hamburger and chips wafting in with him. 'Thanks for being so quick, Aaron. We'll take the Outlander, Bec. Are you happy to drive?

I wondered if it was a test of my driving skills or if he was just pulling rank.

'Sure.' My stomach grumbled as the smell of hot chips filled the room, and I ignored it as the sergeant grabbed the keys from the board and headed to the door.

'I want to be back by six, Aaron, and we'll see if any more information comes in. Just take contact details and jot down anything relevant. If they want to come back, use my diary to make appointments tomorrow. If you hear anything urgent, radio us.'

'Will do, Sergeant Lovatt.'

I followed Mark down the ramp to the Outlander. He clicked it open with the remote and handed me the keys.

'Aaron seems good for a new PC,' I commented once I was in the driver's seat.

'He is. Keen, efficient and bloody organised. He's solely responsible for the tidiness of the public area. He keeps it up to date and even bought the pot plant at the hardware to "improve the ambience," as he said. Mind you, the plant hit the dirt, if you'll pardon the pun when we had a bit of a stoush in there last Friday night. Only the second time I've used the lockup since I've been here.'

'Locals?

'Some. The pub has got pretty rough since the workers have come to town. The mines and the solar plant have stirred up quite a bit of angst in town.'

I backed out of the station and headed down Main Street past the pub. It seemed quiet, and there were only a couple of work utes parked outside. I wondered if Gray was still in the bar, and hoped to hell he wouldn't come looking for me when he ran out of money. Again, I considered telling Mark about him, and again, I pushed it away.

The problem was Bowen River was such a bloody small town that everyone would know my business by breakfast if Gray opened his mouth.

'You know the way out to Valentine's Road?' Mark asked once we were past the pub.

'Yeah. I used to come out here when I was a kid. I guess the road out is still the same one.'

Leanne had asked me to come out and stay one weekend, and I knew it was because she found it so boring staying at the manse. Dad wouldn't approve an overnight stay, but I was allowed out on a Saturday afternoon for three hours until he played the Catholic card. I could picture the gate where Leanne would have waited for her kids because Dad would park there right on the dot of four to pick me up in the afternoon, and woe betide if I was a minute late. That would end in a lecture on godliness all the way back to town. Romans 14:12 was a popular one: *"So then each of us will give an account of himself to God."*

Mark glanced across at me. 'Yep, I can't see the road out would have changed. There's nothing out here. It's quite isolated these days, and the phone service is patchy unless you have a satellite connection. Leanne's place is a fair way out.'

My respect for Mark was growing, even though it was only my first day at the station. I felt comfortable with him, and I liked the way he treated Aaron, a new probationary constable.

'Mrs Purdue seemed convinced that Leanne is missing,' I said. 'She said she was slightly worried yesterday, but when she didn't turn up today, she knew something was wrong. Tell me more about this solar farm stuff. She said that Leanne's been made a good offer for her place.'

'Yes, she's mentioned that at a few of the community meetings I've attended. It's different to mining. I believe she was on a committee that tried to stop Trieste Coal a few years back—it was before my time here—but the legislation is different for mining.'

'She must have been young,' I murmured half to myself.

'Yes. Anyway, I'm sure you're aware that in Australia, coal, petroleum, and mineral resources are generally the property of the Crown rather than the landholder. With underground resources on land, the power to licence and regulate their development lies with the states.'

'Yes, I'm aware of the legislation. One of my friends in Brisbane is a lawyer, and he specialises in that area. The state grants a licence to a person or corporation to explore and potentially develop underground energy and mineral resources. He had some sad stories about fifth-generation farmers who lost their properties.'

'That's right, and in effect, it transfers the property rights in the resources from the state to the licence holder. The coal mine wasn't too bad out here because the land the company took over was pretty much worthless for grazing or agriculture. The solar farms to the west of town are a different story, and Leanne has a lot of our local community on her side. There are a few other groups around the state who've been coming to the community meetings from as far away as Biloela and Childers.'

'How are they different? I don't know a lot about them.' The automatic gearbox dropped back a gear as the vehicle negotiated a steep hill. From the top, we got a panoramic view of the valley out to Suttor Causeway. I drew a breath. 'You know, I didn't appreciate how pretty this was when I was a kid.'

'It is. Sheree and I did a drive one weekend out to the heritage causeways before the road washed away last summer. It's a beautiful place, that's for sure, and I can understand Leanne's—and others'—objections. Wait until you see the first solar panels out here.'

About ten kilometres out of town, a flash on the right caught my eye, and I couldn't help my exclamation as we passed an array of solar panels. Acre after acre of them.

'Shit. Sorry. I had no idea they covered so much land.'

'Apparently, the property has been in her family for a long time,' Mark said.

'I imagine that would make it hard,' I said. Even though I had no personal concept of belonging to a place, I could empathise. 'What are the main environmental issues?'

'Quite a few. I knew nothing about solar farms until I went to the first meeting, and it was an eye-opener. I'm starting to believe that renewable energy isn't as good as it's being made out to be. Chemical runoff to the water table, the impact of air temperature in an already dry environment, fire hazard, and the risk of damage to neighbouring properties in case of catastrophic weather events.'

'Political spin and wealth for offshore countries?' I raised my eyebrows.

Mark nodded. 'You're getting the gist of it. The committee has even raised the need for a larger police presence in the region due to the increased volume of traffic. And we both know the chance of that. We've already seen social issues escalate with the growth in workers who come from outside the district.'

I slowed as I recognised the T-intersection to Valentine's Road ahead and glanced down at the navigation screen. The map confirmed my instinct to take the left turn. 'Not far now.'

I caught my breath as we descended the hill. The land out

here was in the lee of the western foothills of the Great Dividing Range. We'd left behind the dry yellow grass, but I knew from a school excursion back in the day that the land further west deteriorated into dry plains. I shook my head, and Mark frowned.

'What's wrong?'

'Nothing. I'd forgotten all about a geography excursion out here when I was in year nine or ten.'

'Your local knowledge is going to be a real asset to the station.' He pointed ahead. 'Is that the gate to her place?'

I recognised the front gate. A climbing rose grew wild with flowering yellow honeysuckle over an arch beside the main gate. I remembered the long driveway that led to the house that sat in a dip at the bottom of a hill beside a creek. You could just see the house from the gate.

'Looks like fairly recent tyre tracks in the dust,' Mark observed.

I looked ahead and nodded as we drove over the crest of the hill and I looked down at the green paddocks surrounding the house. A few cows grazed at the creek side, and the water glinted in the late afternoon sunshine. A small red sedan was parked beside the house; when I left town, I don't think Leanne even had her licence.

'Is that Leanne's car?' I asked.

'I don't know what she drives. I'll run the plate.'

Mark stayed in the driver's seat, focused on his iPad that was linked to the QPS system as he checked the number plate against the database. His face was set in a steady expression, the kind that let you know he'd been on enough of these calls to make calm his default setting.

Outside of work, I could imagine him being gentle, even kind—but here, he was all business.

The lines around his eyes deepened as he stared at the screen. He was thorough and methodical, fingers moving quickly. Even though I'd only known him a short time, my respect for him was growing. Maybe this job would override the difficulty of being back in town.

Mark tapped his iPad a few times; finally, he glanced up, a slight frown creasing his forehead. 'Yes,' he confirmed, his voice steady. 'Leanne Kerry Delaney, and registered to this address.'

I let out a slow breath, staring at the car in the late afternoon light. It was jarring, almost surreal, to see the car that belonged to the adult Leanne I'd never known. Leanne had once been a big part of my life. But when I'd left Bowen River, I left it all behind—the people, the memories, the small-town routines. I'd tried to erase it, to cut myself loose from the memories that lingered, most of them cast by my father's rigid expectations and constant scrutiny.

Growing up, his rules wrapped around me so tightly I could hardly breathe. I'd clung to the things that gave me a sense of freedom, like school and my friends, but even they'd been under his watchful eye. When I left, I didn't look back. I'd moved to the city and buried Bowen River so deep that even the good memories were left behind, Leanne included.

But now, as I sat there staring at the house I'd visited as a teenager, I felt the consequence of my choice—a sharp pang of regret. I'd let those friendships go too easily without a second thought; I'd abandoned a decent part of myself, too.

Mark glanced at me curiously. 'Nervous?'

'No, just thinking. Memories,' I replied, feeling the familiar knot tighten in my stomach. 'I'm ready.'

He opened the door, and I followed, automatically reaching up to press the activation button on my body camera. A quiet click confirmed it was recording.

'Body camera on,' I said, as per protocol.

Mark gave a quick nod. 'Mine too. Let's keep everything recorded.' He met my eyes briefly, then motioned towards the house.

'Procedure, Sergeant?' I asked.

'Are you familiar with the new procedures since that incident out near Dalby?'

'I'm well aware of them.' I knew exactly what he was

talking about. Since that horrendous incident, we'd all been super vigilant when we went out on calls, whether it was in the city or the country. I knew human nature could turn dark in an instant.

'Stay alert, and remember, no assumptions. We'll wait by the car for a minute to see if anyone comes out.' Mark slowly scanned the area from left to right as I kept my eyes on the house. There was no movement and no sign of life.

'You keep an eye out while I check the car,' he said. My stomach churned as I waited beside the car, my hand on my gun.

He walked over to the car, looked inside and touched the bonnet. 'It's slightly warm.'

'The front door's open.'

'Okay, you take the front door, and I'll go around the back,' Mark said. 'Be vigilant.'

As I walked quietly up the two wooden steps to the small porch, a dog started barking down near the sheds at the back of the house. I stood at the door and called out. 'Police. Is there anybody home? Leanne?'

Silence.

The front door was open, and there was no screen door, which surprised me. There were snakes out here. I reached in and knocked loudly on the open wooden door and called again, 'Leanne? Are you home?'

The dog started barking again, and another one joined in, this time with a deeper, more ferocious bark. The barking sounded aggressive, as if someone was down there; they must have spotted Mark going around the back. I tipped my head to the side, listening. A sound drifted out from inside; for a moment, it sounded as though there was paper rustling inside one of the rooms.

A wind had sprung up, and a sheer curtain was blowing through the open front window. I could see right to the back of the house; the back door was open too, but there was no sign of Mark yet. As I looked down the hall, another door swung shut with an ominous creak.

Was it the wind?

Or was someone there?

Where was Mark? He should have appeared at the back door by now. The hall led straight through the house to the back door at the far end. I remembered running down that hall. On hot days, the timber was warm beneath our feet. We'd put our togs on in Leanne's room and then rush down the hall, out the back door and down the steps to run to the creek.

I took a step into the hall, paused and listened. Nothing. Silence again.

I walked slowly down the hall; the hallstand was still there, a variety of hats and caps hanging off the six hooks. A jumble of papers and keys filled the narrow shelf beneath them.

Along the hall, all the doors were open; the one that had slammed shut was the door to the bathroom at the end. I stood at each door and looked into each room. Beds were unmade in three of the rooms, and clothes were scattered on the floor. The main bedroom—where her parents had slept—was tidy; the bed was neatly made with pretty cushions against the pillows. A desk with a computer sat beneath the window.

'Leanne? Are you home?' I called as I approached the closed bathroom door.

Maybe she was in the bathroom and that's why the bathroom door closed.

Anxiety was clawing at my stomach as I neared the closed door, with no sign of Mark yet. My pulse drummed in my ears, each step forward tightening the unease in my chest. I hovered in front of the door, palms damp, a queasy twist forming low in my belly.

Should I wait here? Or go outside and walk around the back? I took a step back as indecision took hold—but the silence stretched out as all sorts of scenarios flashed through my mind.

I swallowed, brushing off the fear with a shaky, indrawn breath.

Don't be ridiculous, I told myself. Mark was around the back. There was no point yelling for him when there was nothing there.

A great first impression that would make.

But as I reached for the door, I was angry at myself to see my hand shaking. I pushed it open, but the room was empty. The window was open; that's why it had slammed shut. I went back to the hall and moved slowly towards the kitchen, glancing into each room, but there was still no sign of anyone there.

Or Mark.

The living room was on the left, and my eyes widened. I stepped into the room. Dirty plates, cups, and empty food packets littered the floor. I kept walking until I reached the kitchen. A milk carton lay on its side on the floor and the milk had congealed into a yellow sour mess. Empty biscuit packets lay on the floor beside it.

I took out my phone and took a photo of the kitchen before I stepped back into the hall to photograph the bedrooms and living room. My gut was telling me something was wrong. The back door was open, but I was still alone in the house.

Maybe Mark had seen someone near the sheds on his way to the back door. The dogs had stopped barking. I'd go out the front way, walk around to the back and find him.

I was almost to the front door when a slither of movement broke the silence. I went to spin around, my right hand reaching for my gun, but my hand was grabbed before I reached it, and my arm twisted so hard I waited to hear the bone snap. Tears sprang to my eyes as my hair was grabbed, and my head jerked back almost at right angles to my spine. As I looked to the ceiling, something dark came down towards my head, and an excruciating pain blasted through my ears, my eyes, and my neck, and the pain was the last thing I knew.

Chapter 11

Bowen River - Wednesday, 6.30 p.m.
Bec

Despite my protestations that I was fine, Sergeant Lovatt insisted that he call an ambulance and have me checked out before we went back to town.

'I'm fine,' I said. 'I've got a bit of a headache, and I can get checked out when we get back.'

He shook his head. 'Not on my watch.'

The first thing I'd been aware of when I opened my eyes was a large shadow looming over me where I lay on the timber floor beneath the hallstand. I didn't know how long I'd been out. I gasped, but a gentle hand touched my shoulder.

'It's okay. It's me. Mark. Don't move,' the sergeant said as I tried to sit up. I put my hand to my head, and it came away wet.

'It's blood,' he said as he crouched beside me. 'You've got a good bump on the side of your head.' He looked around. 'Who was it? What did you see?'

'I don't know. I was going out the front door after checking the house, and he came at me from behind. He must have been behind one of the doors.'

'He?' he asked grimly.

'I'm just assuming. I don't know. Go and find him. I'll be fine.'

'As soon as I make sure you're safe. I took the keys out of Leanne's car as I came back around the front. He can't get far. I'll call for help from Collinsville.'

'I'm fine, go.'

The sergeant's firm hands steadied my head as he tilted it back, checking my pupils. His fingers pressed gently on the sore spot near my temple, and I hissed involuntarily, the sting sharper than I expected.

'Sorry, Bec,' he muttered, pulling his hand back slightly. His gaze was steady, reassuring. 'What day is it?'

I blinked, needing a second to focus. 'Wednesday.'

'And where are we?'

I glanced around, registering the familiar hallstand. 'Leanne Delaney's place,' I said, keeping my tone even, even though I could feel the throbbing behind my eyes intensifying. 'I'm fine, Sarge.'

He didn't answer; he just studied me for a few more seconds.

'Okay, if you're okay here alone, I'll look for him.'

Before he could move, a distant but familiar sound caught our ears—a car engine revving hard.

Mark turned, and in one smooth movement, he was up and

at the door, his eyes narrowing as he looked out.

'What is it?' I asked, pushing up on my elbows.

'A vehicle coming out of the shed,' he said, his voice clipped. 'Stay there.' He shot me an assessing look, brief but intense, then seeing that I was okay, Mark took off outside, his gun in one hand, phone in the other.

Frustration vied with common sense. I wanted to be out there, so I forced myself to sit up slowly, brushing off the lingering dizziness, and listened to the car roar past, catching only the faint hum of the engine as it gradually faded away.

A couple of minutes later, Mark came back inside, his expression unreadable when he saw me leaning against the wall. His gaze met mine, concerned, before he spoke.

'You should have followed him,' I said weakly.

'Stay right here. I've called the paramedics. They're on the way.'

'I'm all right,' I insisted, sitting up straighter and ignoring the pounding in my head. 'Who was that? What sort of car?'

His jaw tightened, and he hesitated just a fraction too long. 'Don't worry about it. Just sit tight.'

'Don't worry about it?' I echoed, dragging myself up, gripping the leg of the hallstand, ignoring the slight sway of my vision. 'It was probably the person who clocked me.' As I stood, the hallstand rocked, and all the hats fell onto the floor. I bent down to pick them up, and the room spun so much I thought I was going to vomit.

'Leave them,' he said. The flicker of frustration in his eyes told me what I already knew; I was being foolish, and that wouldn't help the situation one bit. He opened his mouth as if to say something more but stopped short.

'Look, Bec, you're concussed. We need to get you checked out,' he said finally, his voice softening just a notch.

'Just tell me what's going on,' I said, lowering my voice and matching his tone. 'Did you see who it was?'

'No, but it was a white ute I saw in the shed. I felt the bonnet, and the engine was cold. He must have hidden in the house when he heard us pull up.'

'No sign of Leanne or anyone else?'

Mark shook his head. 'No, I think he might have been driving her car before. I'm just so bloody frustrated. We're so under-resourced. I can't call Aaron and get him to wait for the offender to go through town. I've called Collinsville and asked for support, but there's only the desk sergeant on duty. The sergeant and the other constable have gone down to Bowen to the races tonight.'

'What sort of car?' I persisted.

He exhaled, his shoulders slumping slightly as he made a decision. 'A white Mazda ute. BT50. An older one knocked around. With no bloody plates,' he muttered, glancing at the door as if he expected someone to be listening. 'He must have hit you and then waited until I came up the side to the front and then raced out the back door back to the shed. I should have been more observant. I'm sorry, Bec. I should have come straight to the house, but I thought I heard a noise down the back. That's what got me down there.'

The knot in my stomach tightened. I focused on my breathing. 'It's okay. I'm fine, and at least we've got a car to chase up. It would have been a lot worse if he'd been in the shed when you went in.'

***

After checking me over, the paramedics loaded me onto the stretcher, and the bright lights inside the ambulance made my head throb harder. I could barely keep my eyes open against the pain, and every jolt and bump on the dirt road on the way to the health centre in town felt like nails being hammered into my skull.

By the time we arrived, my vision was still slightly blurry, and even turning my head left me feeling dizzy. The doctor's face swam above me, asking me questions I could hardly focus on. He checked my pulse, shone a light in my eyes, and muttered something about 'classic signs of a concussion.'

'We'll need to keep you in emergency overnight, Senior

Constable,' he said, scribbling notes as he glanced at my chart.

'Just my luck,' I muttered, mostly to myself, closing my eyes briefly to try to settle the spinning room. 'Is the sergeant still out there?' I managed to ask.

'Yes, he's in the waiting room. I'll send him in.'

Mark was in there within seconds of the doctor leaving.

'I'm pleased they're keeping you in,' he said.

'I'm not,' I snapped. 'Can you do something for me, please?'

'What's that?' he asked.

'Ring my mother and—'

'Yes, I'll let her know you're okay,' he offered, eyeing me cautiously.

'No, don't tell her I'm in hospital. Just say I'm . . . working late. All night. She'll worry if she knows.' My voice sounded weaker than I wanted, and I winced at how easily Mark picked up on it, his expression softening.

'Right . . . working late,' he repeated, eyebrow raised but eventually nodding. 'I understand.'

I looked at him, feeling totally useless.

The doctor came back in and clipped the chart on the end of the bed. He cleared his throat, breaking the silence between us. 'Concussion,' he confirmed, in a tone that allowed no room for protest. 'She stays here tonight. Head injuries can be tricky; we need to monitor her.'

'I want to go back to work tomorrow,' I said to the doctor. 'I have to. We're under-resourced.'

A glimmer of a smile tilted Mark's lips. 'You can come back when the doctor clears you.' He looked across at the doctor. 'John, is it okay if I fill Bec in on some developments?'

'Yes, it is,' I interjected before the doctor could reply. God, Mark was going to think his new senior constable was a shrew, but I wanted to know what was going on. Knowing Leanne made this more personal for me.

The doctor nodded at Mark and walked across to the next cubicle.

'What's happened? Honestly, Sergeant, I'm fine, feeling better every minute.'

Mark ran his hand over his hair. 'I've put an APB out for the car. Couldn't run any plates, of course. But I know it; I'm sure I've seen it in town, and I'm trying to remember where.'

I felt my stomach twist with frustration. First day on the job, and I end up here, concussed and useless in a hospital bed. I bit down on my lip, swallowing a wave of anger, and felt Mark's eyes on me.

'I'm sorry,' he said, his voice quiet. 'You didn't deserve this, Bec. No one should be attacked on their first day.'

I managed a smile to relieve the shrewishness of my attitude. 'Really? Only on the second day?'

'You know what I meant.'

I met his gaze, trying to ignore the ache behind my eyes. 'It's not your fault. I should've been more vigilant,' I replied, my voice hoarse with annoyance at myself.

He nodded, but I could see a flicker of worry in his eyes. 'I've also rung the detectives in Bowen and asked them to come up tonight instead of tomorrow. We need to get moving on this fast. I'm worried about Leanne.'

'Yeah,' I said softly, trying to ignore the creeping sense of dread that settled into my bones. 'Me too.'

'I'm going to see the kids now.' Mark gave me one last nod and headed for the door, leaving me alone in the sterile quiet of the cubicle, the beeps and hums of medical equipment the only sounds in the darkening room.

Chapter 12
Thursday - 7.00 am

Mark sent Aaron to pick me up when I called him early the next morning, as soon as the doctor said I could go.

The doctor finished his examination, his gaze steady as he checked my pulse one more time and made a final note in his chart. 'Well, Senior Constable Whitfield,' he said, giving me a slight smile, 'I'd say you're in the clear. The concussion symptoms have eased significantly, and your vitals are strong. It looks like that good night's rest did you a favour.'

He set down his stethoscope and folded his arms, giving me a serious look. 'However, just because you're feeling better doesn't mean you're ready to go back to full duties straight away. Rest is still essential. Take it easy today, and keep an eye out for any returning symptoms—dizziness, headaches, sleepiness, or anything unusual. If any of that occurs, you get yourself straight back here. They'll give you a fact sheet of what to watch for at the desk as you leave.'

I nodded, relieved. 'Understood. Thanks, Doctor Lane.'

He softened, giving me a knowing look. 'Good. You're free to go, but I'd recommend you keep things low-key for the next twenty-four hours. You're not entirely out of the woods yet, and a little extra caution now can go a long way.'

The drive back to the station was quiet, the dry grass and the streets flashing by, a blur through my still-aching eyes. I kept a hand on my head, trying to stave off the throbbing behind my temples. Rest was a luxury I couldn't afford—not with a missing person and a violent offender on the loose. If there was more manpower at the station, I would have stayed in my new residence and taken the day off, but I knew I could help. I could sit all day and do some research online. Every extra person would help. I'd seen too many cases where delays had resulted in the offender fleeing and often not being caught.

We needed to find Leanne and see if she was alright.

When I walked inside, Mark looked up from his desk, his face a mix of concern and relief. 'Good to see you on your feet, Bec. How are you feeling?'

'A bit battered,' I admitted, leaning against the counter to steady myself. 'But I'll survive. I'm going home for a quick shower, but I'll be back as soon as I can. I'm fine—just need to shake off the hospital smell.'

He gave a small nod, his eyes lingering on me as if he wanted to say more. Finally, he sighed. 'I'd hate to keep you from a shower, but let me fill you in before you head off. It's been a night.'

I shifted my bag onto my shoulder and braced myself,

ignoring the foggy heaviness in my head. 'Go on.'

Mark yawned as he leaned forward, elbows on his desk. 'Further investigation and interviews have established that Leanne's been missing for six days now. That white ute at Leanne's has to be connected, but without any plates or ID on it, we're up against a wall. There's been no sign of it this way or through town. We have some CCTVs on the public buildings, but none captured it. Aaron had a good look through the night.'

Six days. My heart sank. Six days missing, alone—if that was even what had happened to Leanne. The possibilities crowded my mind, each worse than the last. It appeared Mark had been there all night.

'What if he went west?' I asked. 'What's out that way?'

'Lots of tracks that eventually end up at Dalrymple Lake, Ravenswood, and eventually Charters Towers. It's rough country but with plenty of places to hide. He couldn't have got far out that way because the last causeway is impassable. We've interviewed everyone we could find who had contact with Leanne but haven't picked up anything solid. The trail's gone cold,' Mark said, frustration in his voice.

I nodded, feeling my anger about yesterday's ambush grow. Six days, and she'd only just been missed. I swallowed hard, needing to stay focused.

'What about the children?'

Mark shook his head. 'Poor little kids. They didn't know where she was, so they tried to act normally. They've been at home by themselves for six nights, eating whatever was there. Apparently, their father told them last year that he didn't want them, and if their mum ever left them, they'd go into foster care. Sheree managed to get that out of Jonas. He told her he was big enough to be the man of the house. So, they decided to wait it out until their mother came home.'

'That explains the mess in the living room,' I said with a frown. 'But what about the guy who was there yesterday? Has he been there with them too? Did they have any idea who he is?'

'No, but when Sheree pressed them, she said she sensed they were holding something back. We're going to go easy and talk to them again when they're settled.'

'Where are they now?'

'With Jean at the caravan park. They know her well.'

'But of course, only a temporary solution,' I said. 'I'm going to take the doctor's advice and take it easy at my desk, so anything you want me to check today on databases and the like, let me know, and I'll do it.'

'Good, I'm pleased you're being sensible.'

'Sorry if I snapped a bit yesterday.'

Mark shook his head. 'I understand. It's frustrating for you wanting to get to work and to have that happen. The two detectives are on their way. They'll be staying in town for a few days. Detectives Davenport and Chapman are taking over the investigation.'

'Todd Davenport?' I repeated, a faint sense of recognition tugging at the name. I'd heard of him—a sharp, no-nonsense investigator with a stellar reputation for turning up answers in tough cases.

Mark caught my expression. 'Yeah, Todd. He's one of the best. We'll need him with the six days we've lost. We'll go out to the farm as soon as they arrive. Forensics are coming up from Bowen, too.' He put his hand up. 'And before you ask—'

'I know,' I said. 'I know I have to stay here. I'm not on the front desk, am I?' I knew what small towns were like. Everyone would find an excuse to call in today to see what was happening or to give us their ideas.

'No, I won't do that to you. Aaron's on duty.'

'Good,' I replied, relief mixing with my frustration. At least I could get on with some research, and someone with a top-notch reputation would be here, too. 'We'll find her trail. We have to.'

Mark gave a small, understanding nod. 'Go take your shower. Rest up if you need to. I'll update you when they arrive.'

I shot him a grateful look and turned to go, the events of the past day filling me with frustration. I detoured via the bathroom at the station; I didn't even have a cake of soap at the house yet.

It occurred to me then that I hadn't given Gray one thought.

***

I sat quietly, waiting in the station's back office where the morning sun slanted in through the blinds, scattering light over the haphazard piles of folders on the desk. I'd taken painkillers, but my head throbbed slightly where I'd taken the hit. I was focusing on what I'd say to the detectives. I'd heard of Todd Davenport before—everyone had. He was the kind of detective people talked about: tough but fair, with a solid record.

The door clicked open, and two men walked in, tall and broad-shouldered, taking up space like they were used to commanding it. They looked every bit the rugged, seasoned detectives I'd expected.

Mark, who'd been sitting with me, grinned when he saw them. 'Davenport, Justin. Long time!' He stood, extending a hand.

They shook hands, exchanging the kind of grins that spoke of a long-term connection. I heard Mark mention to Aaron that he knew them both from their football days in Brisbane.

Todd nodded, and his gaze turned in my direction.

'You must be Bec.' His voice was deep, but there was also a gentle smile that surprised me. The kind I wouldn't expect from a detective with his record. I nodded, offering a small smile back.

'Yes, Detective Davenport. It's great to meet you,' I replied, trying to keep the admiration out of my voice. I wasn't sure how well I pulled it off.

'We've heard a lot about you too. Mark's been saying you're the next rising star around here.' Todd's eyes crinkled kindly at the corners. 'But first things first—how's that head of yours?'

I hesitated, touching the sore spot gently. 'Just a little headache. Nothing serious.'

'Glad to hear it,' Justin said, folding his arms and studying me with a frown. 'You're sure?'

I nodded. 'I'll be fine, honestly.'

'Good,' Todd said. 'Just don't push yourself too hard.'

Their genuine concern caught me off guard, but it was nice to feel noticed and be acknowledged for something beyond what I'd just gone through. I had to remind myself that Todd and Justin would have seen cases far more brutal, people much worse off than I was after my slight brush with danger.

'Actually,' Mark added, 'these two have been through their own scrapes back in the day. You remember your concussion after that last grand final in Brisbane, Justin?'

Justin chuckled. 'Seems like another lifetime ago. Used to know every trick in the book, didn't we, Todd?'

'Couldn't let the young kids outshine us,' Todd replied with a faint grin. 'We were a good team.'

Their easy camaraderie relaxed me, and I could tell they

worked well together. I watched Todd closely. It was hard to picture someone who exuded such calm authority as a 'gentle giant,' as Mark had put it, yet I could see it in the way he carried himself. I wondered how a man who seemed so laid-back could transform into a detective with such a stellar reputation.

Then the conversation shifted to the case, and I was pulled back to why they were all here.

'Okay, back to work. Leanne Delaney—anything you saw, anything you noticed in that house before things went south?' Todd asked.

I took a deep breath, the memory still painfully clear.

'I walked right through. I thought I checked every room, and the house seemed empty. And the mess that I mentioned gave it a feeling of being abandoned in a way. Does that make sense?' I looked at them, wondering if they'd understand what I was saying.

'Yep,' Justin said. 'Something just not quite right.'

Todd tilted his head, his attention on me. 'Anything specific? Anything that struck you as out of place?'

'Some of her things were there,' I said slowly, 'as though she'd left in a hurry that morning. Her handbag was on the counter, next to a half-drunk cup of coffee. But there was a mess in the rest of the house. Food packets. Food scraps. I noticed it just before—' I trailed off, touching my head again.

'Go on,' Todd encouraged, voice softer now.

'I heard a swishing noise, but before I could turn, it was too late. Someone was there, and the next thing I knew, I was on the floor waking up.' I tried to steady my voice, surprised by how much it still rattled me. 'But there was one thing—I'm sure it was a guy. A big guy. I could smell a male deodorant.'

Todd nodded. 'Good. Anything helps us, especially when a case like this has so little for us at this early stage. We know now that someone doesn't want us out there poking around.'

I looked at him. 'I'll try to remember any other details that I can.'

'Good. Even the most insignificant details add to the picture. We've been doing this long enough to know there's no wasted information,' Justin said.

Todd turned to Aaron, and I sensed it was to give me a bit of space. 'How've you been doing, mate? We hear you've been giving this job your best in the short time you've been here.'

Aaron straightened, clearly a bit shy under the scrutiny, but Todd's smile seemed to make him relax.

'It's . . . yeah, it's been a bit of a challenge. But I've settled in well. Watching you guys work gives me something to aim for. Down the track, that is.' He grinned. 'I've got a lot to learn before then.'

'Hey, we've all been in your shoes, believe it or not,' Justin added, clapping a hand on his shoulder. 'Takes time, but you're doing really well from all accounts.'

A flush ran up Aaron's neck, but he looked chuffed. I was surprised by the collegiality. I wasn't used to that in the stations I'd been in.

The rest of the conversation turned to other case details, and I was interested in the way they approached it. No rush, no pressure—just a determination to understand each part of what had happened already and look for any links. It reminded me why I wanted to be a detective. I wanted that same clear, structured approach to solving a mystery. I would learn a lot from Todd and Justin.

'If it weren't for you needing a quieter day,' he said, 'I'd have liked for you to come out to the farm with us.'

'I'm okay, really,' I replied, but he shook his head firmly. 'I'd like to come.'

'Not this time,' he said gently. 'We need you fully recovered first.' His concern was genuine, and though it frustrated me, I knew he was right.

'Good luck,' I said. 'Are you only going to the farm?'

'At this stage.' He nodded as he walked to the door. I put my head down and went back to my databases.

Chapter 13

Bowen River Police Station - Thursday, noon.
Bec

After I'd settled a bit, I continued combing through the databases, hoping to find anything that could add information to Leanne Delaney's case. But it was hard to sit scrolling through a database when my thoughts kept straying to what they might find. I wanted to be there—see what they focused on, to watch, to learn.

I forced myself back to the screen, letting the names and dates take my focus. Around lunchtime, just as I was beginning to feel I might be closing in on something useful, I heard footsteps approaching. They were back, and I was pleased when Mark motioned for me to join them in his office. I stood and stretched, and the ache in my forehead twinged a little.

As I stepped in, the atmosphere in the room was tense. Todd leaned back against the wall, his arms crossed, while Justin sat in a chair, drumming his fingers on the desk. Mark gestured for me to sit.

'Justin and I swung by the caravan park on the way back from the farm. We asked the kids if they'd had any visitors at home, and Jonas really clammed up,' Todd said. 'Mandy started to speak, but he shut her down too.' He shook his head, his forehead creasing in a frown. 'Poor little mite got really upset. She started to cry and kept asking for her mum. Jean took her out to calm her down, and we tried to talk to Jonas by himself, but he clammed up. I think he knows something, but for some reason, he's not talking.'

'If we had the manpower, we'd station someone out at the farm to watch for anyone,' Mark said with frustration.

'What about a camera at the gate? To see what vehicles come in and out?' I suggested. 'We did that a few times in Brisbane, with some of the child protection cases. We'd need a surveillance device warrant to avoid any case of trespass.'

'That's an excellent suggestion, Bec.' Todd turned to Mark. 'Now that we know an unknown has been out there at least twice, he's obviously after something. It's worthwhile. Mark, there's a security firm we use in Bowen. I'll get the details and get you to organise it.'

'Will do.'

Justin added. 'We'll go back to the kids and try again tomorrow. Sometimes, you need to let them open up at their own pace.'

'Jonas is in denial,' Todd commented, 'but it's obvious there's something he's not saying. He's scared.'

'He's probably missing his mother.' I guessed I was stating

the obvious and looked down.

Mark tossed a glance over at the two detectives. 'I think it's time we took a break. How about heading over to the pub for a hot lunch? It's going to be another long afternoon and night.'

'I'm okay,' Todd said. 'I've got some paperwork to catch up on.'

Justin stood and stretched. 'Good idea. I could go a feed.'

Mark looked at me as they headed for the door. 'Do you want us to bring something back, Bec?'

'No, thanks, I'm fine.'

As the door swung shut behind them, I glanced over at Todd, who was still at a desk, rifling through some files. Just as I was about to turn back to the screen, he looked up, his eyes snagging mine.

'How about breaking for a coffee?' he asked. 'That café doesn't do a bad brew.'

I hesitated; Todd was a colleague, a mentor of sorts, and, to my slight frustration, a man I found myself drawn to.

'Sure,' I said, trying to keep my tone neutral.

Outside, the air was dry, and the heat was building, even though it was well into autumn. We walked together, not speaking until we reached the 1960s-style takeaway on the corner. Todd held the door open for me, and I slipped inside, wrinkling my nose at the smell of stale oil.

He leaned closer to me. 'I hope that enticing aroma isn't indicative of the quality of the coffee.'

I smiled and shook my head. 'Aaron's brought takeaway burgers and chips and coffee back from here, and it was all fine.'

'That's good to hear,' he said as a young girl came from out the back and looked at us.

'Lunch?' she asked with a drawl. Her hair was purple, and there were too many piercings on her face and ears to count. Despite the heat, she wore a hoodie the same colour as her hair. I glanced at her hands. Her fingernails were clean and neatly clipped, which was always a good sign.

'Senior Constable?' Todd asked.

I suddenly realised I was hungry and glanced up at the board. 'A salad sandwich? And a flat white, please. Lite milk.' I reached for my purse, but Todd had a twenty-dollar note on the counter before I could open it.

'My shout. Just a black coffee for me.'

'Thank you. I owe you one,' I said as we moved across to the one table near the front window overlooking the street.

'I'll hold you to that.'

'You're not eating?'

'No,' he said as he held out the chair for me.

The girl brought our coffee to the table quickly, and I waited for my sandwich. Todd leaned back in his seat, studying me for a moment. 'You've been through a lot in twenty-four hours. You doing okay?'

His question caught me off guard, and I took a sip of my coffee, buying time to gather my thoughts.

'Yeah, I'm okay.' I was getting better physically, but I wasn't going to talk about my issues with Gray or my relationship with my father. 'Settling in.'

He leaned back, studying me thoughtfully. 'I hope you don't mind,' he started, a bit hesitantly, 'but Mark told me you grew up here in Bowen River.'

I looked down, turning my coffee cup between my hands. I hesitated, debating just how much to reveal. I'd come back for a fresh start, but I didn't owe anyone my history. Not here, not now.

'It's home,' I said finally, keeping my voice level. 'I left after high school and didn't plan on returning. I guess things worked out differently.'

Todd nodded, his expression interested. But I wasn't ready to offer up my past. I was here to do a job, to prove myself and finally work my way up to detective. The last thing I wanted was for my personal baggage to be known.

I could feel his gaze, assessing, waiting. I didn't speak.

'Guess you're looking forward to a change, then?' he asked gently.

I shrugged, keeping it light. 'Yeah, I needed a different scene. Sometimes it's just time to move ahead, you know?'

Todd's eyes softened a bit, but I quickly looked away. No need for sympathy—I didn't need anyone's sympathy. I wasn't here to dwell on old memories.

'Fair enough,' Todd replied. 'Well, if you need anything as you settle in, let us know. Small towns can take a little adjusting to.'

I nodded, relieved he didn't press. 'Thanks. I'm good. Just here to do the work.'

'I hear you're keen to move up the ranks,' he said with a slight smile.

'That's the plan,' I replied. I smiled up at the waitress as she put my sandwich in front of me. 'Thank you.' It was time to shift the focus away from me. 'What about you? Where did you come from?'

He gave a casual shrug. 'Grew up in a little hamlet on the coast. Small place—you probably haven't heard of it.'

'Try me,' I replied.

'Baffle Creek,' he said.

'Nope. Never heard of it,' I admitted with a smile.

'Told you.'

I was aware of my pulse speeding up, and an odd sense of self-consciousness crept in.

Todd really was easy on the eyes with his tanned skin and sun-streaked hair, cut just short enough to hint at a relaxed, beachy vibe. He seemed so casual—like he could be heading off to a surf break instead of a police station. He certainly had the knack of relaxing anyone he talked to.

I reached up, brushing my fingers over my forehead, suddenly aware of my own appearance. Pale skin, faint bruises under my eyes, and hair that I'd barely managed to run a brush through. After the concussion, it had hurt too much to wash my hair when I'd showered post-hospital.

'You really okay?' he asked quietly.

I dropped my hand and gave a quick nod. 'Yeah, just still a bit shaky at times. I might take the sandwich to the station. I wasn't as hungry as I thought I was.'

He glanced at his watch. 'Time to get back to work.'

I smiled. 'Thanks for the coffee . . . and the sandwich.'

He flashed a grin. 'You owe me now.' For a second, his eyes held mine, and there was no mistaking the interest in them. My heart skipped a beat, and I quickly looked down, clearing my throat.

As I stood, the room tilted slightly. I must've lost some colour because Todd's hand came down over mine. 'Are you sure you're okay?'

I nodded, trying to wave it off. 'Just a bit giddy if I move too quickly. I forgot for a second.'

'Come on. Let's get back to the station,' he said, his voice gentler. 'And I really think you should consider knocking off for the day.'

Before I could stop myself, I shook my head—and the room spun again. But I gritted my teeth, determined to push through. 'No, I won't give in. I'm getting better by the hour. The headache's gone, and the coffee really helped.' I paused, searching for the right words. 'I knew . . . I know Leanne, and I want to do as much as I can to help.'

Todd seemed to hesitate, but then he nodded, and we walked out of the café together, heading back towards the station. We were only a few steps away when loud, angry voices suddenly rang out across the street, coming from the direction of the pub.

I froze, dread tightening in my chest. I'd have sworn one of those voices was Gray's.

I clenched my jaw and turned back towards the station, determined to keep moving, not to look. Todd followed, and I could feel his tension.

If it was Gray, I didn't want to know.

Chapter 14

Strathallyn Station - Spring 1925.
Elspeth

Elspeth found herself drawn to the stables more than ever since the arrival of the new horse trainer. Each day, she sought excuses to visit, her heart racing with anticipation whenever she caught a glimpse of him. He moved with a confidence that was both commanding and graceful, tending to the horses gently and purposefully. There was something in the way he held her gaze that made her feel different—alive in a way she had never experienced. A warm feeling settled low in her belly; a fluttering sensation she struggled to comprehend each time he spoke to her.

In her sheltered life at *Strathallyn Station*, her encounters with men were limited, and her mother carefully monitored her interactions. Yet, for some unknown reason, Mr Delaney stirred something deep within her, igniting a curiosity that went beyond the horses they tended together. Elspeth suspected he was aware of her mother's disapproval and the amount of time she spent in the stables watching him exercise the horses. As much as she tried to limit the visits she made to the work areas, she was unable to resist the temptation. Their social standings felt like an insurmountable barrier: he was the horse trainer, and she was the daughter of the station owner.

As her mother prepared to leave for Rockhampton to visit Aunt Kathleen again, Elspeth felt a mix of trepidation and excitement. Before she departed, her mother issued a stern warning, her tone unyielding. 'Elspeth, do not lower yourself. Stay away from the stables,' she admonished, her eyes narrowing with concern. 'It is not proper for a young woman of your standing to associate so closely with the help.'

Elspeth nodded, but the warning only fuelled her determination to go to the stables whenever she could. The thought of disappointing her mother did bother her a little, yet the allure of Mr Delaney's presence proved impossible to resist.

Elspeth's feet rocked on the bottom rung of the fence as she silently cheered him on as he pushed Babir Boy to the limit. He was a fine rider, and watching him filled her with awe.

Oh, to be able to ride like that.

One day, she promised herself. If she could get her riding to that level, she would be in demand at the most prestigious riding school in England.

Mr Delaney could teach her a lot.

When he stepped down from Babir Boy, it was with the ease of a man who was as comfortable with horses as he was with people. Probably more so with horses in his case; she'd noticed an awkwardness in his conversations.

Elspeth occasionally wondered about that. She couldn't figure out if it was a taciturn nature or simply shyness that limited his conversation. It wasn't just with her; she'd observed his interactions with Mr Burnham, the stud manager, and her father. His conversations were stilted and were never idle chat; his words were always related to the horses.

Mr Delaney led the stallion over, his gaze skimming across the track before finally settling on Elspeth. She could still feel the warmth of his handshake from that first afternoon, and here he was again, calm but somehow discomfited, as if he, too, felt something connecting them.

'I am riding to the back boundary this morning. Would you care to join me for a ride, Miss Valentine?' His words surprised her.

Elspeth widened her eyes and nodded, the word slipping from her lips before she'd even thought. 'Yes, that would be pleasant.'

'It will take a few hours to go out and return.'

'In that case, I shall pack a picnic lunch,' she said. 'I shall return shortly.'

On her return, she carried a picnic basket, and together they saddled their horses, with no words spoken when they were mounted. Nervousness tugged at Elspeth, though she didn't quite understand why. She felt safe in Mr Delaney's company. The path wound along the outer edges of the property, leading to her favourite spot on the river; her father often bragged about this being the best water on *Strathallyn*, where tall trees shaded the dark water, their gnarled roots reaching into the depths, and beyond, grassy hills rose towards the western horizon.

Mr Delaney tensed as a murder of crows flew above them, squawking harshly. She heard him mutter but didn't catch his words.

The sun warmed Elspeth's back as she rode beside him, the steady rhythm of the horses' hooves echoing on the dirt track. In Mother's absence, she wore trousers and a blouse most days, rather than the dresses that her mother insisted a lady wore, even if there were no guests expected. She smiled and relaxed her shoulders as her horse trotted behind Mr Delaney's.

The scent of eucalyptus hung in the air, mingling with the earthy aroma of the ground beneath them as they headed to the back of *Strathallyn*. Elspeth focused on the trail ahead, grateful for the company, though her thoughts drifted to her mother's absence. She realised she had begun to enjoy her days far more when she was alone in the house. It was proof enough that she was ready to leave home and cross the sea to England.

With her mother away in Rockhampton again, the household was more relaxed; even Mrs Revesby, the housekeeper, and

Mary seemed to be happier. Elspeth had once relied on her mother for companionship. Yet, as much as she despised the ladylike pursuits—embroidery, mending, and baking—she knew these were skills she would need at some point, perhaps when she returned from England—if she ever returned.

Mother's cousin Reginald and his wife, Cecilia, had visited *Strathallyn* when Elspeth was fifteen, igniting her desire to travel to England. Cecilia—Aunt Cecy, as Elspeth called her—had warmly invited her to stay at their home. Even then, Elspeth had noticed her mother's lips purse at the suggestion. Mother had other dreams: a good marriage and a life as a station wife in a place as remote as their own.

Elspeth, however, had aspirations beyond the boundaries of station life. Uncle Reginald had brought a few issues of *The Horse and Rider* in his folio case, which he gave to Elspeth that Christmas. She devoured them and, soon after, had persuaded her parents to subscribe. It was frustrating that the issues arrived in monthly bundles, often three or four months after publication.

Despite the delays, the magazine fuelled her passion. Each article deepened her resolve to work in England, far from the isolation of the Australian bush. Her dreams were rooted in England, where she envisioned herself working on a grand estate. Maybe she'd find a way to ride for a living, work as a stable hand or teach at a riding school. England had many prestigious establishments. Elspeth devoured everything she could read on Windsor Great Park, Chatsworth House, and Blenheim Palace.

For now, though, her thoughts returned to the quiet house she had left this morning. She smiled. In her mother's absence, she was her own mistress. Her father was frequently away in Sydney and Townsville for meetings about the soldier land settlement scheme. With Mr Delaney now training the horses to his satisfaction, her father spent much of his time away, freeing Elspeth to wander *Strathallyn* as she pleased. Mrs Revesby was supposed to chaperone her, but Elspeth ignored her, and the housekeeper let her be.

'Is everything all right, Miss Valentine?' Mr Delaney's voice broke through her thoughts as he slowed his horse and waited for her to ride up beside him on Bandy. He glanced sideways at her, concern etched across his tanned face. 'You look lost in thought.'

'Yes, just . . . thinking about the difference in my days,' she replied with a smile. 'It's very quiet without my mother around. And time is going so quickly. Life is changing for me. Or perhaps it's that I crave change.'

Mr Delaney nodded; his expression sympathetic as he again quoted poetry to her.

'The day is come when I again repose

Here, under this dark sycamore and view
These plots of cottage-ground, these orchard-tufts,
Which at this season, with their unripe fruits,
Are but a vain mockery of the past.'

A delicious shiver ran down Elspeth's spine. 'Oh, I am not familiar with those lines. Which poet is that?'

'Wordsworth. He mused on how time moves forward and how this affects our connection to the natural world. Life's impermanence and the inevitability of change.' His deep voice sent another shiver down her back. Mr Delaney had a beautiful voice, but it was often sad. She had never met such a clever man. It seemed that he even knew more than Miss Edmonds.

He spoke again before she could reply. 'It can be hard being a woman, but the war did change things, especially out on stations like this.'

'What do you mean changed things? I was only eleven when the war ended.'

'During those years, the women had to take over—running stations, herding cattle, fixing machinery. They did it all.'

Elspeth adjusted her reins, her brow furrowing slightly. 'Managing cattle and fixing things? I suppose they didn't have much of a choice.'

He nodded, his eyes fixed on the distant hills. 'No choice at all. Some ran entire stations and even handled the finances. It wasn't just about keeping things afloat—they kept the stations running.'

She gave a small, thoughtful nod. 'And when the men came back? Didn't everything just return to normal?'

Thomas shook his head, a hint of admiration in his voice. 'Not quite. Those women proved what they could do. People started to regard them differently and with more respect. And many of their men *didn't* come back.'

Elspeth glanced at him, curious. 'I imagine life must have changed for them, taking on so much and showing they were capable of more than anyone expected. I know how Father is involved with the settlement scheme, giving land to those who came back.'

Thomas's smile was brief and hinted at distant memories. 'It changed things. Women had a say in decisions and how the place was run. Independence, you'd call it.'

'I would like independence rather than my embroidery and household skills being seen as an embellishment to a future husband!'

He smiled and then studied her for a moment. 'You have strength, Miss Valentine. You will see your dream realised one day, I am sure.'

'Please call me Elspeth.'

'And I am Thomas.' His smile turned into a wide grin.

'When I returned . . .' his voice trailed off, and he seemed to catch himself, shifting uncomfortably in the saddle.

Her eyes narrowed slightly. 'When you returned? Where did you go, Mr . . . I mean, Thomas?'

He flashed a crooked grin, though it didn't quite reach his eyes. 'Oh, just further than most. Let's say it gives you a new perspective.'

Elspeth's gaze lingered on him, her curiosity piqued, but she chose not to press further. The silence between them resumed as they rode, the conversation lingering in her thoughts. The scenery shifted from limitless paddocks to dense clusters of tall trees lining the riverbank. The sunlight filtered through the leaves, casting dappled patterns on the ground.

'It is a beautiful day, but Mother worries about my skin,' she said, not wanting to ask him too many questions.

'Ah, but no hat today, I see.'

Elspeth had left her hair loose and had forgone a hat when she left the house that morning. She had been eager to get back to the stable. Luckily, Mrs Revesby had prepared food for Elspeth's meals before she left for the weekend. 'No, the weather is mild today.'

They rode along the distant boundary heading further north.

'There is a clearing ahead on the river where we can have our picnic,' Thomas said. 'Are you ready for a break?'

'I am. I know the place you mean. It's been a long time since I rode out here with Father.'

The river widened, and the sun glinted off the small waves kicked up by the breeze. Elspeth let a satisfied sigh slip from her lips.

'Do you have plans for the future?' he asked, breaking the comfortable silence.

She hesitated, the question echoing in her mind. 'I want to go to England to pursue a riding career,' she said at last. 'But it feels like there are so many expectations weighing me down.'

'Expectations can be heavy,' he agreed. 'But you must find and follow your own path.'

The sound of the river grew louder as they approached the clearing. The water shimmered invitingly in the morning light, and peace washed over Elspeth. For the first time in months, she felt happy.

As they dismounted and led the horses to the water's edge, she let out a breath she didn't realise she had been holding. The serenity of the water soothed her, if only temporarily. She dipped her hand into the cool river, savouring the trickle of water through her fingers.

Another crow flew overhead, its harsh cry slicing through the tranquil evening air. Elspeth shivered, instinctively glancing up at the dark silhouette against the vibrant sky.

'Are you cold?' Mr. Delaney asked, concern flickering in his eyes.

'No, just—the crow's call startled me,' she admitted, shaking off the momentary chill. 'I don't like them.'

'It's a reminder to stay alert, I suppose,' he said lightly, though his expression was serious. 'This land holds many stories, both beautiful and challenging.'

A flicker of determination ignited within her. She would overcome Mother's resistance. Hearing what Thomas said about the change in what women could do since the war reassured her. She *would* follow her dreams.

With that resolve, she took a deep breath, filling her lungs with the fresh, earthy air.

After they ate the simple meal she had packed, Elspeth pointed out landmarks her father had named and the tall eucalyptus he'd always claimed his father had planted. Thomas's lips curved slightly, and a hint of nostalgia softened his face.

'Seems you know this land very well,' he said, his voice low and warm.

'I suppose I do,' she replied, smiling. 'Father's been teaching me about *Strathallyn* since before I could ride. He wants me to love it as he does.' She caught herself, realising she'd shared more than intended. 'Not that I mind that,' she added quickly. 'It's home, after all.'

He nodded. 'You're lucky to have such a place.' Letting out a slow breath, he glanced towards the hills. 'I've never really had . . . a proper home. Not one I could call my own, anyway.'

She looked at him with a newfound curiosity. 'Not at all?'

'No, not in any real sense,' he said, his voice thick with something unspoken. 'I've drifted more than most. Worked on properties and helped raise horses. Came here hoping—' He stopped, as if unsure he wanted to say more.

'Hoping?' she encouraged softly, stepping closer to him.

He exhaled, staring at the rippling water; she sensed he was gathering the courage to open up just a little more, and she hoped that he would trust her. It made her feel more grown up. More a woman than a child.

'Hoping to find a place where I could finally feel settled. Somewhere to feel . . . right.' His voice grew quieter. 'It's strange, though. Since coming to *Strathallyn*, I've started to feel that way, even though I'm only a newcomer.'

A spark of warmth fluttered within her chest. 'I think you might find what you're looking for here, Thomas. *Strathallyn* seems to have a way of making people feel like they belong. Our workers stay for many years. I hope you do, too.'

He looked at her, and the moment stretched between them, charged with the same quiet tension she'd felt since the first day they'd met. The murmur of the trees and the gentle swish of water against the riverbank filled the air as he nodded thoughtfully.

'I think I'd like that very much, Elspeth.'

They turned back towards the homestead in easy silence, the connection between them deeper as they rode side by side. And Elspeth, for the first time in her life, felt something entirely new—a thrill she could neither explain nor suppress. It felt as though the land, her home, had pulled him into its grasp, linking him to her in a way she couldn't resist.

As they neared the house, she stole a final glance at him. 'Thank you, Thomas.'

'For what?' he asked, surprised.

'For sharing . . . and for listening. For understanding.'

He smiled then, a look so warm it reached his eyes. 'The pleasure was mine.'

Chapter 15

Bowen River - Thursday noon.

Bec

Todd and I made our way towards the pub on the corner, and the noise spilling out from inside told me something wasn't right. As we got closer, I spotted Mark and Justin standing near the door. My heart dropped as I saw a man struggling against Justin's hold, but relief hit me quickly when I realised it wasn't Gray—it was a guy in a high-vis shirt.

I took a quick breath, trying to calm my racing pulse, but the shaking lingered. My hand instinctively lifted to my chest as I took another deep breath.

Mark stepped over to me, his expression turning concerned when he looked at me. He put a hand on my shoulder. 'You're very pale, Bec,' he said quietly. 'Go back to the station. We've got this under control.'

'I'm fine,' I forced out, my tone sharper than I intended.

But Mark didn't move. His hand stayed firm on my shoulder. 'Bec, you're off duty as of now. Take a break.'

I bristled at the suggestion, but I couldn't deny the relief that crept in. 'I'm fine, Mark,' I said with a forced smile, trying to push through the weakness I felt. I held up my sandwich bag.

'I'll eat now and see how I go. Okay?'

Mark didn't acknowledge my protest. Instead, he turned to Todd. 'Can you walk back with the Senior Constable and then come back here?' He gave Todd a steady, knowing look.

'She might need to sit down now,' Todd said, his voice calm and gentle. 'Would you rather go into the pub and sit for a while before we head back?'

'No. I told you I'm fine.' I folded my arms tightly across my chest. 'Would you all fuss like this over a male colleague?' My voice was tight, and I could feel the tension rising. The last thing I wanted was to go inside and risk encountering Gray in front of Mark and the detectives. I lifted my chin, trying to stay composed, but the world spun for a moment.

Shit.

Mark's tone softened but remained firm. 'And we know it, Bec,' he replied. 'Doesn't mean you don't deserve a breather now and then.'

I sighed, knowing he wasn't going to let me get away with this. As they turned to leave, I felt a moment of relief—until a flash of movement caught my eye. My breath hitched in my chest, and my muscles tensed involuntarily as Gray stepped out of the crowd gathered outside. He hadn't noticed me, his attention elsewhere, but the sight of him alone was enough to rattle me.

I froze, unable to tear my gaze away. Todd must have sensed the shift in my posture because he looked around, following my eyes until he spotted Gray. I forced myself to breathe, reminding myself that I was here to do my job—nothing more.

A voice came from inside the pub, rough and slurred. 'I'm going to charge the bastard!'

The man struggling against the officers yelled back, 'You're the one who started it, Harry!' His face was flushed, and his glare was fixed on the door like he was ready to charge at anyone who came through.

I glanced over, and recognition hit as another man appeared in the doorway. My stomach twisted—he was one of the guys Gray had been drinking with yesterday. His eyes locked with mine for a brief moment before quickly darting away, tension radiating off him.

I stiffened, holding my breath. Todd's hand stayed steady on my shoulder, grounding me, though my mind raced.

When I looked up again, there was no sign of him or Gray anywhere.

Leaving the tense standoff at the pub, Todd and I made our way back to the station. The quiet streets of Bowen River felt almost surreal after everything that had just happened. We walked slowly, but I could tell Todd was watching me, occasionally glancing my way with concern.

When we were inside, I settled at my desk. I ignored my sandwich and began organising my notes. It wasn't long before I heard voices in the hallway. Mark and Todd were clearly talking about me. It didn't take a genius to figure out they were discussing how I was holding up. Moments later, Mark appeared at my side, arms folded.

'That's enough for today, Bec,' he said, an edge to his voice.

'I'm fine,' I replied, frustration edging my voice.

'No.' Mark raised his hand, cutting off my protest. 'Go home. That's an order.'

I sighed, realising there was no point in arguing. I grabbed my things and slung my bag over my shoulder. I risked a glance at Todd.

'Tomorrow, we'll start interviewing Leanne's friends,' he said, 'especially anyone connected to her environmental causes. We need to piece together who she was spending time with and why.'

I nodded, my fingers still wrapped around my keys. 'Makes sense.'

As he turned to leave, Todd rested a hand lightly on my shoulder. 'Rest, Bec. You did well today.'

Once I was home, I shed my uniform and slipped into an old T-shirt and shorts. I opted for a glass of water instead of coffee; the sandwich was still on my desk at the station. Exhaustion hit me like a wave as I sank onto the sofa. Within minutes, I drifted off, my thoughts swirling between the day's events and everything left unresolved.

I woke suddenly, disoriented. The room was dark except for the faint glow of the streetlight outside. Someone was pounding on the front door, the sound sharp and urgent. My heart raced as I stumbled to my feet, still half-asleep, my dishevelled state a blur as I opened the door.

Gray stood there, his face taut with anger. Without warning, he pushed past me, slamming the door behind him.

'What the hell, Gray?' I snapped, stepping back. 'What do you think you're doing?' I tugged at the bottom of my T-shirt, aware of his gaze on my bare thighs.

'You didn't answer your phone,' he growled, his eyes scanning me with a mix of anger and something deeper. 'We need to talk. Now.'

I was still groggy, my head fuzzy from the abrupt awakening. I steadied myself against the wall, narrowing my eyes at him. 'You can't just barge in here!'

Gray ran a hand through his hair, pacing up the hall, and then turning around to face me. 'I need to stay here,' he muttered, his voice low but urgent. 'Those blokes from the pub—they're after me.'

'What blokes?' I pressed, my mind scrambling to make

sense of his words. I rubbed my temples, trying to shake off the lingering haze from my nap.

'The ones who caused those problems with Harry,' Gray snarled, his eyes darting towards the window as if expecting someone to burst in at any moment. 'They reckon I heard them talking, but I didn't hear anything.'

I crossed my arms, my stance firm despite the disorientation. 'About what?'

Gray's shoulders slumped slightly, but his eyes remained sharp. 'The missing woman. They're dangerous, Bec. If I don't stay somewhere safe, they'll find me.'

I exhaled slowly, weighing his words. The Gray I knew was tough, but this was different. There was real fear in his voice. Still, I couldn't ignore the fact that he had forced his way into my home without warning.

'You need to tell me what you did hear,' I said firmly. 'If you're in that much trouble, I'll help—but not like this. You can't just drop this on me in the middle of the night.'

Gray nodded, his eyes flicking back to the window. 'I'll explain, but please, just let me stay for tonight. I'll be gone by morning. I'll sleep on the sofa. I promise.'

I hesitated, every instinct telling me this was a bad idea. But something in Gray's expression—a mix of desperation and trust—made me pause. I sighed, stepping aside to let him sit.

'One night,' I said, my tone leaving no room for argument.

Gray sat heavily on the edge of the sofa, his hands clasped tightly together. 'Thank you,' he murmured, his usual bravado replaced by quiet relief.

'Now tell me what you heard. And this is in an official capacity. Nothing else.'

Chapter 16

*** Strathallyn Station - early Spring 1925.***
Elspeth

Today, Elspeth and Thomas were only going as far as the billabong. Her pretext was that Bandy needed some exercise and she asked Thomas if he would like to come with her. Mother was due back any day now, and Father, who'd been home for a few days, had gone to Bowen for the races. Babir Boy was racing, and Father and Thomas held high hopes. She was surprised that Thomas hadn't gone with him.

They rode in comfortable silence until they reached the edge of the billabong. The sky above was a serene expanse of blue, dotted here and there with soft clouds drifting lazily in the gentle breeze. The grass around the billabong was lush and green, cushioning their steps as they dismounted, the quiet snorting of their horses the only sound aside from the rustling leaves and the water's soft lapping at the edge. The horses settled nearby, grazing peacefully.

'I thought you might go to the races at Bowen with my father,' she said.

'No, I don't need to see them race. I simply prepare the

horses.' He looked past her as he spoke, and she saw a muscle twitch in his cheek.

'That's unusual.'

This time, he lifted those broad shoulders in a shrug. 'I don't like being in crowds.'

Elspeth took a deep breath. 'I can understand that. I wonder how I will fare in a strange environment with new people when I go to England,' she said, brushing her hand along the tall grass beside her.

Thomas raised an eyebrow, a slight smile playing on his lips. 'And what sort of work would you do there?'

'Working with horses, of course. In the stables of a grand estate.' She glanced at him, slightly embarrassed by her ambitious daydreams. 'But really, that is probably too big a dream. I don't know, exactly. Maybe assist with the breeding or be part of the stable care team. I've read about women who manage estates or keep the ledgers for breeding lines. I'd like to be involved somehow, even if it's only organising the stables or caring for the horses day to day.'

He listened, his gaze steady but holding something she couldn't quite place. 'It's noble work,' he said finally, 'but England's not the place it used to be. It's . . . unsettled. After the war, many places are struggling, and people are—well, people are still picking up the pieces.'

She looked at him thoughtfully. 'Did you see much of that? After the war, I mean. You haven't ever said, but I assume you were over there during the Great War.'

He grew quiet, his gaze drifting over the water. 'I saw more than enough.' His voice was low, a hint of pain slipping through his usually composed tone. 'The trenches . . . the endless days of mud and smoke, friends who—' He broke off, looking out towards the billabong. 'I was lucky to make it home.'

After a pause, he added softly, almost to himself, as though it wasn't meant for her ears, 'Or maybe unlucky.'

Elspeth's heart ached at his words, and she reached out, placing a gentle hand on his arm. He turned, meeting her gaze, his eyes haunted but searching. She didn't know what to say, but the warmth of her touch seemed to reach him. Slowly, he leaned forward, and she let her eyes close as his lips met hers, a soft, lingering kiss that held both comfort and something unspoken.

For a moment, time seemed to hold still around them, the gentle breeze whispering through the trees as they parted, both of them a little breathless, both a little changed.

***

Late summer 1926.

Five months had passed since that first shared kiss by the billabong, and in that time, Elspeth and Thomas had found their way into a quiet companionship. She looked forward to the stolen hours with him when Mother was away, either on trips to town or visiting Aunt Kathleen in Rockhampton. These moments felt like the only time she could be truly herself, sharing laughter and stories with Thomas, watching his features soften, his usual reserved expression giving way to something warmer just for her.

Yet, often, there was a shadow in his gaze, a preoccupied sadness that settled over him in rare, quiet moments. When she asked if he was alright, he'd brush it off with a shake of his head, but she knew it lingered, the past he rarely spoke of haunting him.

Today, the air was thick with humidity, the sun glinting off the water, and they dismounted by the billabong as they always did. She took a seat beside him, her fingers idly trailing through the soft grass. They talked a little, Elspeth laughing at an anecdote she shared about Mrs Revesby before her laughter faded, replaced by a deep silence. Thomas was in one of his darker moods today, and she was trying her best to make him smile. He looked at her with an intensity that made her heart pound, and slowly, almost tentatively, he leaned in and kissed her.

This time, the kiss was different. It was deep, harder and filled with a passion that took her breath away, his hands touching her face, then her shoulders, holding her close. His grip tightened, his hands roaming, and her heart fluttered with both excitement and a sudden shyness. She pulled back, breathless, her cheeks flushed.

Immediately, he looked stricken, pulling away as though he'd broken some unspoken rule. 'Elspeth, I'm so sorry,' he murmured, looking down, his voice strained. 'I . . . I forgot myself.'

Seeing the pain and regret in his eyes, the ache inside her grew; she simply wanted him to be happy.

She reached out, wrapping her arms around him, her cheek resting against his shoulder. 'You don't need to be sorry,' she whispered. 'It is what I desire, too.'

When he turned to face her, she met his gaze, her heart racing. They kissed again, and this time, the kiss deepened, and she didn't want it to end. Being in Thomas's arms made her feel like a woman. The warmth between them grew until there was nothing but his whispered endearments, the soft rustle of the grass beneath them, and the endless blue sky above. What had begun as comfort quickly grew as passion took over, and soon, they were lying together in the soft grass by the billabong, their intense feelings sweeping away any coherent thought.

Only the crows above bore witness to their shared secret as Elspeth completed her passage from girlhood to womanhood.

Chapter 17

Bowen River - Friday.
Bec

The next morning, I woke up feeling surprisingly well. Despite the late night and little sleep, my mind was clear. The dizziness and headache were gone, leaving me feeling much better. I stretched lazily in bed, enjoying the quiet before the day began. It would be hectic as interview transcripts were reviewed, and I ploughed through my databases as we identified potential suspects.

I thought about last night's conversation with Gray. He'd told me what he overheard, and it seemed significant enough to pass on. I probably should've told him to stay in town; Todd and Justin would want to speak to him. I had thought about going to the station last night, but by then, it had been nearly midnight, and there was no point. The place would've been empty. I was going to have to come clean about Gray, too—that I had been in a relationship with him.

As I pushed the sheet back off my legs, the door creaked open. Gray strolled in, his usual swagger back in full force. I instinctively pulled the sheet up, glaring at him. 'What are you doing? Get out!'

He laughed, leaning against the doorframe. 'Oh, for Christ's sake, Bec. Don't play the innocent virgin. You're not at your parents' house now.' He smirked. 'Stay in bed for a bit. That sofa was like a bloody rock. I'll join you.'

'Get out,' I snapped.

He held up his hands, feigning innocence. 'Come on, babe. I said I was sorry.'

'What don't you get, Gray? We're not a couple. It's over. The only reason I let you stay last night was because you were scared.'

'I wasn't scared,' he muttered defensively, though his eyes darted away.

'Just go,' I said firmly, my voice cold. 'And close the door on your way out. I'm having a shower, and then I'm going to work.'

His tone shifted, turning wheedling. 'Want to save some water? I could use a shower, too.'

I narrowed my eyes, looking at him with disgust. Not only with him but with myself too, because I'd let him con me and live with me for eight months. I should have been strong and refused to listen to him when he said he'd come here with me.

He must have finally realised I was serious because he walked over to the door. When he turned to face me, his smirk had been replaced with anger.

'All right,' he said, raising his hands again. 'I'm going. Don't want to stay in this shithole of a place anyway.'

The door closed behind him, and I exhaled, shaking my head. I swung my legs out of bed, determined not to let his presence ruin my morning. A hot shower and a clear head were what I needed before heading back to the station.

When I was headed out to the kitchen in my uniform ten minutes later, he'd gone.

Good.

I was proud of the way I'd dealt with Gray. It looked like he'd finally accepted that I was serious. Maybe coming home to Bowen River had brought back some of the strength I'd once had. I'd keep working on that. A new Bec Whitfield; I wasn't going to be controlled by anyone again.

I arrived at the station just before seven. The early morning light bathed the town in a softness that wasn't there when the sun was high. I pushed the door open and called out. 'Anyone here yet?'

Aaron's head popped up from behind the front desk, a wide grin spreading across his face. 'Morning, Bec. You're looking much better today.'

'Takes a lot to knock me down,' I said, leaning against the counter. 'You want a coffee? I'm going over to the café. I'm starving.'

'I wouldn't say no to a bacon and egg roll, and a chocolate milkshake would hit the spot, too,' he replied, his grin widening.

'Right,' I said with a laugh. 'Where's everyone else?'

Aaron held the back of the desk chair and pushed it closer to the computer chair. 'Sarge headed over to see Jean at the caravan park, something about last night's disturbance. Todd and Justin went out to the mine a couple of hours ago to catch some bloke coming off the night shift.'

'And here I was thinking I was early to work!' I nodded. 'Anything urgent I should know about? What happened with that guy yesterday?'

'Sarge gave him a warning, and he went back to the dongas at the caravan park. He's one of the workers from the solar farm. It's been pretty quiet so far this morning,' Aaron said.

'Okay, I'll be quick, and then I'm going to get back to those files I was looking at when Sarge sent me home yesterday.'

To my surprise, Todd was standing at the counter in the coffee shop when I walked in. I hadn't noticed the unmarked car outside. His eyes lit up as he spotted me.

'Well, don't you look a lot better,' he said, his voice warm.

'So Aaron tells me. I'm feeling back to normal,' I replied with a quick smile.

The girl behind the counter, a different one from yesterday, handed Todd two coffees. 'Ten dollars, please.' Her eyes lingered on him, giving him a once-over that was anything but subtle.

'Where's Justin?'

'Outside in the car on a phone call.'

I hid a smile as he pulled out his wallet, oblivious to the attention. He handed over a note and glanced back at me. 'Do you want a lift back?'

'No, I'm fine, thanks.' I shook my head. 'I'll be a while. I'm grabbing breakfast for Aaron and me.'

Todd nodded. 'He was at the station all night.'

'I didn't know that,' I said, turning to place my order. 'He didn't say.'

'He's doing a good job,' Todd added, his tone genuine.

I glanced at him, appreciating his praise for my probationary colleague. 'He is,' I agreed, then gestured towards the door. 'Go on, I'll see you back there.'

Todd hesitated for a second as if he wanted to say more but then nodded. 'See you soon.'

As he walked out, I caught the counter girl watching him again, a wistful look on her face. I chuckled to myself and sat at the table, flicking through the news on my phone as I waited for my order. Nothing about Leanne's disappearance had yet been given to the media, but I imagined there would be a media release today. The Queensland Police Service's centralised Media and Public Affairs Unit handled media releases, especially for cases that needed widespread attention. I'd been involved with a few releases when I was with the Child Protection and Investigation Unit, and I knew the importance of information being accurate, appropriately framed, and consistent with QPS policies.

By the time I got back to the station, the enticing aroma of bacon and egg rolls I carried was making my mouth water.

I held up the takeaway bag for Aaron, who was still at the desk. 'Want me to put this in there?' I asked, nodding towards the kitchenette.

'Yeah,' Aaron said with a grin. 'Not a great look to eat out here. I'll microwave mine when I'm done. Sarge said I have to go home. Break regulation.'

'Todd said you pulled an all-nighter.'

Aaron nodded. 'We all did.'

As I made my way down the short corridor, I could hear voices coming from the kitchenette—Mark, Todd, and Justin were all back. The low hum of conversation filled the air.

'Central Media has advised us to hand local media over to them if they approach us first, but they agree that we need to get something out today. Brian Cochrane said that the media might sensationalise this case, and we don't want the fallout from that if it turns out that Leanne has just gone away of her own accord.'

I knew Brian Cochrane from my time in Brisbane, and he was great at his job.

I hesitated in case I was walking in on something private, but then I reminded myself—this was the lunchroom, not a private meeting space. No need to overthink it.

Mark turned as I entered, his eyebrows lifting slightly. 'Wow, you look—'

'Better,' I finished for him with a grin.

He chuckled. 'Yes, much better.'

'I'm fully recovered and looking forward to getting back to work properly this morning and putting a full day in. I'm starving. Do you mind if I eat in here while you talk? I can get a plate and take it to the workroom?'

'No, have a seat,' Mark replied, gesturing to the table.

I placed Aaron's roll on the counter and moved to the table with my breakfast. 'I'd like to bring you up to speed anyway, and I've got something to tell you too—something I heard.' I took my roll out of the paper bag and sat down, the smell of bacon making my stomach rumble.

Todd frowned as he leaned back in his chair. 'At the café?' he asked.

Heat flashed up my cheeks. 'No, last night. I had a visitor.' I looked at Mark. 'I didn't mention this before because it's personal, and up until now, it was irrelevant. I came to town with my partner—well, now he's my ex-partner.'

Todd's eyes stayed on me, sharp and unreadable. I spoke quickly. 'When I got the transfer, I didn't want him to come, but Gray insisted.'

'Gray Cameron?' Mark interrupted, his brows lifting.

I felt my stomach tighten. 'Yes. Why?'

Mark exchanged a glance with Justin. 'His name came up last night—and again this morning at the mine.'

I blinked, momentarily thrown. 'Anyway, we split up as soon as I arrived,' I continued, my voice steadier now.

Mark's eyebrows rose again, and his tone held a bit of doubt. 'That was Thursday?'

'Yes. That's why I was going to Bowen. To take him to the bus, but Gray went to the pub when I called in here, had a few beers and refused to leave. That's why I could come straight in.' I was kicking myself for not mentioning it before. Now, it made me look like I was hiding something. 'It feels like days ago, with everything that's happened,' I admitted. 'We should've split months back.'

Justin held up a hand. 'Bec, that's your business. What we need to know is what he heard that might be relevant to the case.'

I nodded, taking a moment to gather my thoughts. 'Well, he turned up late, pounding on my door; it was almost midnight. He was scared and said some guys were after him.'

'Do you believe that?' Todd's jaw tightened, and his gaze was intense. 'Why would they be after him if he just hit town?'

'That's what I asked,' I said. 'He wouldn't give me a straight answer. Just said he overheard something at the pub, and it made him a target.'

'Target of who?' Mark leaned forward; his expression was serious. 'Did he say what he overheard?'

'He did, but if his name has already come up in your interviews, there's possibly more to this than he was telling me.'

Todd's eyes darkened. 'We'll find out soon enough. So, what did he overhear?'

I met his gaze steadily. 'Something about Leanne—although he didn't know her name,' I continued, my voice steady. 'He said the guys were talking about "the woman who got murdered".'

The room fell silent for a moment.

'Interesting,' Mark said, leaning forward. 'Go on.'

'I asked what he knew, but he denied knowing anything beyond what he overheard,' I explained. 'Remember, he arrived in town with me. So, he can't be involved. Anyway, he said he was at the bar when these two guys started talking about her. When they realised he was listening, apparently things got ugly.'

Todd's frown deepened. 'And he left?'

'Exactly,' I said. 'He didn't stick around to hear more or

confront them. Just bolted and came to my place.'

Mark exchanged a look with Todd. 'Did he describe them?'

I shook my head. 'No, no names either. Knowing Gray, he was too focused on getting out of there to pay much attention. He'd had quite a bit to drink, too.'

I was uncomfortable with Todd's assessing gaze.

Justin leaned back in his chair, rubbing his chin. 'Still, if he can identify those guys, it's a good lead. Don't you talk to him, Bec. To ease your mind, his name came up only by association with some persons of interest from the solar works, but seeing he's only just arrived in town, we'll only be asking him who they were.'

I felt sick from guilt; even though I had nothing to be guilty about, I knew what it sounded like.

Todd nodded. 'We'll need to find out who else was at that bar last night. Might be time for another visit to the pub.'

Mark stood. 'Agreed. Let's view the CCTV footage while we're there to see the interaction and find out who they were. This could be the break we're looking for.'

I watched as they shifted into action. Gray might have stumbled onto something, and now it was up to them to piece it together.

'What do you want me to focus on today, Mark?' I asked as they headed for the door.

'Keep digging into those local records. See if there are any other groups Leanne was affiliated with. Jean said to take a close look at the minutes of the meeting of the group that was against the solar development. She said it got quite heated at times, and she was the secretary, so it's all recorded.'

'Okay. I'll get straight onto it.'

'Eat your breakfast first. When we get back from the hotel, I'll take you with me to talk to the kids again if you're up to it.'

'I'm back to normal, Sergeant,' I said crisply, pushing away the now-cold breakfast roll, the fat congealing in front of me. I sensed a slight distance in Mark's tone and I silently cursed Gray Cameron.

Chapter 18

Bowen River – Friday.
Bec

As Mark and I walked up the hill to the primary school later that morning, I looked down at the town below. It was so different from working in the city. Here in Bowen River, just about everything was within walking distance of the police station.

Mark was deep in thought, and I waited a while before I spoke.

'Did you find out anything about the two guys who allegedly threatened Gray? Any footage?'

He raised an eyebrow when I said, 'allegedly.'

'Do you doubt what he said?'

I shrugged. 'I shouldn't have added that. He did seem genuinely scared.'

Mark adjusted his collar, his expression guarded. 'We've got two names and saw the footage. Your Gray was telling the truth. The footage backed up what you told us.'

'Not *my* Gray, please, Sergeant.'

His nod was brief, and again, I kicked myself for bringing Gray to town.

'Todd and Justin are out at the mine, interviewing them to see what they know.'

I nodded, letting the information sink in. 'Two names.'

'Yes, hopefully, something comes out of the interviews. We'll see what they turn up. Things are moving slowly, and we can't rule out anyone at this stage. That "murderer" comment has me worried.'

'Do you need to talk to Gray again?'

'No. It was as he said. His name came up a couple of times. He chose to drink with a couple of rough-and-ready blokes. Anyway, it appears he's left town.'

'Good.'

There was a brief, uncomfortable pause before Mark shifted the conversation. 'How did you go with the minutes of the anti-solar group meetings? Did you spot anything unusual?'

I exhaled slowly. 'Yes, I did. There's one name that keeps coming up. And it's not just in passing—it's like every time Leanne suggested something, this person was against it. Almost ... too vehemently.'

Mark's eyebrows lifted, clearly intrigued. 'Really? Who is it?'

'A guy called Murray Reid,' I said. 'I asked Aaron if he'd heard of him, and he said he was a local who worked at the mine.'

'What do you mean, "vehemently"?'

I hesitated. 'Well, Jean recorded the language he used, and it was pretty offensive. Her notes were very clear about his opposition to Leanne's suggestions, even though they were just passing points. The words "anti" and "selfish" came up frequently, along with some pretty nasty swearing. Jean made sure they were noted. It stood out.'

'We'll have a chat with him, too. Jean's got a sharp eye, even if she doesn't show it. I've been to meetings where she's taken the minutes,' Mark said, his tone softening with quiet admiration. 'She doesn't just write bland minutes; she spots the nuances. If she's saying someone's pushing back too hard, we might want to pay attention.'

I frowned, thinking it through. 'It's strange. Leanne was trying to move things forward, but this Reid guy, every time, there was pushback. It's not something you'd expect to see on paper. Jean caught it, though.'

'Well, Jean knows the value of keeping an eye on things. She doesn't miss much. Looks like we might have another angle to pursue. Good work.'

I met his gaze, a flicker of determination in my eyes. 'I'll go over the minutes again. Maybe there's more in there. We can't overlook any detail.'

Mark's expression held frustration as we reached the office

door. 'Exactly. Keep digging.'

As I stepped into the school foyer, my boots echoed against the polished floor. It looked the same as when I was at school. I looked up at the honour board and smiled when I saw my name listed as school captain in 2006. Mark followed me in, his usual easy demeanour still holding subtle tension.

It was early, just after the lunch bell, and the school hummed with the noise of children heading back to their classrooms.

Sheree was waiting by the front desk, her smile welcoming. She stepped forward to greet us, her heels clicking on the floor. 'Morning,' she said quietly, her eyes flicking to Mark before settling on me. 'Thanks for coming.'

Mark introduced us. 'Bec, this is Sheree, my wife.'

'Good to meet you.' Sheree's hand was soft, and I caught a whiff of floral hand cream. I nodded, hearing the undercurrent of concern in her voice. 'We'll head straight to the office,' she said, gesturing for us to follow her down the hallway. Her voice dropped a little as she spoke again. 'I wanted to fill you in on a couple of things before you speak to them.'

I nodded, sensing her concern. 'Of course,' I replied.

When we reached the office, Sheree opened the door and led us inside. The children were sitting quietly at a small table in a room next door. A window in the wall allowed Sheree to check on them from the office. The boy, maybe eight or nine, was dark-haired. He looked up and watched us warily. The girl, much younger and small for her age, was a picture of innocence, her golden curls framing a delicate face with pink cheeks. She was drawing, her crayon moving furiously across the paper, her concentration intense.

'Jean has been looking after them since we discovered they have been out there by themselves,' Sheree said quietly, sitting behind the desk. Her hands rested on the table; her fingers intertwined. 'For now, they're coming to school to keep some normality. They'll stay here until child services step in.'

I nodded, my heart heavy for the children. 'So, what happens now?' I asked.

Sheree's gaze flicked to Mark before she spoke again, keeping her voice very low. I had to lean forward to hear what she was saying. 'Well, until we make contact with their father or his family, Jean is going to care for them. But—it's not easy for her. She's been great, but at her age and running the business, it's probably unlikely for her to do it for more than a few days.' She glanced at Mark. 'I offered to take them at our place, but Mark made me see sense. Being a teacher at the school and Mark on the investigative team leaves us open for criticism.'

I absorbed the information, running through possible scenarios in my mind. 'What happens in a case like this?'

Even though I'd worked in child protection, I hadn't

encountered a missing parent case before. I lowered my voice and tried to remove the concern from my expression when Jonas looked over at us. 'If we can't track down their father and their mother is missing?'

Sheree sighed, her voice softening. 'Hopefully, there will be some relatives on their father's side.'

'Bec, I'll get you onto that as soon as we get back, too,' Mark said.

I nodded and added it to my notebook.

'If there is no family to take them, they'll be placed into foster care. And given the circumstances, they'll probably be split up. We're doing what we can, but it's hard.' Sheree hesitated before adding, 'They'll likely be separated if they're not kept together here.'

My heart sank at the thought of them being split up. 'Do you think they'll stay together for now?' I asked quietly, watching the boy protectively keep his gaze on the girl. 'How about I call my former boss at Child Protection? There might be something we can do, seeing we're fairly remote.'

Sheree looked at the children, then back at me. 'I hope so. But we can't make any promises. For now, Jean's taking care of them, but as I said, with everything she's juggling, that's not sustainable.' She paused and added, 'It could be months before there is an outcome.'

My mind raced. 'Maybe my mother could help,' I suggested, almost without thinking. 'She's got a bit more time now, and I know she'd be willing to help out Jean, at least for a while.'

There was a brief, significant pause. Mark and Sheree exchanged a look that didn't escape me. My stomach tightened, but I held their gaze, not backing down.

Sheree smiled faintly, though there was an edge to it. 'I'll talk to Jean about it. We can't ask too much of her.'

Mark nodded, though his expression remained distant. 'Thanks, Bec,' he said. 'A kind suggestion.'

I turned back to the children. The boy still watched us cautiously, his dark hair falling in front of his face while the girl continued to draw. For a brief moment, I caught the boy's gaze—something there, a silent plea, maybe—and my heart twisted.

'We'll figure something out,' I said firmly, my voice full of resolve. 'I'll talk to Mum.'

Mark and Sheree exchanged another look, one that left me with more questions than answers. But for now, I had to focus on the children. I glanced at the young girl, still lost in her drawing, and the boy, who was starting to settle, a little of the tension leaving his shoulders.

Sheree stood and walked across to the door between the two rooms. She went in and crouched beside them; her voice, gentle but firm, reached us at the table.

'Jonas, Mandy?' she began. 'I have some more people here who'd like to talk to you. They're trying to bring your mum back home as fast as they can.'

Amanda's face brightened, her eyes wide with hope, but Jonas kept his head down, his jaw tight. He muttered something under his breath that I couldn't quite catch.

Sheree gave him a patient smile. 'Would you like to stay here, and they can come in while you keep drawing? Or how about you sit with us at the big table? What would you prefer?'

Jonas's reply was low and defiant. 'I'd rather go home to our place.'

Sheree sighed softly, placing a hand on his arm. 'I know you miss your house, Jonas, but we need to find your mum before you can go home to stay. These are the people who are going to help us do that.'

Jonas let out a huff of frustration, but after a moment, he stood, tugging his sister up with him. His hand reached for Mandy's, and I saw him give it a reassuring squeeze. Her lip quivered, but she blinked and followed her brother into the office.

We moved to the large table adjacent to the desk, and Mark and I sat down across from them. Sheree stayed close, leaning slightly on the edge of the table as she kept an eye on the kids.

I started carefully. 'Jonas, Mandy, can you tell us how many nights you were at home by yourselves before Jean took you to her place?'

Jonas's face tightened. 'Dunno,' he said, his voice clipped.

Mandy opened her mouth, her small voice piping up, 'We weren't by ourselves all the time. Uncle—'

'That was another time.' Jonas shot her a warning look and cut her off. 'We were okay,' he said firmly. 'We don't need anyone checking on us.'

'Uncle who?' I asked.

Jonas shook his head.

Mark exchanged a glance with me, then leaned in slightly. 'Have you seen your dad at all? Or heard from him?'

Jonas shook his head quickly, his expression hardening even more; he was a strong little boy. 'No. It was just us.'

Mandy's eyes darted nervously between her brother and me, her little fingers fiddling with the edge of her school shirt.

I tried a different approach. 'We'd like to help you get some things from your house,' I said gently. 'Would you like to do that today after school?'

Jonas's lips pressed into a thin line. 'I want to go there now.'

Mark nodded thoughtfully. 'How about this? After school, we'll pick you up, stop for milkshakes, and then head to your house. Does that sound okay?'

Jonas hesitated, then gave a reluctant nod. His grip on

Mandy's hand tightened, and she stayed silent, her wide eyes filled with a mixture of fear and uncertainty.

'It'll be okay,' I said softly, trying to reassure her. 'We'll take care of everything.'

Mandy didn't respond, but she clung to Jonas; it was clear she trusted him. I wondered what these kids had seen in their young lives. Or was it fear about their mother that was making Jonas resist?

Sheree gave them both an encouraging smile. 'Are you ready to go back to class?'

They both jumped up.

Mark and I walked back to the station; it wouldn't be long before we headed out to the farm with the kids.

Chapter 19

Strathallyn Station - April 1926.
Elspeth

Elspeth could still feel the warmth of the sun on her skin from that day by the billabong, the feel of Thomas's fingers on her bare skin. A blush heated her cheeks as the memory lingered, both vivid and distant, like a half-forgotten dream. But Thomas Delaney had changed. His demeanour hardened, and every glance in her direction was laced with something unspoken—anger, regret, perhaps even hatred.

The morning after, Elspeth found herself in the stables, brushing down her mare. The rhythmic stroke of the brush was soothing, though her thoughts were anything but. Thomas entered, his taciturn presence filling the space. He didn't acknowledge her, walking straight to his horse with a grim set to his jaw.

'Good morning, Thomas,' she ventured, her voice trembling slightly.

He grunted in reply, not meeting her eyes.

'Do you want me to check the girth on Babir Boy?' she asked, attempting to lighten his mood. 'Father said he is going to ride him later.' Their horse had run last at Bowen; maybe that's why Thomas was in an extra bad mood.

'No need,' he said curtly, tightening the strap himself. 'I can manage.'

Elspeth bit her lip and returned to her work, the silence between them as oppressive as the midday heat until her father came into the stables and Thomas's voice lightened as he and her father discussed a new training regime. She pushed away the ache in her throat as tears threatened. She was the problem; he didn't want to be in her company. He had enticed her and seduced her, and he had got what he wanted.

This time, she let the anger build in her. The sooner she left for England, the better; she could get away from him, and she would never forget what he had done. He had taken advantage of a naïve girl and taken the one thing that should have been precious to her. She vowed never to forgive him, but each time she saw him from afar, the warmth of her attraction to this complicated man would not leave her.

In the weeks that followed, Thomas's indifference grew into outright avoidance. He spoke to Elspeth only when necessary and never spoke on the rare occasion they were alone. His laughter, once so easy in her company, was now reserved for others on the rare occasion he did laugh. Each day, Elspeth's unhappiness deepened.

Her mother, ever observant, took note of her quiet demeanour.

'Elspeth, you've hardly said a word lately,' she remarked one evening, setting down her sewing. 'Is something troubling you?'

Elspeth shook her head, feigning a small smile. 'Just tired, Mother.'

Her mother wasn't convinced. 'You've been tired a lot lately. You're not unwell, are you?'

'No, I'm fine,' Elspeth insisted, her hands tightening around the fabric of her dress.

But she wasn't fine. Her body betrayed her with waves of nausea in the mornings and an unrelenting fatigue. She counted the weeks since that afternoon by the billabong. Ten weeks. The realisation struck her like a thunderclap.

Could she be carrying Thomas's child?

##

That night, unable to sleep, Elspeth rose quietly to go to the outside lavatory. The house was silent, save for the faint murmur of her parents' voices drifting down from their bedroom window. She paused, curiosity piqued by her father's troubled tone.

'I'm worried about Thomas, Amelia,' her father said. 'I

found him in the stables last night, drunk as a lord. It's not like him.'

'Has something happened?' her mother asked, her voice tinged with concern.

'I don't know. He's been distant lately and irritable. I've had to speak to him a couple of times about his rough handling of Babir Boy. It's almost as though he has it in for that horse. And then there's Elspeth.'

Elspeth's breath caught in her throat. She stopped and pressed herself against the wall of the house.

'What about Elspeth?' her mother pressed.

'She's been so quiet. I wonder if something's happened between them.'

Her mother sighed. 'She's of an age where emotions run high. He is a fine-looking man. Perhaps she's had her heart broken.'

'Maybe,' her father said. 'But I'll keep an eye on him. He's a good trainer, but if this continues . . .'

Their voices faded as Elspeth made her way to the lavatory and then retreated to her room, heart pounding. Tears streamed down her face as she lay in bed, the enormity of her situation pressing down on her. What would she do? Regret wrapped around her like a heavy blanket. All her dreams of England, of a life filled with promise, were now in ashes. And Thomas—the man she had loved so fiercely—looked at her as if she were a stranger.

She had been so foolish.

The following days were a blur of routine. Elspeth kept her head down, avoiding both her parents' probing questions and Thomas's scornful glances. But the silence was unbearable. She needed to confront him, to understand why he had turned so cold.

She found him in the paddock one afternoon, repairing a fence. Summoning her courage, she approached.

'Thomas,' she called softly.

He straightened, wiping sweat from his brow, and fixed her with a hard stare. 'What is it?'

'We need to talk.'

'There's nothing to talk about,' he said, turning back to his work.

'Please,' she pressed, her voice breaking. 'You can't just pretend it didn't happen.'

He shook his head. 'It was a mistake, Elspeth. One that never should've happened.'

'A mistake?' she echoed, pain lacing her words. 'Is that all it was to you?'

He didn't answer, his silence speaking volumes.

Tears welled in her eyes, but she refused to let them fall. 'You don't even care, do you?'

'Elspeth, I can't do this,' he said, his voice low. 'It's better if we leave things as they are.'

She turned away, her heart shattering anew. As she walked back to the house, she realised she was truly alone in this.

That night, Elspeth lay awake, her mind racing. She placed a tentative hand over her stomach, the enormity of her situation sinking in. She was carrying a child, a part of Thomas that would forever tie them together, no matter how much he tried to distance himself.

Her mother's voice echoed in her mind: 'You're not unwell, are you?'

No, not unwell. But changed irrevocably.

She couldn't keep this secret forever. And when the time came, she would have to face the truth—no matter the consequences.

A time very soon.

Chapter 20

Bowen River - Friday.

Bec

Todd was waiting at the station when we walked in, and he gestured to the door. 'Will you take me up to the caravan park, please, Bec?'

'Sure. It'll have to be quick, though. Mark and I are taking the kids out to the farm after school.' Too late, I realised *I* was telling the head of the investigation team what we were doing. 'I'm sure Mark will talk to you about it; he's outside taking a phone call.'

'Good, I'll go out there with you, too.'

Relief flooded through me. I had lost my confidence with my place in the team over the past few hours.

Mark was still on the phone when we walked outside, and he nodded when Todd gestured in the direction of the caravan park. He nodded and kept talking.

'How did it go with the kids?' Todd asked when we were in the Stinger. 'Any more information?'

'They wouldn't tell us how long they'd been by themselves.'

'So, the first day she was missing was Tuesday, according

to the IGA boss and Jean. The little girl, Mandy, tried to say something about an uncle, but her brother cut her off.'

'Maybe being at home in a familiar environment will get them talking more.'

'That's what Mark thought.'

I turned into the caravan park. It was so different to when I was a kid. The neat rows of dongas and cabins nestled among well-tended gardens. I assumed Jean had staff; she certainly wouldn't be able to do it all herself. Workers milled about, most heading back to their rooms after the day's shifts. I parked beside the office, and the familiar figure of Jean Purdue emerged before we even stepped out of the car.

She waved us in with a nod, a clipboard tucked under her arm. The office was cool, and the hum of the air conditioning was steady in the background. I had already talked to Jean about the children once, but I could tell from her furrowed brow that she had more to say this time.

'Rebecca, Detective,' she greeted us, her tone professional but warm. 'Back again? Thought you might be.'

'We're following up on a few things,' Todd said as we took seats by her desk. 'Are you familiar with two workers from the mine—Terry Clegg and Mike Henson?'

They must be the two from the fracas at the pub last night that Todd and Justin had been out to interview.

Jean consulted her clipboard, flipping a few pages. 'Yep, both of them are in Cabin 14, but I haven't seen them all day. That's not unusual, though, with shift work.' She set the clipboard down and folded her hands.

'Any issues with them? Bad behaviour? Fighting?'

Jean shook her head. 'The workers come here to eat and sleep. We rarely have any issues. On their time off, most of the workers fly home. Some go down to Airlie Beach or Bowen for a break.'

'Thanks.' Todd nodded. 'We're trying to find out more about any visitors Leanne might have had. Do you know who she was dealing with from the solar company?'

Jean's eyes narrowed slightly, thoughtful. 'I don't know what his name was. She did say she'd spoken to him a few times, and she had a letter from him with the offer for her place. From memory, he was always referred to as the representative of the company. If you call the company, I'm sure they'll give you the name of the local contact.'

She stared at me, and I could see her thoughts ticking over. 'Is there something else you've thought of, Jean?' I asked.

'Yes, there's something else you should hear.' Her gaze shifted to me, and her expression softened, tinged with apology. 'Rebecca, this might be hard for you to hear, but I think you need to know. I've been thinking about it since you were last here.'

I braced myself, the familiar tension returning. 'What is it?'

Jean sighed, glancing out the window before meeting my eyes again. 'Leanne told me she'd been meeting your father. Said she ran into him at the library, of all places. They got talking—family history stuff. She was trying to track down relatives, and your dad offered his . . . perspective.'

Todd's pen hovered over his notebook. 'What kind of perspective?'

'The usual,' Jean said, her tone wary. 'He told her the past didn't matter as much as how you live now. That faith could give her peace and help her let go of the things she couldn't control. At first, she seemed to appreciate it. She said he was a good listener.' Jean paused, her lips pressing into a thin line. 'But then he started going out there to visit her, and that's when things went a bit . . . off.'

I felt my stomach twist. 'At her place?'

Jean hesitated, then sighed deeply. 'Look, I know he's your father, Bec, and I'm sorry to say this, but he's always had a way of focusing his attention on young women. Trying to "guide" them, as he puts it. Leanne didn't say much, but I could tell she was starting to feel uneasy. She mentioned feeling pressured to accept his views, and it didn't sit right with her.'

Todd's face remained impassive, but I knew he was working through the implications. I, meanwhile, was struggling to deal with the growing dread in my chest. My father—a man I'd always seen as righteous—had crossed a line. And now, his involvement with Leanne was becoming more troubling by the second.

'Did Leanne ever say why she stopped trusting him?' Todd asked.

Jean shook her head slowly. 'No, but she got quieter after his last few visits. I told her to trust her instincts and tell him to leave her in peace. That was the phrase she used to me. She said she didn't want to make a fuss. I'm sorry, Rebecca. Your father's not well-liked in town.'

'Oh, I know that well,' I said. 'One of the reasons I knew it would be hard coming back here.'

'Anything else you can tell us?' Todd asked Jean.

She shook her head. 'No. Did you want me to tell Terry and Mike to go to the station when they knock off?'

'No, that's all good.' Todd stood. 'Thanks for your time, Jean. I appreciate your candour.'

The room seemed to close in on me as I headed for the door. Jean's words wouldn't leave me. My father's zeal had always been a point of pride for him, but I knew how inappropriate he could be. I had no idea he'd go that far.

How far? I wondered. Going out to her home, he'd stepped over a line, considering he was no longer a member of the clergy with cause to visit anyone. What else had he done that I didn't know about? And what did it mean for Leanne's disappearance?

Jean reached out and squeezed my arm as I walked past her. My smile was tight.

Todd was quiet as we walked across to the Stinger. The only sound was the crunch of gravel under our boots. My mind was spinning, trying to make sense of what we'd just heard. I reached the car first, heading straight for the driver's side and climbing in without a word. Todd slipped into the passenger seat, and for a long minute, there was silence stretching thin, taut like a wire about to snap. Unease sat in the pit of my stomach, and the back of my neck prickled.

Finally, he broke the silence. 'Are you okay, Bec?'

I gripped the steering wheel, my knuckles white. 'If you're asking whether I can stay impartial, yes, I can,' I said, my voice flat. 'I do not want to be taken off this investigation.'

'Good,' Todd replied. 'I wasn't going to suggest that anyway.'

I gave a bitter laugh. 'Mark might.'

Todd turned slightly to face me. 'I'm the leading detective on this case, and I believe we need your help.'

I nodded but didn't reply. My stomach churned with a mix of anger and disbelief. The thought of my father being mixed up in this made my skin crawl.

'How long since you left town? How close did you stay to your father? I saw your reaction.'

'Twelve years, and I've probably seen him three times since I left.'

'I don't have a problem with that.'

Back at the station, Mark was waiting in the workroom, leaning against the edge of the table. He straightened when we walked in.

'How'd it go?' he asked, then without waiting for an answer, his gaze shifted to me. 'Bec, what kind of car does your father drive? Someone in the community has come forward and said he had been visiting Leanne.'

I stiffened immediately, my temper flaring. 'Why? Are you suggesting it was him out at the house? That he—' my voice caught, but I forced the words out, 'that my father clouted me and gave me a concussion?'

Mark held up his hands, his tone calm but firm. 'I'm not accusing anyone. I'm asking because we need to follow up every lead.'

'I know. Jean told us too.' I stared at him, my jaw tight. 'He drives a white sedan. Not a ute. And even if he did visit Leanne, he wouldn't hurt *me*. He's my father.'

Mark didn't respond. Todd, as usual, stayed quiet, his gaze flicking between us.

After a long silence, Mark said, 'I know this is hard, Bec. But we're not ruling anything out. We need to consider every possibility.'

I crossed my arms, leaning back in my chair. 'Fine. Consider every possibility. But my father isn't a violent man, and he wouldn't hurt Leanne or anyone else.'

Mark nodded; his expression neutral. 'Noted.'

Todd cleared his throat. 'Let's focus on what we know and keep digging. We've got more pieces of the puzzle now, but we're not there yet.'

I forced myself to take a deep breath, trying to suppress the frustration bubbling inside me. I needed to stay composed, to keep my focus on finding Leanne. But the doubts about my father's involvement gnawed at me, and I couldn't shake the uneasy feeling that things were about to get a lot more complicated.

Chapter 21

Bowen River – Friday.

Bec

Mark's phone buzzed and broke the silence. His expression darkened. 'On the way.' He put the phone in his pocket.

'Trouble at the pub, Todd,' Mark said, his voice low. 'Bec, stay here with Aaron. Tom is on his way in before the bus run. I'll get you to talk to him.'

'Tom?' I raised an eyebrow. 'What's happened?'

Mark shook his head. 'Not sure. Maybe he's finally got onto his driver. He wanted to come here and talk to us. Any issues, lock the station door.'

What the hell was going on?

Todd and Mark headed out fast, and I sat at my computer, trying to clear my head. I didn't even have a chance to log in before Aaron appeared in the doorway and told me Tom was waiting out the front.

I followed Aaron back to the foyer. Tom was sitting next to Aaron's potted fern, tapping his fingers on the side of the chair.

'Hi, Tom,' I said.

'Hey, Bec.' His brow furrowed as his gaze flicked to the ground, then back up to me. 'I finally got on to Marty on a call. Want to pass on what he said.'

I gave him a nod and led him into the interview room, closing the door behind us.

'Are you happy if I record what you say?' I asked, taking a seat across from him.

'Yeah, not a problem,' Tom replied, his voice steady, but his eyes flicked around nervously. 'What he said—'

I put up my hand before he could continue. 'Wait until we're settled, Tom. Thanks for coming in. I know you've got a busy schedule.'

Tom glanced at the clock on the wall. 'I've only got ten minutes before I need to collect the bus and head to the primary school. But I knew I needed to tell you this sooner rather than later.'

That meant Mark and I had ten minutes to get to the school, too.

'We'll be quick,' I said, trying to keep my voice calm, though my heart was pounding. We sat at the table, and I hit the record button on the recorder. The beep seemed to echo in the room as I looked up at Tom.

'Thank you for coming in, Tom,' I began, my voice steady. 'I know you've got a busy afternoon. What additional information do you have for us?'

Tom took a deep breath before speaking. 'Marty, our casual driver, called me back. He's been away and didn't get my message until he arrived home around lunchtime today. He told me that Leanne wasn't at the bus stop either morning or afternoon last Friday. He said she must have driven the kids in as there was an excursion, because he did pass her car coming back out of town about a quarter to nine. The kids were on the bus at the end of the day, but he said she wasn't waiting at the gate. He didn't worry because he could see her car at the house. He dropped the kids off.'

I felt my stomach drop. My eyes widened, and my breath caught in my throat. *That meant the kids had been out there alone for almost a week.*

I don't think any of us had considered it being that long. It also meant that the trail could be cold by now.

'Wait,' I said, trying to keep my voice steady. 'Last Friday? Is he sure of the day? That's the first time she wasn't waiting for them?'

Tom nodded gravely. 'Yeah, that's right. I had him double-check. He was certain because it was the day of the excursion.'

I pressed my lips together, trying to process the likely possibility that the kids had been out there for almost a week by themselves.

'When I told Marty that we needed to be sure of the day, he mentioned that he saw an unfamiliar car at their place that afternoon. A white ute. When he saw Leanne's car near the house, he assumed she had a visitor, and that's why she wasn't at the gate.'

The white ute. Another connection to it.

'This is important, Tom,' I said after a moment, my voice soft but firm. 'Are you sure she wasn't at the bus stop early this week?'

'I'm sure,' he replied, his face drawn. 'I thought it was strange on Monday morning, but when I asked Jonas where she was, he said she was a bit busy. When she wasn't there that afternoon, I wondered. I could see her car parked outside the house down the dip, so I figured that she was letting them walk down to the house by themselves now. Country kids. You know how it was. We knew about snakes and not being allowed to go to the creek and all that country stuff.'

'What about the car Marty saw?'

'No, I've never seen a white ute there,' he said, glancing at his watch. 'I'd better get going.'

'Thanks, Tom,' I said as he stood to leave. 'Don't hesitate to call if you think of anything else.'

'I'm sorry about what the kids are going through. My heart breaks for them. If there's anything Lacey and I can do to help, don't hesitate to ask.'

'Thanks, we appreciate that. I'll pass that on, too.'

He nodded grimly. 'Do you think she's okay?'

'We can only hope,' was all I could offer in reply. My words felt hollow.

As Tom left, I stood there trying to shake off the fear that Leanne wouldn't come home.

Chapter 22

Bowen River – Friday.

Bec

My mind kept racing back to those kids—how scared they must have been alone in the house at night. I wondered why they wouldn't tell anyone. Someone had said something to them, or someone had frightened them into silence.

I was heading back to my desk when I heard a commotion in the foyer. The voice hit me like a punch to the gut.

Jesus Christ.

It was Gray's voice yelling out. 'Let go of me, pig. I said I'd come with you.'

What the hell was going on now?

I froze, every muscle in my body locking up. I didn't have to see him to know it was him. His voice—shouting, furious, filled with anger—came through to the workroom. I heard a string of expletives, and the slurring of his speech made it clear he was drunk.

Mark said he'd left town. Obviously not.

I hesitated, wondering whether I should go out there. Every instinct told me to stay here, to avoid the confrontation, but I knew sooner or later I'd have to deal with it. Still, I stayed at my desk, forcing myself to keep calm. The last thing I needed was to inflame the situation further.

I could hear the clang of the cell door being opened and then slammed shut. Gray's voice echoed through the building, now muffled but still full of rage, as his objections filled the air. I squeezed my eyes shut for a moment and put my head in my hands, my mind a swirl of thoughts I couldn't organise.

Footsteps approached, sharp and quick. I dropped my hands and began pretending to focus on the open database in front of me, anything to appear as if I wasn't listening to the mess unfolding out the front.

The door to the office opened with a soft creak, and Mark stepped in, his face grim, Todd close behind him.

'Bec,' Mark started, his voice low as he glanced at the Q Prime screen I had just logged into, 'I need you to check something for me.'

I nodded quickly, still trying to steady my breath. 'What's up?'

'Gray Cameron's been arrested,' Todd said, his expression tight.

'I heard him.' I held my voice steady.

'He assaulted Justin; he's at the health centre. His nose is broken, and it looks like he'll have to go to Townsville for facial surgery. Ross, the publican, called because he said he saw

Cameron passing over a wad of dope to one of the guys at the bar. So, we need to know if he's got a record. Can you check Q Prime, please?'

Q Prime is the Queensland Police Records Information Management Exchange. It had been in existence when I started in the force, and I couldn't imagine what it must have been like before it was built, integrating with a single point of access to intelligence and data. In the field, we had Q Lite, a fleet of iPads. I never thought I'd be looking up Gray.

I clicked away at the keyboard, trying to push everything else from my mind as I typed in Gray's details. I didn't want to think about him, about what he was doing here, or why he was in this state. But as I pulled up his record, my stomach sank.

His name popped up on the screen immediately: Gray Larson Cameron.

'Shit,' I muttered under my breath.

I clicked into the file, and my stomach dropped as I read through his record. The entries were clear, striking a deep chord of unease in me. Gray, the man I thought I knew, had a past I had never known. My fingers shook slightly as I scrolled down the list of offences—assaults, public disorder charges, and something much more disturbing: a history of violent behaviour, especially when drinking.

I turned around to look at Mark and Todd. 'I had no idea,' I whispered. 'Absolutely no bloody idea. Please believe me.'

Mark didn't say anything right away, just watching me with a steady, unreadable expression. He seemed to sense my shock and stepped closer. His hand gently squeezed my shoulder.

Todd, his voice calm but betraying a note of disbelief, started reading aloud from the screen. 'Public disorder charge, 2018. Convicted . . . 2019—intimidation charges, Domestic Violence Act. Several incidents involving alcohol . . . another arrest for assault in 2021 and breaching probation.'

I watched the words scroll by, the reality of Gray's past sinking in. I had always known there were things about him I didn't understand, but this was far beyond what I could ever have imagined.

'Two years ago,' Todd paused, glancing at me, 'conviction for assault. Served three months and was released, but there's more. His name has also come up in a couple of drug importation investigations, but no charges have been laid yet.'

My stomach churned as I thought of the parcels, the trips to the post office. How could I have been so stupid not to ask him? The couple of times I had shown interest in his business, he'd waved me away.

The evidence in front of me made it impossible to believe that the man I knew—the man I had lived with—was not who I thought. I knew he had his problems, but I had never imagined anything like that.

I nodded slowly, trying to keep my emotions in check. It didn't matter how I felt right now. What mattered was the investigation, the children, and finding out what had happened to Leanne. Everything else had to be put aside for now.

I closed the screen with Gray's details on it. I was going to stay at my desk and not go anywhere near the cells.

Mark spoke, his jaw tightening. 'Bec, we need to talk. Come to my office, please.'

I didn't argue. It was clear that he needed to talk to me even though I was still trying to process the two big shocks of the day: my father and my ex.

Chapter 23

Strathallyn Station - May 1926.
Elspeth

The marriage of Elspeth Valentine and Thomas Delaney took place on a dull day at the end of May. Rain had swept across the station for days, turning the paddocks into a quagmire. The ceremony, originally planned for the garden under the sprawling gum tree, was hastily moved to the veranda of the homestead. The minister, a stoic man from Bowen River, performed the rites as the rain drummed softly on the iron roof.

Elspeth stood with her hands clasped tightly around her small bouquet of white wildflowers. Her wedding dress, hastily sewn by Mrs Revesby, was simple yet elegant—an ivory frock with a modest lace collar and sleeves that grazed her wrists. Her hair, usually free to tumble down her back, was gathered into a low chignon under a delicate veil. She was the picture of a bride, but inside, it was the last thing she felt herself to be.

Thomas stood beside her, looking uncomfortable in a navy blue suit that did little to hide his discontent. He kept tugging at his stiff collar, and each time he adjusted it, Elspeth bit her lip, fighting the urge to scold him. Not today. She couldn't let her frustration boil over during the ceremony.

The only witnesses were her parents, Mrs Revesby, and her daughter Mary. Elspeth caught Mary's eyes lingering on Thomas, her gaze laced with a quiet longing. A knot of suspicion tightened in Elspeth's stomach. Had he been with Mary, too? The thought churned her insides, disgust creeping in where joy should have lived.

As the minister spoke, Elspeth's heart thudded against her ribs. She had always imagined her departure to England to be the next big celebration at home. Her father's booming voice wished her a successful journey. In her imagination, her mother beamed with pride, congratulating Elspeth on securing a place among the well-heeled society of a grand English estate. She envisioned her daughter being courted by a man of refinement, perhaps an heir with a fine lineage. A man whose hands were not rough and scarred like Thomas Delaney's, but a man whose life revolved around fox hunts and summer balls.

Instead, on this bleak May afternoon, the air was heavy, thick with disapproval. To his credit, Father had been kind to her when her mother had called him in when Elspeth finally told her of her fear that she was having Thomas's child. Mother had been distant and had not spoken to her since that day three weeks earlier.

Still, there was a small flicker of hope deep in Elspeth as Thomas solemnly recited his vows. His voice, though low and hesitant, carried a sincerity that momentarily softened her resentment. Her voice was steady as she pledged herself to him, though she couldn't ignore the quiet sobs of her mother behind them.

##

After the ceremony, the small party moved into the house for the wedding breakfast. The dining room, usually reserved for special occasions, was set with fine china and silverware. A simple feast awaited: roast lamb, fresh bread, and fruit preserves with custard. Despite the intimate setting, an uneasy quiet hung over the table.

Her father raised a toast. 'To the newlyweds,' he said gruffly, lifting his glass. 'May your life together be prosperous.'

And happy, Elspeth hoped.

Thomas barely touched his food, his discomfort as palpable as the rain outside. Elspeth forced down a few bites, the horror of the day making her throat tighten. Her mother, pale and withdrawn, dabbed at her eyes with a handkerchief, her gaze avoiding Elspeth's.

As Mrs Revesby cleared the plates away, her father cleared his throat. 'Thomas,' he began, leaning back in his chair, 'I've given some thought to where you and Elspeth might settle. I'll be giving you one of the settlement blocks—about twenty miles west, near the boundary line on Suttor River.'

Elspeth's stomach dropped. The settlement blocks. The place was remote, cut off from the rest of the station by rugged terrain and dense scrub. There wasn't even a proper road leading out there.

'That's very generous of you, sir,' Thomas said, his tone neutral. 'I will make it a home.'

Elspeth stared down at the slight bump that had appeared over the past weeks, her stomach churning. She had dreamed of a life in England, far from the isolation of the bush, and now she was being sent deeper into it. Her father's words felt like a cruel twist of fate, as though he were punishing her for her sin. She lifted her chin and stared at him and he had the grace to look away.

Later that night, as she lay beside Thomas in his bed in the staff quarters, the events of the day replayed in her mind. The joy she had once imagined was nowhere to be found. Her dreams of escaping to England and working on a grand estate were shattered. Instead, she was bound to a man who barely acknowledged her in a place that now felt more like a prison than her home.

Hot tears rolled silently down her cheeks, and she put her hand on her stomach. How would she ever love this child?

Wasn't that what a mother was supposed to do? This child had destroyed her dreams.

Her thoughts drifted to the old superstition her mother often spoke of: marriages held on rainy days were cursed with misfortune. She had dismissed it as an old wives' tale, but now, lying alone in the dark, she couldn't shake the feeling that her mother was right. The rain had soaked her wedding day and, with it, her hopes for a happy future.

Thomas snored beside her; he hadn't said a word to her or touched her after they had left the homestead.

Perhaps she could make him love her. It was her only chance at salvaging something from the ruins of her dream. When the child was born, she would try to make a happy family. But as the rain continued to fall outside, her resolve wavered. The path ahead seemed as bleak as the stormy sky.

Chapter 24

Bowen River Police Station -Friday 3.30 p.m.

Bec

My thoughts were churning and bleak as I sat opposite Mark's chair. He closed the door and my spirits plummeted lower. I was worried about my place in the investigation team a while ago; now, I worried that my job at Bowen River could be in jeopardy.

Mark pulled up a chair beside me, his expression serious but kind. 'Bec, we need to talk before we go.' His voice was low and steady.

'School will be out already,' I said. I looked up at him. 'I guess I won't be going with you now.'

'It's okay. Todd's gone to pick them up in the patrol car, and Sheree is coming with the kids too. If you're up to it, we'll go out in the Outlander.'

My head flew up, and I forced a smile I didn't quite feel. 'Of course, I'm up to it.'

'You looked so worried after all that's happened this afternoon. I want you to know that it's not you who's responsible for another's behaviour.' He leaned forward, resting his arms on his knees. 'I just want to check you can deal with it and provide any support I can. After everything—the assault on you, the fight at the hotel, your dad, and now Gray's history, I need to know if you're okay to keep going. You've had a bloody rough week.'

Taking a deep breath, I clasped my hands together, grounding myself. 'Thanks, Mark. I appreciate it, but I'm fine. I'm not going to let any of that throw me off. This investigation is too important, and I'm not stepping back. I'm strong enough to do it. Trust me.'

He studied me closely, and I held his gaze steadily. 'Please, I'm fine.'

'Right. If you're sure. Just remember, you don't have to shoulder everything alone. We're a team, plus you can get some support through Priority One.'

I rolled my eyes. 'I don't need any employee counselling. I need to get on with the job, Sergeant.'

'Right, the offer's been made, and I'll document that in my diary.'

I stood. 'Are we meeting them at the school or the farm?'

'The farm.'

'What about Gray?'

'He's already had bail posted. He'll be gone by the time we get back.'

'I wonder where he got the money for that.' My voice was

cold.

'Someone from Brisbane posted it for him. Whoever it was has a hire car being driven up for him to go back to Brisbane.'

'Good. I hope I never see him again.' I shook my head. 'I cannot believe how he sucked me in.' My voice trembled. 'He's been living in my apartment for almost a year. I could have been drawn into the investigation about the drugs. It could have been the end of my career.'

'Well, you weren't, and it hasn't been. Like I told you, your sergeant at Bayside spoke very highly of you. I'm sure it was flagged if it was even known who your partner was, but your record's clean, and he's gone now.'

'Probably not. I always tend to keep personal stuff out of the workplace.'

'Well, it works differently up here. We look out for each other.'

'I know. I can see that, and I appreciate it,' I said, my voice shaking a little. 'And thank you for checking on me. I'll let you know if I need anything, but I'm sticking with the investigation if you'll have me, but I guess it's up to Todd.'

'We've already spoken. You're not going anywhere.' Mark leaned back, a faint smile breaking through his concern. 'And listen, when we get back, Sheree and I are having an easy barbie tonight. Aaron's coming over. We'd love you to join us. A late one, seven thirty.'

The invitation caught me off guard, and for a second, I hesitated. 'That sounds nice. Thanks, Mark. I'll be there.'

'Good,' he said, standing. 'Now, let's get moving.'

##

Mark was quiet as he drove, his gaze fixed on the road. I refused to let my thoughts dwell on anything apart from the two children. As we passed a new array of solar panels glittering in the late afternoon sun, I broke our silence.

'Those weren't here last time,' I remarked, watching the panels disappear in the rearview mirror as we passed.

'Nope,' Mark replied, his tone clipped.

We arrived at the farm just behind the others. Jonas climbed out of the back of the Stinger and looked at Mark and me with wide eyes. 'That was way cool. I've never been in a police car before. Todd put the siren on for us.'

I managed a smile, though my heart ached for him. 'That's pretty special.'

Once Mandy was out of the car, the children rushed to the front porch. Mandy called out, 'Is Mummy back now?'

Sheree and I exchanged a glance; the hope in Mandy's voice set off an emotional reaction in both of us. Todd unlocked the front door, and the kids shot off with Sheree behind them.

I could hear her asking them what they wanted to pack to

take back to town.

Meanwhile, Mark, Todd and I moved methodically through the empty house, every creak of the floorboards adding to the tension. Forensics had been in and done their stuff: fingerprinting, DNA collection, and evidence of disturbance with inspection, enhanced by luminol or other chemical sprays to detect blood or bodily fluids not visible to the naked eye. Todd was still waiting for the report to come back in.

Todd, Mark and I started in the kitchen, opening drawers filled with neatly stacked utensils, then moved to the pantry, where shelves were lined with jars of preserved fruit, with labels in writing that I recognised as Leanne's all these years later. Nothing was out of place, but the absence of the person who had created them was palpable.

In the living room, we searched the cabinets beneath the television. A few photo albums and stacks of magazines were neatly arranged, but nothing to raise our alarm came to our attention. Moving on, Todd and I entered the master bedroom while Mark went to check on Sheree and the kids. Todd opened the wardrobe, rifling through neatly hung dresses and jackets while I turned my attention to the bedside tables. Forensics had taken her laptop to look for digital information that could timestamp her presence and to look for any emails that might raise flags.

'It's so intrusive,' I said quietly.

'But necessary,' Todd replied.

The drawers revealed a mismatched collection of books, a small wooden box containing old letters, and a pair of reading glasses. On the dresser, I noticed a faded photograph of the family, Leanne smiling with her two children when they were a couple of years younger, her arms wrapped tightly around them. There was no photo of their father in sight.

Jonas appeared in the doorway, his voice high-pitched. 'Where are our dogs?' he asked, his voice filled with quiet concern. 'Have you taken them too?'

Poor little mite; it seemed he held the police responsible for Leanne's absence.

Mark appeared behind him, placing a hand on the little boy's shoulder. 'It's okay, mate. Tom's taken them to his place to look after them until Mum comes home.'

Jonas's eyes dropped to the floor, and he nodded solemnly. 'Okay. As long as they are getting fed. That's usually my job.'

I could tell Mark's smile was as forced as mine.

'How about you and Mandy show me around outside? I'd love to see this creek I've heard about.'

With a reluctant nod, Jonas followed Mark and Sheree out, his little sister trailing behind. Their voices faded as they stepped onto the verandah. Todd and I exchanged a brief glance before resuming our search.

I moved to the desk in the corner of the room, where a pile of folders sat neatly stacked. I flipped open the top one, scanning the contents.

'Todd, take a look at this,' I said, holding up a few sheets. 'It's photocopies of marriage, birth, and death records—looks like a detailed family history. Leanne must be looking into it. I wonder if there was a reason other than for general interest.'

Todd stepped over, peering at the documents. 'Hmm,' he muttered, flipping through a few pages. 'She must've been working on this for a while. It makes me wonder why when most of her energy seemed to go into environmental stuff. Why would she be focusing on family history?'

Underneath the family history folder, another one caught my eye, this one marked with a plain label. I opened it and found reports, maps, and assorted correspondence. 'This is interesting,' I said, holding it up. 'It's about the solar company.'

Todd took the folder from me, flipping through its contents with a frown. 'Looks like detailed negotiations had taken place with her,' he said. 'Might be worth digging into. Could be relevant. Jean mentioned the letter of offer. It's probably in this lot. We'll take both of these back with us,' he said, stacking the folders into one pile and picking them up.

I headed down the hall when Todd put the folders on the hall stand. 'Let's keep going. There are still a couple of rooms to go.'

We moved to the bathroom and linen closet, but everything was neatly organised, and nothing stood out. In the children's rooms, toys were scattered on the floor, evidence of Leanne not being there to tidy up. Sheree had put some items in a bag in the hallway. It was hard to believe that the kids had looked after themselves for a week and pretended everything was normal. If only they'd told someone, the search for Leanne could have started days ago.

By the time we finished, the house felt cold, the silence depressing. Todd crouched by the children in the front yard, holding the hat out. 'Is this your dad's hat?' he asked gently.

Mandy shook her head. 'No, that's Uncle Teddy's.'

Todd glanced at me, his brow furrowing slightly. 'Uncle Teddy?' he prompted, keeping his tone light.

Mandy nodded. 'He's Mummy's friend. He told us he's our uncle, and he's going to get rich and take care of us.'

Todd pressed on. 'Do you know his other name, Mandy? Does he live around here?'

Before she could answer, Jonas cut in sharply. 'No, we don't. Stop asking her stuff. She's too little.'

Mandy's eyes filled with tears, and she choked out, 'I want my mummy. I want her to come back.'

Todd crouched lower, his face softening. 'We'll do

everything we can to bring her home soon,' he promised.

As we packed up and prepared to leave, Todd and I shared a glance. Whoever Uncle Teddy was, he was now a prime suspect in our investigation.

'He's going to get rich and take care of us.'

##

After we dropped the kids back at the caravan park and Sheree at their house, we went back to the station; Mark called a team meeting. His expression was serious as he gathered us around the conference table.

'There have been some significant developments today,' he began, glancing between Todd and me before he walked to the whiteboard. 'First off, we now know that Leanne hasn't been seen for a full week. Todd has confirmed that she spent some time the week before with Gerald Haynes, the CEO of Strathallyn Solar. Apparently, he's taken her out driving a few times. He confirmed that today by phone.'

Mark paused, leaning forward. 'They'd made an offer on her land—five million dollars—and she refused. She said the place had been in her family for four generations, and there was no way she was selling.'

He gestured to Todd, who took over as Mark began to write names on the board.

Uncle Teddy.

Murray Reid.

Gerald Haynes.

Terry Clegg.

Mark Henson.

'According to her friend Jean, Leanne was very vocal in her opposition to the solar arrays. She felt the negatives—like disruption of the land and potential damage to the ecosystem—far outweighed the benefits. When Jean heard about the offer, she was floored. But Leanne told her it would happen over her dead body. She was also really upset that they were using the name of the original station for their company: Strathallyn Solar.'

Mark nodded. 'We're very interested in talking to Mr Haynes face to face. Todd and I are going to Townsville to interview him tomorrow.'

Todd's tone shifted slightly as he continued. 'Then there's a mine worker we've been told was seeing Leanne. He's one of the guys who went missing after the first disturbance at the pub. We're still trying to track Terry Clegg down. He's on the five-day fly-out part of his roster. We'll speak to him as soon as he flies in tomorrow. And then there's,' his gaze shifted towards me, 'Jim Whitfield.'

I kept my face blank as my father's name was added to the list. My stomach roiled but I didn't move a muscle.

I fought the urge to react as Mark spoke. 'I interviewed him earlier today. So far, everything seems above board. He claims he was helping Leanne find her way "back to righteousness".'

Mark cleared his throat but quickly grew serious again. 'The librarian backed up his story—that he was helping Leanne with her family research, which led to the documents we found at the farm. Still, we'll keep digging.'

Mark continued, his eyes scanning over some notes he had pulled from the case files. 'There's also the guy named Murray Reid. We don't know yet if he's a genuine local or a plant working for one of the companies. He's been obstructing a lot of the meetings, according to the minutes. He's been really vocal in his opposition to Leanne's stance on solar energy, even more so than anyone else in the community. There is some valid opposition when people talk about jobs and benefits to the community, but his responses to some of the points Leanne raised were harassment. We need to know if that continued outside the meetings.'

Todd pulled out a file from the stack on the table. 'I was reading some of the meeting minutes from a session a few months ago. Leanne was quite clear on her position.' He read from the page:

'She said, "Strathallyn Solar says their valuable infrastructure for our region will provide jobs, reduction of greenhouse emissions/assisting emission reduction targets, and diversification of the agricultural economy in the region. Her objection was based on fact, according to the local research. However, in our meeting with them, it was suggested that they would be using the Cairns-based company that constructed their solar farms there. How will this benefit our region, other than flooding available accommodation?"'

Bec nodded. 'We've seen that ourselves with the caravan park and the pub.'

Todd continued. 'She says, "They say they are "excited to work with the local community to create a positive outcome for Strathallyn Solar and Bowen River for many years to come," and yet once the solar farm is operational, only about five staff are required for maintenance. It is at the expense of our town and our residents. And not only that, every country that has significantly introduced solar and wind technologies into their electricity generation has not only significantly increased their electricity prices but also destabilised their electricity grids. This leads to more expenditure on transmission infrastructure, more expensive electricity grid management, and more ad hoc unproven solutions being pursued. Do we want that for our town?"'

'That's some strong opposition,' Mark said, looking over at me.

Todd nodded. 'Leanne didn't mince words in that meeting. But it wasn't just her stance on the issue that seemed to trigger Reid.' He flipped through the minutes again, his finger stopping at another section. 'Here's where things got heated. Reid, according to the minutes, started verbally attacking Leanne. He called her "misinformed" and "living in the past" and even went as far as saying, "You're just an old-fashioned, stubborn bitch who doesn't understand the future. You're standing in the way of progress and economic growth. And you'll be sorry one day."'

Mark raised an eyebrow. 'That's harsh. Did he attack her like that in front of everyone?'

'According to the minutes, yes,' Todd replied. 'The atmosphere got tense. Reid was angry, maybe even frustrated, with the local opposition to the solar project. Leanne was calm, though. She stuck to her points, but Reid kept pushing. Jean has noted the swear words he used in the minutes with asterisks, but it's clear from the minutes how vicious his response was.'

'I can imagine that,' I said, rubbing my forehead. 'Leanne was passionate, but Reid's attack probably felt personal. If he had been so aggressive at the meeting, maybe there was more to his hostility than just professional disagreement. He could have felt threatened or maybe had a vested interest in the solar project. Either way, it's worth looking into.'

Mark nodded. 'We need to track down Murray Reid and see

if we can make a connection. His behaviour in the meetings—and the fact that he's still been obstructing things—makes him a person of interest. If there's anyone who has it in for Leanne, he might be a key player in that story. The problem is, he's not home, and no one seems to know where he is.'

'Married? Family?' I asked.

'No, but a local from way back and a bloke who heads off in his four-wheel drive and camper for months at a time, according to his neighbour. I've already flagged him on Q Prime, and if he turns up somewhere, they're pulling him into a station.'

Finally, Mark leaned back, folding his arms. 'And that brings us to the elusive Uncle Teddy. Bec, that's your priority on the databases. See if you can find him, who he is and where he lives. If he is related or if the term "uncle" is just used for a friend.'

'Yes, I'll get onto that first thing in the morning. Are you sure I can't work tonight, Mark?' I said, my mind already racing through the notes and records.

'Yes, I'm sure. You'll be fresher in the morning. Time to call it a day, and don't forget dinner at our place.'

Chapter 25

The Lovatts' barbeque – Friday 7.30 p.m.
Bec

The dry streets of Bowen River stretched ahead of me, the brittle yellow grass crackling under my sandals. A shower and a change of clothes had lifted my spirits, and I was determined to stay upbeat, refusing to let this afternoon's revelations drag me down. The late afternoon heat lingered, casting long shadows across the road. I wiped a bead of sweat from my temple and slowed my pace, the stillness of the town settling over me. Children had gone inside for dinner, leaving the streets silent.

As I passed an elderly man mowing his footpath, he looked up and grinned, his smile gappy from missing teeth.

'Wasting me time, hey, love, but it fills in the evening,' he called out.

I smiled back, glancing over my shoulder as I continued walking, sensing his gaze following me until I turned into the gate. By now, everyone in town would know who I was. But how many of them knew what my father had been doing? Had he been acting outside of the law?

I tried to brush the thought aside, though it stuck like a burr in my mind. Maybe it was all innocent. I might not agree with his relentless religious fervour; he'd always been that way. Still, unease gnawed at me.

My thoughts shifted to Todd as I walked. I wondered if he'd be at Mark and Sheree's tonight but quickly dismissed the idea. He'd probably be working late, as usual.

The pull I felt towards him was undeniable, but acting on it wasn't an option. Not after Gray. The sting of *his* betrayal was still fresh, his lies too sharp in my memory. Trusting someone again felt like a risk I wasn't ready to take. Relationships were off the table for a long time.

When I walked up the front steps to the door, Sheree was waiting for me.

'Come on in, Bec. I'm so pleased you could make it,' she said, pulling me into a warm hug. 'If you ever need a shoulder, don't hesitate,' she added softly.

'Thanks, Sheree. That means a lot.' Her kindness caught me off guard, softening my usual reserve and I hugged her back. My gaze shifted to the food spread across the benchtops. 'How did you do all this? You've been at school all day, out with us this afternoon, and still managed to put together a feast.'

Sheree waved off my amazement. 'Just some easy salads and a potato bake in the oven. Mark's in charge of the barbecue.'

The tension in my body eased as we walked through their

welcoming home.

'Mark and Aaron are out the back,' Sheree said with a smile.

The warm, smoky aroma of a barbecue hit me before I even saw the grill, and when we stepped outside, the space opened up into a lush little oasis. Green everywhere—hedges, flowerbeds, and a big, sparkling pool set in pale stone. I could almost feel the cool water on my skin as I glanced at it longingly.

'Wow,' I said. 'This is gorgeous.'

'All Sheree's work,' Mark called from the barbecue, flipping what looked like thick steaks. 'I just mow the lawn and clean the pool.'

'It was a bit bare when we moved in, but Mark helped me dig all the flower beds.' Sheree rolled her eyes, but she was smiling. 'He undersells himself,' she said, gesturing towards the table set with salads and drinks. 'Come on, let's sit down. Everything's nearly ready.'

We settled in as Mark brought over a platter of meat, Aaron taking the seat beside me. I glanced at him as we began to help ourselves to the food. He looked a lot younger out of uniform and was relaxed, maybe thanks to the Lovatts' easy hospitality. I could feel myself relaxing more, too.

'Help yourselves, please.' Sheree pulled out a chair and poured juice for each of us from a large glass jug rattling with ice cubes.

'So, Aaron,' I started, spearing a piece of tomato. 'Where are you from originally?'

'Longreach,' he said, looking up with a quick grin. 'Born and bred. My family's still there.'

'A long way from here,' I said, nodding, but then I paused, realising what might come next. People usually ask the same thing in return. Where are you from? And I wasn't ready to delve into my own past over steak and salad. Before Aaron could say anything, I rushed to steer the conversation in another direction.

'This garden's incredible,' I said quickly, turning to Sheree. 'It reminds me of Mum's. She loves gardening too—though she sticks to vegetables. Beans, tomatoes, that kind of thing. Are these your tomatoes?'

'They are, and my cucumber, and lettuce and asparagus. I love growing our own food!'

I reached for the asparagus that sat in a shallow bowl in what looked like white vinegar. 'My mum always says a garden's not a real garden without at least one tomato plant.'

'Does she grow much?'

'Enough to keep herself busy.' I smiled as Mark came and sat down, and he sat back, sipping a beer.

'So, you're settling in okay, Bec?' Mark asked, his tone casual but warm.

'I think so,' I said, glancing around. 'It's a great town.

Friendly people and a good community. And places like this—' I gestured towards the garden and the pool, 'definitely don't hurt.'

Sheree winked. 'Well, you know where to come for a swim if you're ever sweltering after work, especially in summer. You too, Aaron.'

When we finished eating, Aaron got up to help Sheree with the dishes, leaving Mark and me sitting outside. The night air was cooler now, and the sky was an indigo canvas dotted with brilliant stars.

'Quite a day today,' Mark said, his voice low.

'It's been a long one,' I admitted, offering a faint smile.

Mark nodded, leaning back in his chair. 'I'm glad you came tonight. Didn't think you would, but you deserved to relax.'

'How's Justin doing?' I asked, turning the conversation.

Mark's face darkened. 'He's in surgery in Townsville. Quite a few broken bones in his face.' He shook his head. 'Gray will be charged with that, of course.'

'Serious assault of a police officer, causing grievous bodily harm.' I nodded grimly. 'That charge sheet's only going to grow.'

'Fourteen years maximum.' Mark straightened, his tone shifting. 'Anyway, enough of that. A quick bit of shop talk—now that Justin's out, I want you to formally step up into an acting investigating role.'

I froze for a moment. 'Even with my father in the spotlight?' I asked cautiously.

'We can navigate that,' Mark said firmly. 'I need you to focus on the documents you found at Leanne's house. My gut says there's something important in there. They have to be connected to her disappearance.'

'And we still need to identify Uncle Teddy,' I added.

'Exactly,' Mark agreed, just as Sheree reappeared, carrying two glasses of wine. Aaron was behind her with another two. She handed me one and shot us a mock, stern look. 'Come on, you two, no shop talk. You've earned a break.'

I chuckled, sinking back into my chair and taking a sip of chilled wine, grateful for the moment of calm. Sheree turned to Mark. 'Todd couldn't come tonight, love?'

Mark nodded. 'I asked him, but he wanted to keep working.'

Sheree sighed, her expression softening as she glanced at me. 'You might not know Todd's wife passed away last year. Breast cancer. She was only thirty-nine.'

A pang of sympathy lodged in my chest. 'That's so sad. I didn't know.'

'I didn't know either,' Aaron said. 'That sucks.'

Mark nodded. 'He's thrown himself into work since. Solved quite a few cold cases, actually. On top of the current caseload.'

'I've heard of his reputation, even down in Brisbane,' I said. 'It's an honour to work with him. I know I'll learn a lot.'

Mark's eyes twinkled, and he leaned forward. 'Well, you might get to Bowen. Word is, Justin's planning to move back to the Gold Coast in a few months. Maybe earlier now that he'll be on sick leave. A relieving position might even come up there.'

I raised an eyebrow. 'And?'

'And,' Mark said with a grin, 'you should apply. You've only just joined us, but I know what your aspirations are. Your sergeant in Brisbane spoke highly of you—predicted you'd get that promotion and start detective training sooner rather than later. I was worried you might not stay here long.'

Heat rose to my cheeks. 'I didn't know that.'

'Now you do,' Mark said, raising his glass. 'To new opportunities.'

I hesitated, then clinked my glass against his. Maybe Bowen River had more to offer me than I'd thought.

Chapter 26

Strathallyn Station - November 1926.
Elspeth

Elspeth's world had shrunk to the dim, familiar confines of her old bedroom. The storm outside had raged through the night, rain drumming against the roof in a relentless rhythm. She lay in the bed she had known since childhood, gripping the sheets as another wave of agony coursed through her. Mrs Revesby, pale but steady, dabbed a cool cloth against her forehead. Mother was in Rockhampton; she spent more time there than she did at *Strathallyn.*

'It'll be all right, love,' the housekeeper murmured, though her eyes betrayed a flicker of concern. 'The doctor's on his way.'

Thomas was miles away at their small house near Suttor River, fixing the roof before the storm worsened. He hadn't known the child would come so soon. Even if he had, Elspeth doubted he would have been of much comfort. He'd been distant since their wedding; sometimes, she wondered how she would endure the rest of her life. The afternoon she sat by the billabong where it had all begun, and the water called to her. She imagined stepping beneath the murky surface and letting the cool green water go over her face, her hair floating around her head. She pulled herself out of those wicked thoughts as the baby kicked. That was the cowardly way out; she deserved every moment of unhappiness.

But sometimes, she looked at Thomas, wishing they could recapture the feelings she knew they had shared, the poetry he had recited to her. Perhaps her misery was stopping him from being kind to her. Her hope left her as another excruciating pain gripped her from front to back; she curled her toes and screamed when it seemed to last longer than the others.

When Dr Hargrove finally arrived from Bowen River an hour later, he wasted no time. 'The baby's early,' he said, his tone brisk but kind. 'This will be hard, but you're strong, Elspeth. Where is your mother?'

'She is away,' she said dully as the pain eased. Mrs Revesby gently wiped the perspiration from her face as the doctor examined her. She didn't care what he did.

'Just get it out of me,' she muttered.

Dr Hargrove straightened, his expression calm but determined. 'The pain is making her tense and slowing the baby. We must help her relax.'

He moved to his black leather bag resting on the dresser. Unclasping it, he rummaged through its contents until he removed a small amber bottle. He drew it out and held it up, the label catching the dim light of the kerosene lamp.

Mrs Revesby's eyes widened. 'You think ether is safe, Doctor?'

He nodded. 'In small doses, yes. It'll dull the pain and help Elspeth through this last stage.'

He reached for a clean square of muslin cloth from the bag and carefully tipped the bottle, letting a few drops of the liquid soak into the fabric. The sharp, medicinal scent filled the air instantly. Elspeth blinked. If it took the pain away, she would welcome whatever it was.

Turning back to Mrs Revesby, he held out the cloth to her. 'Now, listen carefully to me. Hold this just over her nose and mouth—lightly, mind you. Don't press down. She needs to breathe normally. Only keep it there for a few seconds at a time, then lift it away to let her take in some fresh air.'

Mrs Revesby took the cloth with steady hands, nodding.

'Only a little at first—she'll settle once it takes effect,' Dr Hargrove assured the housekeeper. 'If she shows any signs of distress—if her breathing becomes shallow, or she seems confused—pull it away immediately. Do you understand?'

'Yes, Doctor.'

Elspeth cried out again, her back arching as another contraction wracked her body. Mrs. Revesby hurried to her side, murmuring soft encouragement. She gently placed the cloth near

Elspeth's face, following the doctor's instructions.

Elspeth flinched at first, her eyes fluttering open as panic gripped her. Mrs Revesby glanced over her shoulder at the doctor, who gave a small nod of reassurance. 'It's all right, dear,' she said soothingly. 'Just breathe. You're doing so well. It won't be long now, and you will have a fine baby to hold.'

Moments later, Elspeth began to relax, her breathing slowing. Her grip on the bedsheets loosened, and her head sank back into the pillow as calm filtered through her.

Dr Hargrove moved closer, checking her pulse and the rise and fall of her chest. 'Good,' he said quietly. 'Let's keep going. She's almost there.'

The hours that followed were a blur of pain and exertion. Elspeth fought against the exhaustion pulling her under, each contraction a mountain she had to climb. When at last, with a final push, the baby entered the world, she collapsed back onto the pillows, trembling.

The room was quiet except for the baby's thin, wavering cry. The doctor cleaned him and placed the tiny bundle in her arms. 'A boy,' he said with a small smile. 'He's early, but he's strong and healthy.'

Elspeth looked down at her son, her heart swelling with a fierce, protective love. His skin was pale, and his cries were weak, but he was alive. She traced a finger along his delicate cheek, tears blurring her vision.

The doctor spoke softly to Mrs Revesby. 'He'll need careful tending. Keep him warm, and feed him often.'

Elspeth barely registered the words. She was already lost in the tiny, miraculous life she held. Despite the pain, the fear, and the loneliness of Thomas's absence, she had brought their child into the world. She whispered softly to him, promising to keep him safe.

When Thomas finally arrived the next morning, soaked and haggard, he paused in the doorway, taking in the sight of Elspeth and the baby. For a moment, his usual reserve faltered.

'A boy?' he asked, his voice hoarse.

Elspeth nodded, her exhaustion giving way to a faint smile. 'Yes, Thomas. Your son.'

He approached hesitantly, as if afraid to step into the room. His hand hovered over the baby before finally resting lightly on the small, blanketed form. Elspeth searched his face, hoping for some flicker of joy or connection. But Thomas's expression was unreadable.

'Please, Thomas,' she said quietly. 'Hold your son. Take him from me.'

'You should rest,' Thomas said softly, but instead of stepping back, he hesitated. His gaze shifted to the small bundle in Elspeth's arms, his expression a mixture of awe and uncertainty.

Elspeth bit her lip, her heart tightening as she offered the baby towards him. For a moment, Thomas didn't move. Then, with a deep breath, he stepped forward and carefully took the child into his arms. His hands, calloused from years of work, cradled the baby with a gentleness that surprised Elspeth. But she knew from the past that this man could be gentle. Her heart filled with hope—and love.

The tension in the room softened as Thomas gazed down at his son. A smile—tentative at first—broke across his face, and a quiet laugh escaped him. 'He's so small,' he murmured, wonder in his voice. 'Much smaller than a foal.'

'Of course he is,' Elspeth said softly. 'He is a little boy.'

Thomas's eyes shone as the baby stirred, a tiny hand peeking out from the blanket to grasp at the air.

Elspeth blinked away tears, overwhelmed by the sight. The storm outside had passed, leaving the world still and fresh. Inside, a different kind of calm was settling over her heart.

Thomas's expression grew fierce and protective as he gently rocked the baby. 'I'll take care of you,' he said, his voice low but resolute. Then he looked up, his gaze locking with Elspeth's. His voice was deep and low, and as he recited to her, joy filled the empty space in her heart.

'He who binds to himself a joy,

Does the winged life destroy;
But he who kisses the joy as it flies,
Lives in eternity's sun rise.'

'And you too, Elspeth,' he continued. 'I'll look after you for the rest of my life.'

Tears slipped down her cheeks, but she smiled through them.

Elspeth reached out, her hand resting lightly on Thomas's arm. 'Thank you,' she whispered, her voice breaking.

Chapter 27

Bowen River - Monday 3.00 p.m.
Bec

The next few days passed in a blur. Mark and Todd were constantly in and out of the station, following up on leads and interviewing persons of interest. Aaron kept things steady at the front desk, supported by Jenny Enright, a constable from Collinsville. Meanwhile, I was glued to my desk, combing through the police database, determined to find something—*anything*—that could explain Leanne's disappearance. There had to be more family somewhere. Surely, no one could be so alone in the world.

Then, again, I thought of my situation. Mum and Dad were both only children, so I had no cousins. A vague memory of an elderly aunt visiting when I was a child was the only family I was aware of, so it wasn't unreasonable to think that Leanne was in the same situation.

I had yet to find out who Uncle Teddy was. While Jenny manned the front desk, Mark had Aaron looking at the electoral rolls in a hundred-kilometre radius, looking for Edwards and Theodores.

The children's father, Randall Simms, was back in jail and had been for three months, so he had been discounted for the time being. Mark had notified the Department of Children, Youth Justice and Multicultural Affairs, and they had agreed to temporary foster care of Jonas and Amanda with Jean.

Mid-afternoon, my phone buzzed. It was Todd. My heart rate slipped up a notch as I picked up. Had something happened?

'Detective Davenport.'

'Bec, any luck with the family connections so far?' His voice was calm but had an undertone of urgency.

'I've found a few mentions of extended relatives in her notes, but I think they are all from way back,' I said, leaning back and stretching my aching shoulders. My stomach grumbled as I moved, and I realised I'd had nothing to eat since a coffee mid-morning. 'I think I'll need access to the Births, Deaths and Marriages records to piece more together, but I couldn't log in.'

'Yeah, that system's restricted. I'll send you the login details for the department-wide account. Just keep a record of what you access—the oversight auditors want the paper trails.'

'Yep, I know accountability, transparency, audits, and legal compliance.'

'You'll make a good detective, Bec. Mark tells me that's your plan.'

'One day.' I scribbled a note on my pad, reminding myself

to screenshot when I logged in to each database. 'Thanks, Todd. How are you and Mark going? Any luck?'

'We're up in Townsville and about to interview the guy from Strathallyn Solar. Just wanted to touch base.'

'Fingers crossed.'

'And Bec? Good work. Keep at it. See you later.'

I hung up, a faint smile lingering. Todd's encouragement was steadying and reminded me that it was usually methodical legwork that led to breakthroughs. Within half an hour, I had access to the database and was tracing Leanne's family history through old records. I spread Leanne's notes across my desk, letting them guide me with dates and names.

The name Delaney caught my attention. Elspeth Delaney—Leanne's great-grandmother—had inherited part of the *Strathallyn Station*. The deeper I dug, the clearer the family tree became. Dates and names swam in front of me, connecting pieces of Leanne's story. Her notes mentioned her grandfather Robert's pride when Jonas, her son, was born, knowing the Delaney name would live on.

Then there was Edward. Or *Teddy*, as he was called in Leanne's notes. He was the brother of her grandfather, Robert Delaney. Was that a coincidence? A forbear called Teddy and an Uncle Teddy in the present. My pulse quickened. A connection? Uncle Teddy, who said he was coming into money?

Was the contemporary Uncle Teddy really part of this family or an outsider weaving himself into their legacy? Whoever he was, did he know of the offer from Strathallyn Solar to buy her land? I needed to find him in the records, but it was impossible when I didn't have a surname. Maybe he was an innocent visitor and didn't even know she was missing. But if he was the owner of the white ute, he was the one responsible for my concussion.

That's when Dad's words from the other afternoon came crashing back. How had he known Leanne was missing? The way he said it was too smooth, too deliberate. A knot of unease tightened in my chest. Was I reading too much into it, or was there something more sinister beneath the surface? Could my own father be hiding something? I would mention that to Todd and Mark when they came back later today.

And then there was Mum—her silence spoke volumes. She hadn't reacted when Dad mentioned Leanne. Not outwardly. But I'd seen her knuckles tighten around her cup. What did she know? Had she been covering for him, or was she just as much in the dark—and worried—as I was?

The tap at the door startled me. Aaron entered, carrying a coffee and sandwich. 'Jenny thought you might need a break,' he said, setting them down with a smile. 'You've missed lunch.'

'Thanks, Aaron,' I said, managing a weak smile.

'You okay?' he asked, leaning casually against the

doorframe.

'Yeah. Just . . . a lot to do.'

Aaron nodded, his easy-going attitude a comfort. 'You'll get there. One step at a time.'

I watched him leave, then turned back to my screen. But the questions about my father lingered, shadowing every move I made.

Chapter 28

Strathallyn Station - October 1927.
Elspeth

Elspeth and Thomas sat together on the veranda in the house at Suttor River, the late afternoon light casting a golden hue over the yard. She rarely went back to the homestead at Strathallyn. Mother had not been home from Rockhampton for over a year, and Mrs Revesby looked after Father. More often than not, Father stayed out at their small house on the river near Suttor Causeway so he could spend time with his grandson.

Edward, now a sturdy little toddler, tottered on unsteady legs a few feet in front of Elspeth and Thomas.

'Come on, Robert,' Elspeth called softly, her hands outstretched. 'You can do it, sweetheart.'

Thomas leaned forward in his chair; his usual stoic expression softened by a trace of a smile. 'He's stubborn,' he said. 'Like his mother.'

Elspeth shot him a look, half-amused. 'And his father, don't forget.'

Robert wobbled, his tiny feet shifting precariously before he took another hesitant step, then another.

Elspeth gasped. 'Thomas, look!'

Their boy laughed, a giddy sound of triumph as he crossed the small gap between them and fell into Elspeth's arms. She hugged him tightly, her eyes bright with pride.

'You did it, Robert! You walked!' She glanced at Thomas, whose face was lit with rare joy.

'That's my boy,' Thomas said, his voice thick. He reached out, ruffling Robert's hair.

'Dadda,' the little boy said, laughing as he grabbed hold of his father's knee.

Elspeth swallowed when she saw the glint of tears in Thomas's eyes.

Later that evening, as the house grew quiet and Robert slept peacefully, Thomas and Elspeth sat in their bedroom. Thomas seemed restless, his hands fidgeting as he stared out of the window. Finally, he spoke, his voice low.

'I'm sorry, Elspeth.'

She turned to him, confused. 'For what?'

'For everything,' he said, his eyes glistening. 'For taking your dreams away, for dragging you out here to this life. And for the man I've become . . . the damaged man I am.'

Elspeth reached for his hand. 'Thomas—'

He shook his head, his voice breaking. 'I see them, Elspeth. Every night, in my dreams. My friends—John and Will—falling beside me in the trenches. I can't escape it. No matter how hard

I try, it's always there.'

Tears slid down his face, and Elspeth pulled him into her arms. 'Perhaps talking about it will help,' she whispered. 'You don't have to carry it alone.'

For a long time, they sat like that, his sobs gradually easing. That night, for the first time in months, they lay together as man and wife, finding solace in each other. A smile tilted Elspeth's lips, and Thomas's grip on her hand remained firm as sleep claimed them.

He woke before her the next morning, and by the time Robert called to her, Thomas was already out with the horses. She worried about him as the day passed and was reassured when she heard the clatter of hooves outside late in the morning.

She hurried outside, but it was her father; his smile was wide, and the words tumbled from his lips as he dismounted. 'Your mother's home, Elspeth, and she wishes to see her grandson.'

Elspeth's smile faded as her thoughts turned to her mother. 'She's been away for so long,' she said bitterly, her voice tight. 'I don't see why she deserves to meet Robert now.' She turned to her father, who stood quietly, his hands gripping the reins. 'Where was she when I needed her? Where was she when Robert was born?' The words tumbled out, the anger at her mother overwhelming her. Her father sighed, leaning forward. 'Elspeth, she's here now. She wants to make amends. Don't let anger rob you of the chance to heal.' His steady gaze softened her defences.

After a long pause, she exhaled. 'Fine,' she said quietly. 'I'll come home tomorrow. But today, I've got chores, and Thomas will be home soon for his midday meal.' She stood, her resolve tempered by the lingering sting of her mother's absence.

##

Elspeth's pulse raced as she glanced at the empty chair by the fireplace. Robert was finally asleep, but her worry for Thomas kept her pacing through the quiet house. The clock ticked steadily, each passing minute deepening her fear. He hadn't returned to Suttor River since he had left that morning and the storm rolling in making the darkness outside threatening.

She tried to busy herself, setting a kettle on the stove and folding clothes by lamplight, but her hands shook too much to finish. The thought of him lying injured—or worse—on some desolate track filled her with dread. Every creak of the house made her glance towards the door, hoping, praying it would open. She knew she loved Thomas; she had loved him from the moment he had first recited poetry to her. She wouldn't be able to bear it if anything had happened to him.

By midnight, exhaustion weighed on her, but she dared not sleep. She sat by the window, wrapped in a shawl, her eyes fixed on the black horizon. The lightning lit up the darkness, and she peered towards the track, hoping to see Thomas and his horse appear. The storm eased as dawn approached, and the faint light of morning began to seep through the curtains. Suddenly, the sound of horses' hooves broke the silence.

Elspeth sprang to her feet, her knees weak beneath her. She steadied herself on the door, peeking into Robert's cot. He was still curled up, his rhythmic breathing soothing her for just a moment. She hurried to the front door, ready to welcome her husband home.

Through the haze of the rising sun, she saw her father and Mr Burnham dismounting their horses. Their grim faces stole the air from her lungs. Her father stepped forward, his boots crunching against the gravel, and without a word, he pulled her into his arms.

'It's Thomas, Elspeth. He . . . he's gone.'

Elspeth's breath caught, and she clutched his coat, her worst fears firming in his silence. Tears spilled down her cheeks as she whispered, 'No . . . no.'

Her father held her tighter, his voice trembling as he spoke. 'We found him in the stables when we went to tend to the horses at dawn. He took his own life. We couldn't get to him in time.'

The words hit Elspeth with the force of a great wave, leaving her unsteady. She clung to her father, her breath coming in ragged gasps. 'No . . . no, you must be wrong.'

Her father's voice broke as he continued, his grip tightening around her. 'I'm so sorry, my girl. We did everything we could, but he was gone long before we got there.'

The realisation tore through Elspeth's heart. Her knees buckled, and she collapsed into her father's arms, the loss pressing down on her heart and taking her breath away. Her mind raced, trying to make sense of the man she had loved, the man who had so suddenly and completely slipped away. The life they had started together, the family they were making, now seemed a distant dream, shattered in one fell swoop.

Mr Burnham, standing a few paces away, spoke quietly, his voice heavy with sympathy. 'He was . . . he was a troubled man, Elspeth. We didn't know how deep it went. He'd been carrying it for too long.'

Elspeth nodded numbly, her hands trembling as she pulled away from her father. She stared at the horizon, the first light of day creeping over the land, but it did little to chase away the darkness that had descended on her heart.

'Come, I will gather up Robert and take you home to *Strathallyn*.' Her father's voice reached her through the shroud of grief that surrounded her.

'Please wait,' she replied, her tone flat but resolute. 'I will pack up some clothes.'

She knew she could never return to this house.

Chapter 29

Bowen River Police Station -Monday 7.00 p.m.

Bec

I was still at the station at seven p.m. when I heard Mark and Todd's voices out the front. Aaron had clocked off, and Jenny was holding down the fort at the front desk until eight. Mark had explained earlier that the station's hours had been extended when the influx of workers hit town. It made sense, but I was starting to feel the strain of the long day. I needed to eat or at least have a coffee before I walked home. I'd spent barely any time in my new place and hadn't even managed to stock the kitchen with groceries. I'd recovered from my concussion, but poor diet and lack of exercise were making me sluggish, and I knew I needed to lift my game.

Ha, in my spare time.

I looked up as Jenny greeted them, her voice carrying down the hall. Moments later, Mark and Todd appeared in the doorway of the back room where I'd been stationed for hours. I'd moved here earlier, commandeering the bank of computers to keep all my research in one place. Three databases were running simultaneously, and I was cross-checking everything, pursuing leads with a single-minded focus.

'Bec,' Todd said, his tone a mix of tired and impressed as he took in the chaos of screens and printouts spread around me. 'How's it going?'

I glanced up as he pulled out a chair, spun it around, and straddled it, arms resting on the back. Mark logged onto one of the other computers, his face illuminated by the screen's pale glow.

'You've put in a long day, Bec,' Todd said, his voice low but kind.

'Still at it.' I tapped a key to bring up another search. 'Figured I'd make the most of the quiet. I've made some progress.' I leaned back in my chair and stretched. 'But still no sign of the elusive Teddy.'

Mark glanced over at the screen.

'How was the interview in Townsville?' I asked.

'Productive. Haynes has an alibi. He was overseas for the last two weeks,' Todd said, typing something into his phone. 'We got a few more locals to look into. A few who've been hassling Strathallyn Solar. Might be worth talking to. Especially the one we don't have a name for.'

'What do you mean?' I prompted, raising a brow.

'The guy we spoke to mentioned a couple of anonymous calls claiming family connections,' Todd explained.

'Anonymous?' I sat up straighter.

Mark nodded, his hands pausing on the keyboard. 'Yeah, someone digging, saying the land Leanne supposedly owns isn't hers.'

'What?' I frowned. 'Who would claim that?'

'According to the caller, he's entitled to half of any sales,' Todd added. 'Said he was her cousin.'

I blinked, processing the information. 'And no name?'

'No, he wouldn't give it. He just said he's family. A man,' Todd replied.

'No luck here. The land title is in her name alone.' Mark shrugged as he stared at the screen. 'She owns all the land.'

'Interesting,' I murmured. 'You think it's our Teddy?'

'Could be,' Todd said, his expression thoughtful. 'We really need to find him.'

I glanced at the screen where I'd been digging into Randall Simms. Something about him didn't sit right. He came from a big family, which could be significant. If we confirmed he was tied to Leanne in some way, his family might step in to care for the kids. It was a stretch, but I couldn't leave any stone unturned. The children didn't have anyone else—at least, no one obvious.

Mark stood and leaned over my shoulder, scanning the list of names and connections I'd pulled up. 'Simms, huh?' he murmured. 'What are you thinking?'

I hesitated, biting my lip. 'If we can't locate a direct family member for the kids, this might be our next best bet. Simms has a long list of relatives—aunts, uncles, cousins. Someone who might be willing to take them in.'

'Is there a Teddy or Edward in that family?' Mark asked. 'Maybe Simms knows about the offer and has got someone from *his* family involved.'

'Or a mate on the outside might be working with him while he's inside?' Todd offered.

'That's an avenue we haven't explored,' Mark said.

'I've been down the family route of both,' I said. 'No Edwards or Teddys in the Simms or Delaneys. Only a great uncle called Edward back in the nineteen twenties.'

'Maybe it's time to interview Simms. He needs to know what's happening.' Mark pulled a face. 'Another day on the road. I'll do that tomorrow.'

'You've been thorough, Bec.' Todd stood and stretched. 'But I think it's time you knocked off. You've put in a long day. Have you had dinner?'

'No. I was just thinking about eating.'

'We haven't either. Do you eat pizza?' Mark asked.

We both nodded.

'I'll ring up the pub and walk over and get it. Any preferences?'

'Whatever comes,' I said.

'I'm easy,' Todd agreed.

When Mark left, Todd moved across to the other computer and logged on. 'I'm going to have a look at some of Simms' associates. You never know.'

'I'm still looking at the family. His parents live in Cairns. Maybe they need to know Leanne is missing before they see it in the media. Mark's managed to keep it local, but a news article is going out from the media unit tomorrow.'

I hesitated. 'That reminds me, Todd. There's something I want to tell you. Something I remembered. When Mum told me about Leanne being missing the day I arrived, Dad seemed to know that already, too. Mum looked surprised and asked him where he heard it—she got it from next door—and he said she'd told him. Mum had a strange look on her face. I don't think she did tell him, and that worries me.'

'Thanks, I'll find out how he knew.'

'I feel as though we're walking sluggishly through quicksand,' I said, stretching my arms above my head.

Todd nodded. 'I know. The kids won't leave my thoughts. I want this sorted before too much longer.'

'I can't shake the image of their little faces, trying to act brave but clearly terrified. How do you explain to two kids that their mother's missing and their father's locked up? And the worst part—how do we promise them it'll all be okay when we're not sure of the outcome?'

'We work methodically, and we do our best, Bec.'

I took a deep breath, shaking off the thoughts. 'I'll keep digging. There has to be someone.'

I wasn't going to think the worst. We *would* find Leanne. We had to. Still, the nagging uncertainty sat heavy in my chest.

I exhaled slowly, tapping my pen against the desk. 'I've narrowed things down as much as I can. If there's a cousin, and he's legitimate, he has to come down through Elspeth's side. She had another son called Edward, but I can't find him in any database under Edward Delaney.'

'He has to be somewhere. Have you tried variations of the surname?' Todd asked.

'I've tried everything,' I said, exasperation creeping into my voice. 'Even military records. Robert, Leanne's grandfather, has a service record from World War II, but Edward was born in 1929. He would have been too young at the time. None of it adds up.'

Todd glanced over from his screen; his brow furrowed in thought. 'You know,' he said, 'it wasn't unheard of back then for young guys to lie about their age. Maybe Edward enlisted under a different name and used an older birth date.'

'That's a possibility,' I admitted, leaning forward. 'But why change his name?'

Todd shrugged. 'Could have been a lot of reasons. Maybe he was running from something, or maybe it was just to get into the army early. People did what they had to back then.'

'So, if he used another name, we'll need to cross-check aliases or enlistment records under similar profiles. It'll be tedious, but it might be the only way to trace this line,' I said, pulling up the database again. 'I'll widen the search parameters. If Robert's there, I'll find him.'

Todd gave me a small nod of approval. 'Good thinking. Go for it.'

Chapter 30

Strathallyn Station – January 1928.
Elspeth

Elspeth watched, heart heavy, as her mother completely ignored her grandson, Robert, as he toddled around the homestead. Amelia's coldness seemed to spread with each day that passed, her eyes never softening when she looked at the child whose father had suffered from the same darkness that had claimed his life.

Amelia's belief that Thomas's mental health was hereditary hung over Elspeth like a storm cloud, a shadow that she couldn't escape. Amelia, with her narrow view of the world, had always feared this. She feared that the "weakness" Thomas had displayed would somehow pass on to her grandson. It was a concept Elspeth found unbearable.

She tried to explain, once again, 'Mother, you don't understand. Thomas's depression wasn't something he was born with. It was the war . . . it broke him. The things he saw, the things he did—that's what changed him.'

But her mother simply shook her head, her jaw tightening. There was no room for understanding in her mind. All she saw was a man who had failed, committed a grave sin by taking his own life and leaving a son who might inherit that same darkness.

'Perhaps,' Elspeth continued, her voice shaking with frustration, 'if you could see Robert as a child, not a reminder of his father's faults, you might not be so quick to judge.'

But Mother turned away, ignoring her daughter's words, her silence a sharper rebuke than any of the harsh words she could have spoken. Elspeth clenched her fists, the helplessness rising inside her. She knew her mother feared for Robert's future, but her refusal to even acknowledge him was unbearable.

Elspeth struggled with the heavy burden of this rejection. In her mother's eyes, Thomas had been nothing more than a dangerous legacy. Every day, it felt like those fears were becoming her own, and the burden of it left Elspeth feeling as though she was drowning.

'I'm trying,' Elspeth whispered to the empty room, her words lost on the stillness. She was trying to make sense of it all—trying to heal, trying to protect her child from the same fate that had befallen Thomas. But with her mother's indifference and her own grief still raw, Elspeth wasn't sure if she could ever truly escape the past.

She had not told her mother she was expecting another child. She simply wished Mother would leave again. But as the months passed and the baby grew within her, Elspeth could no longer hide her condition. When Edward was born—a quick and almost painless birth—her joy was fleeting. Her grief returned, heavier than ever, dragging her into a deep, unrelenting depression. Her days blurred into nights, the cries of her newborn and little Robert fading into the background of her desolation.

Her grief was overwhelming, but even that was not enough to shift her mother's coldness. Mother, sharp-eyed and quick to judge, soon lost patience. She ignored the children, her focus narrowing to the housework and her embroidery as if detaching herself from the chaos that was in Elspeth's heart.

Mrs Revesby and Elspeth's father stepped in, tending to Robert and the new baby with quiet devotion, while Mother kept her distance, her face a constant mask of disapproval.

A year passed, and Elspeth's grief was still such that she was unable to look after the two boys without assistance. A decision was made.

'This cannot go on,' Mother said, her tone as icy as the dawn air. Unable to bear their presence at *Strathallyn*, she removed the boys from Elspeth's care. They were sent to her sister, Kathleen, in Rockhampton. 'They'll be better off there,' Mother said, her gaze unyielding. 'A child should not be raised by a woman whose husband succumbed to weakness. It's a risk we will not take.'

Elspeth watched in numb silence as her sons were taken from her, the sound of Robert's laughter fading as the car drove down the road, the happy sound growing fainter with each passing moment. The emptiness left in their wake was suffocating, like the stillness that followed the storm the night Thomas had taken his life. She wanted to cry out, to run after them, but her desolation made it impossible to move.

Mother had made the decision, and it was final. Her decision had been cold and unyielding, a stark reminder that in this house, Elspeth's grief was an inconvenience to be dismissed.

The hollow silence of the house deepened, Elspeth's heart sinking as she knew she had lost more than just her husband and children. She had lost her way and didn't know what to do. She tried to escape the despair, already a black curtain that separated her from the everyday world, but it was hard to face every day.

When the letter came from the Rockhampton solicitor two years later, informing Elspeth of the tragic drowning of her two sons, her guilt overtook her. The words on the page blurred together, the ink turning into a dark stain that spread into her heart, suffocating her. The grief she had buried so deeply within her now surged to the surface, more overwhelming than anything she had known before. It wasn't just the loss of her children—it was the painful realisation that they had been taken from her; their lives ended before she could ever make amends, before she could even attempt to be the mother they deserved.

And that was the hardest thing to accept.

Chapter 31

Bowen River Police Station - Monday 7.00 p.m.
Bec

The station was quiet, save for the rhythmic tapping of keys as Todd and I scrolled through database entries. The smell of coffee from the empty takeaway containers in the bin was a testament to our long hours and lack of attention to anything but the task at hand. I glanced up at Todd; he looked as tired as I felt, brows furrowed in concentration.

Mark called from the front of the station, 'Pizza man!'

The scent of tomato, garlic, and melted cheese wafted through the room, cutting through the stale air of the workroom. I stretched my arms over my head and looked at Todd. His eyes met mine, and we both knew it was time to call it quits for the night. The databases could wait; we weren't going to find Leanne tonight.

Mark appeared in the doorway, holding two boxes in each hand. 'I grabbed four pizzas after I called Sheree,' he said. 'Two for me to take home and two for you pair.'

'Thanks, Mark,' I said, standing and rubbing my lower back. I really needed to hit a gym or go for a run the instant we had a spare hour.

Mark set the boxes down and grinned. 'Two large in there. Figured you both could use a solid feed.'

I looked around the small workroom, its clutter of case files, empty coffee cups, and discarded sticky notes closing in on me. 'Todd, how about we eat at my place? I need to get out of here before these four walls drive me insane.'

He grinned, the fatigue momentarily lifting. 'That sounds like a fine idea. But forget the coffee—got any beer at home?'

I grimaced. 'Would you believe I don't even have milk for coffee, let alone beer? Too busy to shop.'

Todd chuckled. 'Tell you what. I'll grab a six-pack on my way over. Pizza and beer sound perfect.'

Mark watched Todd leave, then turned to me, his smile fading to a softer expression. 'You try to get a good night's sleep, Bec. I know how hard it is when a case takes over your life.'

I nodded, but he wasn't finished. 'I was a detective in Brisbane, you know.'

That caught me off guard. 'Really? I didn't know that.'

'Yeah,' he said, leaning against the doorway. 'I wanted to escape the grind, thought station life in the country would be easier.'

'Your wish hasn't exactly come true,' I said with a wry smile. 'This case is anything but easy.'

Mark sighed. 'You're right. And I hate leaving it like this tonight, but we don't have the manpower to search the region in the dark, and we're not even sure Leanne didn't just walk away.'

'I don't think she would have,' I said softly. 'Not from everything we've heard. How could she leave her kids?'

Mark placed a hand on my shoulder. 'Go home, Bec. Take a break and try not to talk shop with Todd. You both need a breather. We'll pick it up fresh in the morning.'

I gathered my things and headed out, leaving the station lights on as we always did. At home, I left the door unlocked, stripped off my uniform, and stepped into a quick, hot shower. The water was a welcome reprieve, washing away the grime of the day and some of the tension that clung to me like a second skin.

Dressed in jeans and a T-shirt—the autumn nights in Bowen River had turned chilly this week—I was just pulling plates from the cupboard when Todd knocked at the front door.

'Come in!' I called.

He stepped inside, a six-pack in hand, and looked as relieved as I felt to be out of the station.

'Pizza's in the oven,' I said. 'Want to wash up? Bathroom's down the hall to the left.'

'Sounds good,' Todd said, taking his jacket off and throwing it on the sofa. Before he went to the bathroom, he reached for a beer, opened it, and passed it to me. 'I'll catch up in a minute.'

The water ran for a while, and when he came out, his hair was damp, his tie hung from his hand, and his shirt was unbuttoned at the top.

I'd set the table with plates but no cutlery. 'Fingers work for you?' I asked, pulling the hot pizza boxes from the oven.

'Perfect,' Todd said, grabbing another beer and cracking it open. 'Cheers,' he said, and we clinked beer bottles. 'Thanks for the invitation. Even though it's a police house, it still has more ambience than the station.'

My place wasn't much, just the standard issue: pale beige walls that seemed to drain the light, a government furniture-issue sofa that was more utilitarian than comfortable, and a lack of any personal touches. No photos, no paintings. Nothing to indicate this was anyone's home, least of all mine.

'Home sweet home,' I said, more to myself than Todd, as I looked around. The words came out with a bitter edge. It was a box, a place to sleep, eat, and work when the station got too much. But it wasn't home—not the kind you felt in your bones.

Todd chuckled, following my gaze around the room. 'It's got a certain charm.'

'Yeah, if charm means being one step above a holding cell.' I sighed, taking another sip of my beer. The cold drink was a small luxury after the day we'd had. 'Honestly, I should probably think about decorating. Maybe get a plant or something.'

'A plant? That's bold,' Todd said, smirking. 'You'd need to be home to water it.'

'True. Probably end up dead in a month.'

He leaned back, stretching out his legs under the table. His tie was draped over the back of a chair, his shirt hanging open at the collar. I looked away at the glimpse of bare skin. Not going there. For the first time all day, he looked relaxed, even if only slightly. I envied that ease, the way he seemed to shake off the focus on the case, even if temporarily.

'Are you staying at the pub or the motel?' I asked.

'Motel.'

'Doesn't bother you? Being away from home, I mean?'

Todd shrugged. 'I've stayed in places like this on and off for years. After a while, it just becomes part of the job. As long as it's got a decent bed and hot water, I'm good. Mind you, I love my apartment down at Bowen; it's on the beach, and I can sit for hours watching the water. Best debriefing there is. You'll have to come and visit one day.'

And with his words, our relationship switched from professional to friendship. No more. Just an offer of simple friendship.

'I'd like that. Once this case is over, I know I'll struggle with being in Bowen River when I'm off duty. You know, the parents, the gossip and all that.' I put my hand up. 'I'm not mentioning the case there. Just the way parents can be, you know. Honestly, I couldn't believe it when my transfer brought me here. Out of all the places in Queensland, I came home.'

Todd smiled faintly. 'Brisbane's where I started too. Took my first detective posting in Cairns.'

I tilted my head. 'Cairns? That's a bit of a distance.'

'It was,' he said, his voice quieter now. 'I met Clare, and we got married the same year. She had to put up with the crazy hours I worked. Yep, families,' he said. 'We all have them.'

I nodded. 'Feels like I should make more effort with mine, you know?'

Todd's eyes softened, and he didn't rush to respond. He was good at that—leaving a moment for words to process. 'You'll find your place again,' he said eventually. 'It takes time.'

I knew he was referring to my break-up with Gray. I hadn't given him a thought today. We fell into a comfortable silence, the kind that didn't need to be filled. I reached for another slice of pizza, the warmth and richness a stark contrast to the databases I'd been poring over all day.

'I get why you came back,' Todd said after a while. 'This region has an attraction. Even for someone who didn't grow up here.'

'You seem to have settled in well,' I said, watching him closely.

He nodded. 'Yeah. After everything with Clare—' His voice trailed off, and for a moment, I thought he might not continue. But then he took a deep breath. 'I needed a fresh start. This place gave me that.'

'I'm glad you found it,' I said. I hesitated, then said softly, 'Mark told me you lost her recently.'

Todd nodded, his jaw tightening. 'Yeah. Bloody breast cancer. Aggressive form. She fought hard, but—'

'I'm sorry,' I said, unsure if it was enough.

'We tried for kids,' he said, his voice distant. 'Didn't happen. And then, before we knew it, she was sick.'

I reached for another slice, giving him space. 'Did you take time off?'

'A month,' Todd said. 'After that, I found it easier to work. Sold our house and moved into an apartment to be more mobile. Eventually, I started taking cases down here. Fell in love with Bowen. It's one of the prettiest spots on the coast.'

'It is,' I agreed.

'When a transfer came up, I didn't hesitate,' Todd added.

We sat in silence for a while, lost in our thoughts. The pizza was almost gone, and we were on our third beer each. I studied Todd's profile, seeing the sadness he carried but also a strength

I admired.

'He raised his beer, and I clinked mine against it. 'Here's to Bowen River,' he said.

'To Bowen River,' I echoed.

Chapter 32

Strathallyn Station - April 1936.
Elspeth

Each morning, as the sun began to stretch across the land, Elspeth would make her way to the small graveyard at the side of the homestead before she went to work with the horses. The gravestones, weathered by time yet sturdy in their place, bore the names of her two sons, their lives cut short by the river's cruel hand. Though they did not lie there, it felt as though a part of them had taken root beneath the soil, and it was here she would stand, speaking to them as though they could hear.

It had become a quiet ritual, a way to gather herself before the long day ahead. Her father had insisted she work with him in the stables after the loss of the boys, sensing her need to find some purpose, some way to lift herself from the depths of despair that had threatened to swallow her whole. The grief had nearly destroyed her—had made her want to turn away from everything, to hide from the world that had taken so much from her. But Father had been relentless, pushing her gently but firmly back into the rhythm of daily life.

Gradually, the stables became a sanctuary, a place where she could lose herself in the familiar work of feeding and grooming the horses. As Father added to the stock, and *Strathallyn* became known for its fine horseflesh, the stables filled with life again, and with it, Elspeth's own spirit began to rekindle. She started to feel the warmth of the horses' breath on her hands, the steady thump of their hooves against the earth, and it was as if, for the first time in years, she could breathe again. The motion of riding, once a joy, now became a healing process—each gallop, each careful turn, reminding her of the woman she had once been before the shadows of tragedy had crept in.

Her mother's death was a blessing; it was the end of the harsh reminder of what had happened. If Mother hadn't sent them away, her sons would be working here with her on the family property.

For a short time, Elspeth considered going to England to follow the dream she had once cherished; it had seemed like a way out. She thought of the faraway shores, the promise of something different, something that might ease the ache in her chest. But whenever she imagined leaving, she saw the gravestones—those two small white markers surrounded by the wrought iron fence near the creek—and the idea of leaving them behind felt like a betrayal she could not bear. Her father, ever watchful, had known she would never truly leave, not while the memory of her sons still lingered in every corner of the homestead.

And now, years later, Father had come to rely on her again.

She had taken over from him, supervising the stables and the work of the property as he became frail. It was no longer just a matter of survival, of getting through each day. She had found her strength in the rhythm of life, in the steady routine of taking over the breeding program.

The pain of loss would never leave her, but in her work, she had found something to keep going for. Something worth living for. She touched the rough stone of their memorials, the cold surface a reminder of the warmth she would never feel again.

'Robert, Edward,' she would say softly, her voice raw from the grief that still clung to her heart. 'I don't know if you understand, but your father was a good man. He always tried to do what was right, even when the world seemed to turn its back on him. Sometimes, I think the war broke him inside; it was too much. He couldn't find peace after it.'

She would sit down on the grass between their gravestones, her thoughts heavy and slow. Her voice softened as she leaned her forehead against the cold stone. 'I didn't know how to help him . . . and I couldn't help you. It's my fault you're gone. But I promise I'll never forget you. I'll never forget him, either.' She would pause, then add, almost in a whisper, 'And I'll never leave you here alone. Not while I breathe. You'll always be with me, my boys. Always.'

Her father's voice would break through the silence, calling

her back to the house, to the work that awaited her. But Elspeth, with one last look at the gravestones, would stand slowly and walk away, her thoughts of the day ahead forcing away the grief that still held a piece of her heart.

Chapter 33

Bowen River - Tuesday.

Bec

Todd left around midnight, and I headed straight to bed. After three beers—two more than usual—keeping my eyes open was like fighting a losing battle. I walked him to the door, and he stood on the step for a moment, looking up at me.

'You get a good night's sleep,' he said. 'I'll see you in the morning.'

I smiled, watching as he turned at the gate and gave a quick wave before disappearing into the dark. Within minutes, I was under the covers, slipping into a deep, dreamless sleep.

But it didn't last. In the early hours, I woke groggily and stumbled to the bathroom before crawling back into bed. That's when the dreams started—fragments of conversation, faces I hadn't seen since school. I was on the old school bus, and beside me sat a grown-up Tom, his familiar grin oddly reassuring. The bus rumbled to a stop outside Leanne's house, and suddenly, I was running up the path in my old school uniform, calling out.

'Leanne! Where are you? Don't be silly, it's time to come home.'

Inside, the hallway felt endless, dark shadows stretching in every direction. I reached the hallstand, and as I passed, it toppled over. Hats—dozens of them—spilled onto the floor. The sight jolted me awake from my dream, my heart pounding. I sat up in the dark, my breath ragged.

The hat. The kids said it belonged to Uncle Teddy, and we hadn't given it more than a passing glance. Maybe it wasn't just a hat. Maybe it was something unique, something that could lead us closer to Leanne.

The thought sent a jolt of energy through me. I rose early, letting the hot water of the shower clear my head. After washing and braiding my hair, I quickly pulled on my uniform. By seven, I was at the station, making do with a bitter cup of instant coffee as I waited for Todd and Mark.

When Todd finally walked in, looking as tired as I had the night before, I practically jumped out of my seat.

'We need to go out to Leanne's place,' I said, barely able to contain my urgency. 'The hat.'

He blinked, confused. 'The hat?'

'Uncle Teddy's hat. We didn't look at it properly.'

'Right, I'm following you. Do you want to go now?'

'Yes. I'll call Mark and let him know,' I said as we headed out the door.

Aaron arrived just as we were heading to the car. 'We won't

be long,' I called back, buzzing with energy and keen to get going.

The trip to Leanne's farm was quiet. We exchanged a few glances as we passed the vast solar panels stretching for hectares. It wasn't long before we turned into the driveway.

The house loomed ahead, the doors shut and locked. Mark had kept the keys we'd taken from the hall stand to the station. It was dark inside as we unlocked the door. Todd flicked the light switch, but nothing happened. A shiver ran down my spine, remembering the moment I was struck just inside the front door.

He moved ahead, pausing to lift the man's hat off the stand. The band was lined with teeth set into a leather strip. He turned the hat over in his hands, his eyes narrowing as he examined the teeth lining the brim. 'Crocodile teeth,' he said, his voice low. 'You don't see this kind of thing every day.'

I stepped closer, my pulse quickening. 'Do you think they could tell us something? Maybe there's a unique pattern or marking.'

Todd nodded thoughtfully. 'Could be. If these teeth were taken illegally, they might be traced back to a specific place or even a poacher.'

I glanced around the hallway, still feeling unsettled. 'Let's bag it and take it back to the station. We'll see if forensics or wildlife authorities can help. Plus I'll take a photo and do a reverse image search. You never know; it might come up with the guy wearing it.'

Todd carefully placed the hat into an evidence bag, sealing it with practised efficiency. 'You're an optimist, I'll give you that.' His cheeky smile lightened the mood.

We moved methodically, checking the rest of the house, but nothing else stood out. As we locked up and headed back to the car, I couldn't shake the feeling that we were finally onto something.

Todd must have sensed my energy. 'It's a good lead, Bec. Let's see where it takes us.'

Back in the Stinger, I glanced at the horizon. The morning sun cast a pale glow over the land, and hope flickered through me. Maybe, just maybe, we were getting closer to finding Leanne. I hoped wherever she was, she was okay.

Todd's expression shifted as he tilted the hat to catch the light. His brow furrowed, and then his eyes widened. 'Holy shit, Bec. Look!' He turned the hat so I could see inside. 'You've cracked it.'

My breath caught as I leaned over. There, faint but unmistakable, were the initials T.V. scratched into the inner lining of the brim.

'T.V.,' I whispered. 'T for Teddy. Uncle Teddy! This could be the link we've been missing.'

He nodded, his face a mix of excitement and caution. 'If these initials match anything in our records, we might finally have a direct tie to Leanne's disappearance—or at least to someone in her family who knows more than they've been letting on.'

A surge of adrenaline rushed through me, but a wave of doubt quickly tempered it. 'What if it's just a coincidence? Lots of people could have those initials.'

'True,' Todd said, folding the evidence bag carefully. 'But with the kids saying it was Uncle Teddy's and that it appears to be secretive for some reason makes me very suspicious. It's too specific to ignore. We've got a trail now, and we're going to follow it.'

I took a steadying breath, my thoughts racing.

Todd gave a firm nod. 'Let's get this back to the station and run those initials through the system. And I'll contact Parks and Wildlife about the teeth. If they're tied to a known case, we'll have more leverage.'

As we drove back, my mind kept circling around those initials. T.V. What did the V stand for? I was going to get straight on the family tree when we got back.

My thoughts whirled as I drove back to Bowen River. Todd sat beside me, holding the evidence bag as though the hat were the most delicate piece of evidence he'd ever encountered. I couldn't help but notice how methodical he'd become—more so than usual.

As we stepped into the station, the quiet hum of the air conditioning was soon replaced by Mark's booming voice. He was standing near the whiteboard, where timelines and photos of Leanne Delaney were pinned in a chaotic mosaic.

'Tell me you've got something,' he said, eyes lighting up as Todd held up the evidence bag containing the hat.

'Oh, we've got something,' Todd replied, his tone calm but the glint in his eyes betraying his satisfaction. He placed the bag on the table. 'T.V. Whoever this belongs to, they've been in that house. And they didn't leave this behind by accident; I think Uncle Teddy, whoever he is, was quite at home there.'

Mark leaned in, squinting at the worn felt brim. 'Crocodile teeth, initials—it's like something out of an adventure movie. Harrison Ford, move over.' His delight was evident from his wide grin. 'This is it. Now all we have to do is identify and find him.'

I barely heard them as I hurried over to my desk, my pulse quickening. This wasn't just a lead; it felt like *the* lead. Logging in, I navigated straight to the case database, fingers flying over the keys. Every second felt critical.

Todd nodded. 'Bec's already on it—running the name and searching for connections.'

Mark chuckled. 'Looks like she's got the detective fever, Todd. You'd better watch your back.'

'Come on, come on,' I muttered, pulling up archived files and cross-referencing names. The initials T.V. could mean dozens of things, but I was determined to narrow it down. My breath caught as I pulled up the case notes. 'Mark, Todd, quick, I think I've got it already.'

They both turned and hurried over.

I pointed to the screen. 'Look, the family name. Elspeth married into the Delaney family, but the founding family's name was Valentine! Do you think that could be it?'

Todd nodded. 'Let's run it through some databases.' He sat beside me. 'I'll do Q Prime. You go to Births, Deaths, and Marriages.' He caught my eye as he logged on. 'Good catch, Bec. That dream of yours—weird as it was—might just be the breakthrough we needed.'

I ignored his direction and went straight to Google and typed in Teddy Valentine.

My satisfaction was complete when I clicked on the first link and an article's headline filled my screen.

Crocodile Hunter from Alva Nabs a Big Un.

The best part was the photo of Teddy Valentine wearing the hat that now sat beside us in the evidence bag. I cleared my throat. Mark had gone back to the whiteboard, and Todd was intent on Q Prime.

'Ah, guys, you might like to take a look at this,' I said, unable to keep the smugness from my voice.

Chapter 34

Bowen River - Tuesday 3.00 p.m.

Bec

I was surprised when Mark called me into his office a couple of hours later. My morning had been productive; I'd traced the family lineage and confirmed that Teddy Valentine and Leanne were third cousins. I suspected Teddy might have been the anonymous caller to Strathallyn Solar, but that was something Mark and Todd would have to address during his interview.

'Yes, Mark?' I asked as I stepped in, trying to keep my tone neutral.

He gestured for me to sit. 'We're sending you and Todd to Alva tomorrow to interview Teddy Valentine. We've tracked down an address, and there are a few minor infringements under his name on QPrime.'

'Me?' I blurted, my voice catching. I could feel my heart skip a beat. *Why me?* My palms felt clammy, and a knot tightened in my stomach.

Mark nodded. 'You've been invaluable to this case, Bec. You've done the groundwork, and your insight could make the difference. Plus, you've earned it.'

I swallowed hard, trying to mask my nervousness. My mind raced—part excitement, part dread. *What if I mess this up? What if I ask the wrong question?* But alongside the nerves was a flicker of pride.

Mark continued, 'I've already spoken to the local police. They've confirmed he's at his residence, and they've done a drive-by to ensure he's still there. They'll provide backup for you and Todd tomorrow.'

I nodded, doing my best to seem composed. 'Right. So, tomorrow?'

'Tomorrow morning. Take the evening to prepare. And Bec?'

'Yes? I stopped in the doorway

'His vehicle is parked in the driveway.'

I frowned. 'And?'

'It's a white ute with new number plates ordered by him and a dent in the front driver's side. He reported the other plates as stolen.'

'I'd say if we searched, we'd find them somewhere on Leanne's property,' I said.

'I agree.'

As I left his office, the reality set in. I was going to be face-to-face with a potential key player in the case. It was a mix of apprehension and determination—my chance to step up.

Todd was waiting for me in the workroom. He'd obviously been filled in by Mark.

'Well done, Bec.'

I shook my head. 'This week has been amazing. A huge learning curve and very different to what I imagine my work would be like here. All we need now is to find Leanne.'

I sat on the edge of my desk, my arms crossed tightly as Todd leaned against the doorway. His expression was serious, but there was a softness in his tone as he spoke.

'We have to prepare for the worst outcome, you know,' Todd said quietly, his eyes steady on mine.

I nodded, swallowing hard. 'I know. I've been in policing long enough to learn that. But this is personal, Todd. I knew her. And I hate to think that something's happened to her.'

Todd stepped closer, his voice dropping slightly. 'Look, we've been digging into Teddy Valentine's background, and something stands out. If Leanne is dead, he has a clear motivation—he'd probably inherit the property unless she made other arrangements in her will.'

My stomach twisted. 'Inherit? That would explain why he'd want her out of the picture.' My mind raced, piecing together fragments of memory and possibility. 'I wonder how long she's known him. Was he always in the background, or did he show up recently?'

Todd shrugged. 'That's something we'll need to pin down. But it makes you think, doesn't it? If they've only reconnected recently, that could be a red flag.'

I frowned, my thoughts pulling me back to my teenage years. 'We talked a lot back then, as girls do. I'd have remembered if she'd ever mentioned a Teddy. She never did.'

Todd gave a slight nod. 'Then maybe he's a recent addition to her life. Someone who saw an opportunity.'

The stakes were clear, and time felt like it was slipping away.

'Let's hope tomorrow gives us some answers,' Todd said, his tone resolute.

I nodded, my jaw set. 'It has to.'

Chapter 35

Bowen River - Tuesday 5.00 p.m.
Bec

I stood outside my parents' modest home, unease in my chest. I hadn't been here since before I was attacked, and the familiar sight of the place stirred up a mix of memories I wasn't ready to deal with. Taking a deep breath, I stepped up to the open door and called out, 'Mum, are you home? Dad?'

Footsteps echoed down the hallway, and Mum appeared, her face lighting up with a mix of surprise and worry. 'Bec, what a lovely surprise. Come in, darling.'

I stepped inside, immediately spotting Dad in his usual chair, the Bible open on his lap. His gaze lifted, sharp and disapproving.

'Honour thy father and thy mother,' he said in that familiar, measured tone. 'Good to see you're finally obeying the Word, Rebecca.'

My jaw clenched. 'I'm here because we need to talk.'

He closed the Bible with a deliberate thud, placing it on the table beside him. 'Talk? Or are you here to question my faith again? You always did have the spirit of rebellion in you. "Pride goeth before destruction."'

Mum hovered in the doorway, wringing her hands. 'Please, Jim, let's not start—'

'Quiet, Peggy,' he snapped, his voice slicing through the air. 'This is between me and my daughter.'

The anger simmering inside me flared to life. I stepped forward, squaring my shoulders. 'No, Dad, it's not. Don't you dare speak to Mum like that.'

His eyes narrowed. 'A wife must submit to her husband.'

That was it. My patience snapped. 'And a husband is supposed to love and honour his wife, not belittle her,' I shot back. 'How dare you use Scripture as an excuse to treat Mum this way?' I crossed the room to stand beside her, wrapping a protective arm around her shoulders. 'You don't get to twist the Bible to suit your own ego.'

His face flushed red, but for once, he didn't fire back. Instead, he slumped back in his chair, his hands trembling slightly. 'I'm ashamed,' he muttered, his voice softer now. 'Ashamed that I let my pride blind me. I'm supposed to lead this family in righteousness, but instead…' My throat closed as my father buried his face in his hands, his shoulders sagging. 'I can't believe they suspect me of being involved in that girl's disappearance.'

I ignored the sympathy that tried to overtake my anger, and

I kept my tone firm. 'Then tell me what really happened, Dad. Not as a police officer but as your daughter. I deserve the truth.'

He lifted his head, and I was startled to see his eyes wet with unshed tears. 'I was counselling a young woman, trying to help her get back on the right path. I met her at the library one day—she was sitting at a computer, swearing. I couldn't let that go.'

Of course he couldn't.

His voice cracked, and he took a shaky breath. 'She'd been struggling. Her ex-husband was harassing her, and a relative had turned up, causing trouble for her and her kids.'

My interest sparked, and I focused on his words.

My father paused, his voice full of regret. 'I visited her at her farm a couple of times. She was very receptive to what I read her from the Bible.'

I couldn't believe that of the Leanne I had known. She would have been being polite.

'The day she disappeared, we were supposed to finish our conversation, but even though her car was there, she wasn't. I didn't tell anyone I'd been there because I didn't want to betray her trust. It was foolish, and it made me look guilty.'

I studied him, my heart heavy with a mix of frustration and pity. 'You should've been honest from the start. Keeping secrets has only made things worse.'

'I know,' he whispered. 'I thought I was protecting her, but all I did was bring shame to myself and my family.'

'If we'd known that earlier, we could have found him. And maybe found out where she is.'

'Him?' Mum asked. She had walked over and put her hand on Dad's shoulder, and I fought back the tears as I saw his hand go up and hold hers.

'A person of interest,' was all I said.

Mum's voice was gentle but firm. 'We'll get through this, Jim. No one would ever believe that you would hurt someone.'

'You need to change your attitude, Dad. Stop hiding behind the Bible. Show some true compassion. Be a nicer person. Get rid of the anger and drop the fire and brimstone act.'

Dad nodded slowly, the seriousness of his actions finally seeming to sink in. 'You're right,' he said hoarsely. 'I can do better. I'll try.'

I exhaled, the tension in my shoulders easing slightly. 'Good. Now let's start afresh.'

'Your mother and I are going to move. We've discussed it.'

'That's a good idea. A new beginning. Where to?'

'We're not sure. Maybe you could help us decide,' Dad said meekly.

I almost had to bite my tongue. I almost said, "and the meek shall inherit the earth." My religious upbringing had left me with more Scripture than I'd realised.

My smile was wide. 'I'd love to do that.'

##

Back at the station, I found Mark and Todd in Mark's office, poring over files. I knocked lightly on the doorframe.

'Got a minute?' I asked.

They both looked up, and Mark gestured for me to come in.

'I talked to my dad,' I began, sitting down. 'He swears he wasn't involved in Leanne's disappearance. He admitted he was counselling her, trying to help her through some tough times. Apparently, a relative had been harassing her, making her life miserable. He didn't want to betray her trust, which is why he didn't tell anyone.'

Mark nodded, rubbing his chin thoughtfully. 'It's all coming together,' he said. 'If this relative was harassing her, it could be the key to what happened.'

Todd leaned forward, his brow furrowed. 'Did he say anything about being there the day she vanished?'

'He said he went out to the farm to see her that morning, but she wasn't there.'

Mark exchanged a glance with Todd. 'Okay, that gives us a clearer timeline. Let's think about how we approach Teddy tomorrow. If he's connected, we need to get him to talk.'

We spent the next hour strategising; Todd jotted down potential questions.

'How long have you known Leanne?' Todd suggested, writing it down. 'And what was your relationship like?'

Mark added, 'Were you aware of any threats or harassment she was facing?'

'And we'll need to probe into the inheritance,' I said. 'We can ask if he knew about her will or if they'd ever discussed the property.'

Todd nodded. 'Right. If he thinks there's a financial motive, we'll watch for any cracks in his story. Also, where was he the day she disappeared? And can he account for his movements since?'

By the time we finished, we had a solid game plan. I pushed my chair back, ready to call it a night. 'Sounds good. I'll see you both in the morning.'

As I reached the door, Todd's voice stopped me. 'Bec, wait a sec.'

I turned back, curious.

'Justin's just got his transfer,' Todd said, leaning back in his chair. 'He's heading back to Brisbane. That leaves a vacancy for a detective in Bowen.'

My heart skipped a beat. 'And?'

Todd smiled slightly. 'What do you think? You've got the skills. And you've been invaluable on this case.'

For a moment, I was speechless. A mix of excitement and

nerves fluttered in my chest. This was what I'd been working towards, but it felt surreal hearing it out loud. 'I—I'd love that,' I finally said, my voice steady despite the rush of emotions. 'Thank you, Todd. That means a lot.'

I couldn't help myself. On an impulse, I leaned over, touched his arm, and kissed his cheek. 'I think that's the nicest thing you've ever said to me, friend,' I teased with a grin.

Todd laughed, colour creeping up his neck. 'Don't let it go to your head, Whitfield.'

Mark chuckled from his desk. 'Alright, let's get some rest. Big day tomorrow.'

I left the office, a smile lingering on my face. For the first time in a while, I felt like things were falling into place.

Chapter 36

Strathallyn Station - April 1948.
Elspeth

The man stood outside the gate of *Strathallyn,* watching the horses grazing in the front paddock. Elspeth, riding towards the stables, pulled on the reins, frowning. She blinked, wondering if she had had too much sun. It was as though Thomas stood at the gate, and she was nineteen years old again.

They weren't expecting anyone. She turned the horse around and took it back to the stable, but when she came out, the man was walking towards the house. She blinked, her heart pounding in her chest as she stared at the man before her. His face—those dark eyes—had such a familiarity to them, like a ghost of the past walking before her. The world seemed to tilt, the edges of her vision blurring as her thoughts swirled. She shook her head, trying to clear the fog that seemed to cloud her mind.

For a moment, she thought she might be imagining things. Perhaps she had spent too much time in the stables, too long in the company of the horses, that the line between reality and memory had become blurred.

It's as though Thomas stands there at the gate, she thought numbly, as though a part of him had come back to her. She blinked again and took a deep breath.

Perhaps I've died, and he is waiting for me, she thought, the notion so strange and heavy she almost believed it for a moment.

But no, that wasn't possible. She wasn't dead. She was here, on *Strathallyn*, standing on the hard, dry earth. Still, the pull of memories—the impossible pull—made her hesitate, and she looked down, desperate to distract herself, to ground herself in the familiar motions of care and routine.

He was still there, the stranger, walking towards the house. Her breath caught in her throat as she quickened her steps, her heart racing. Her mind, racing ahead of her, tried to make sense of it.

Could it be? Could it really be him? Perhaps it was Thomas's brother, someone she had never known existed. She had never learned of Thomas's family; he'd never spoken of them. The thought seemed too distant, too fanciful, but still, it gnawed at her.

She hurried to the gate, her legs unsteady. He turned as she approached, and she drew in a sharp breath. His presence felt like a force pulling at her, something beyond her control.

'Hello,' she called out, her voice trembling slightly. 'How may I help you?'

The stranger's eyes met hers—dark, almost too familiar— and a sharp pang gripped her chest, her breath momentarily catching. The air around her seemed to shrink, the shortness of breath pressing down on her.

'Are ... are you, Elspeth Delaney?' The young man's voice was hesitant, unsure, but the words struck her like a blow. She couldn't breathe. Her legs wobbled, and she reached for the gate to steady herself.

'I am,' she managed to say, her voice barely above a whisper, her frown deepening in confusion. 'Are you here to look at some of our horses? I'll get my father—he still handles the sales.'

But he stood still, staring at her with an intensity she could not understand. His gaze dropped for a moment, and his feet shuffled, betraying a discomfort. Then, in one long, agonising pause, he spoke again, the words tumbling out, raw and unguarded.

'I don't know how to say this,' he began slowly, then swallowed hard. 'But I think I just need to come out and say it. I am your son. I am Robert.'

Elspeth's world tilted, this time so violently that the ground shifted beneath her boots. The dizziness hit her in waves, her thoughts spiralling out of control.

Robert? Her heart seemed to stop, and the air around her grew thin. She stared at him, the words echoing in her mind.

Robert? My son? But how could it be? How? He was dead.

But the boy—the man—before her was real, his presence undeniable, but her mind refused to make any sense of it.

Her vision blurred, and the colours of the sky, the ground, and the gate all ran together, and she felt herself falling. She couldn't catch her breath. Couldn't find her footing. Her legs buckled beneath her, and the last thing she remembered before the darkness took her was the sensation of her body collapsing towards the ground, the air suffocating, and her heart racing with disbelief—and hope.

Chapter 37

Strathallyn Station - April 1948.
Elspeth

The sharp, oppressive weight of silence surrounded her as Elspeth slowly regained consciousness. She blinked, her eyelids heavy, the world swimming around her like a fog. She could hear the distant murmur of the wind and the soft rustling of the trees, but nothing seemed quite real yet. A familiar smell—clean air, the scent of the stables, and something faintly medicinal—filled her senses.

She let out a shallow breath, her chest tight as she tried to move, but something—or someone—stopped her. She opened her eyes slowly and was met with a blur of figures and shapes. Then, as if the world was gradually coming into focus, she saw him—her father. His worried face hovered above her, his hands wringing with a mixture of relief and uncertainty. His lips were moving, though she couldn't catch the words at first.

'I thought you were having a heart attack,' he said, his voice thick with concern.

Elspeth blinked, struggling to sit up, her head spinning. She felt the coolness of the verandah beneath her. The thick wooden beams of the homestead loomed above her, and she realised she was lying on one of the old beds set up on the high verandah.

But then she heard it again—the sound of a voice she had longed to hear, one she thought had been lost to her forever. A voice she never thought she would hear again. It was Thomas's voice.

'Please look at me,' he said.

Her heart skipped, and with effort, she turned her head. There, standing just beyond her father, was a young man, his face familiar yet so different. She felt a jolt of recognition so powerful it almost made her gasp.

'It wasn't a dream,' Elspeth whispered, her voice trembling. 'You're real. Are you really Robert? Are you really my little boy?'

The young man—her son, Robert—shifted awkwardly on his feet. His face, now marked by age and experience, carried the same eyes, and the same shape of his smile that had haunted her memories. He laughed nervously, almost apologetically.

'Not so little anymore,' he said, his voice laced with uncertainty but also the beginnings of a tentative hope.

Elspeth's breath caught in her chest as she processed his words. Her mind scrambled, trying to piece together what had just happened, trying to comprehend how he could be standing here in front of her, so alive, so real.

'But I don't understand,' she stammered, her voice faltering.

'You both drowned. You and Edward. I remember the letter. I still have it. Aunt Kathleen had her solicitor write it. You and Edward drowned at the beach on holiday—' Her voice trailed off as she struggled to make sense of the painful memory. Tears began to spill from her eyes, the grief she had buried for so long surging to the surface.

Robert looked at her with a deep sadness in his eyes. 'It was a lie,' he said softly, shaking his head. 'I can remember bits of Aunt Kathleen's house in Rockhampton, but . . . I don't know how long we were there. We were sent to an orphanage in Brisbane after that. She told us our parents were killed in a train crash and that she couldn't care for us any longer.'

Elspeth blinked, her mind reeling, the breath caught in her throat. 'No,' she whispered, 'I thought—I thought you were both dead.'

She reached out instinctively, her hands trembling as she took his. Robert squeezed them tightly in return, his face twisting with emotion. It was then that she saw the tears running down his cheeks, and she felt the truth in his touch. He was her son, standing here before her, the child she had lost, now returned.

'Where is Edward?' she asked, her voice raw. 'Is he with you? Where is your brother?'

Robert's expression darkened. He shook his head slowly, and Elspeth's heart faltered.

'He didn't come back from the war,' he said, his voice thick with sorrow. 'I'm sorry. Edward didn't come home.'

Elspeth felt a sharp pain cut through her chest. She staggered, trying to sit up, her body betraying her as grief coursed through her again. 'Oh God, no,' she whispered. 'Not war again? Another loss?' She felt the ground shift beneath her, her son's words crashing over her.

'Have you been to war too? Just like your father did?' she asked, her eyes wide with horror. 'You were young for that. I can't—I can't believe it.'

Robert took a breath, his face clouded with sadness. 'I had only just enlisted when peace was declared,' he said softly. 'I went to Borneo in the last months, and after the war ended, I couldn't find him. No news, nothing. I've searched, tried to find out, but nothing.'

Elspeth closed her eyes, her heart breaking all over again. Edward, her other son, her boy, lost to another war. She had lost him once, and now she must grieve him again. Her heart felt as though it would shatter again, but through it all, she clung to the fact that Robert, her Robert, was here. Alive. And she would never let him go again.

That night, they sat for hours on the veranda, the conversation flowing slowly but steadily. Jack joined them for a while, but the mention of Robert's story and the cruelty of his wife and her sister had overwhelmed him. He had embraced Elspeth before making his way down the hall to his room. 'I'm sorry, sweetheart,' he had murmured, his voice heavy with regret. 'I should have stopped her from sending them to Kathleen. She assured me it would only be for a short while.'

'No, Father,' Elspeth had replied, shaking her head. 'It wasn't your fault. You can't take any blame. I'll always tell myself that Mother was thinking of me, that she was trying to protect me.' Her gaze had flickered over to Robert. 'When your father committed suicide, my mother was frightened that it would pass onto you. It was what she believed, and she worried about me. She thought she was doing what was best. I blame Aunt Kathleen for sending you away,' Elspeth said. 'And for lying about your deaths. That, I will never forgive.'

Jack had dropped a kiss on the top of her head before he walked down the hall, leaving her and Robert alone. For the first time, Elspeth had seen her father look like an old man. Robert's return and the story he had brought had hit him hard. She felt her heart squeeze as she watched him go, but she forced herself to stay strong. She turned to Robert and sat beside him on the swing chair.

'Your father loved you very much, but he was so damaged by the war. I was unable to help him. If Edward is alive, we will find him,' Elspeth had said, her voice steady now as the shock of Robert's return eased. The joy that she now carried in her heart would feed her hope of finding her other son, the one she barely remembered. Her memories of Thomas and Robert were joyful.

Robert nodded, his gaze intense. 'We will, Mum. We'll make sure of it.'

Elspeth took a deep breath, the dark enclosing them in a safe cocoon. 'We have to remain strong,' she said, her voice resolute. 'For Edward. For Father. For each other.'

Chapter 38

Strathallyn Station - May 1948.
Elspeth

The sun had just dipped behind the hills, bathing the stables in golden light. Robert was working with the young foals, his hands steady as they coaxed the animals into a comfortable rhythm. He had inherited the family skills for working with horseflesh. Elspeth was nearby, checking the feed and ensuring the stables were secure. The work on the farm was demanding, but it was the kind of hard work Robert had always known. She watched him, proud of the man her son had grown into.

He walked over to the fence where she stood and put his arm around her. 'It is so good to be here, Mother,' he said as Elspeth leaned against him.

'You know we want you to stay, don't you? To work with us and to build the stud up. Tell me how you found your way home. Perhaps it will help us find Edward.'

'Mother,' Robert began, his voice steady but with a trace of something softer in it. 'When I was in Borneo, I never thought I'd see a day of peace. The jungle was thick with tension, the air heavy with the smell of smoke and the sound of gunfire.'

Elspeth paused in her work and looked at him. 'You've never spoken much about it,' she said softly, wiping her hands on her apron.

Robert gave a small smile, though it didn't reach his eyes. 'The day peace was declared, I remember the feeling. It was so surreal like the ground had shifted beneath us. But when I came back, I tried to find my brother. I searched everywhere, thinking maybe he was in some far corner of this country. But he was gone. I've always assumed he's buried in some unmarked grave somewhere, one of the many we left behind.'

There was a long silence between them, Robert's words hanging in the air. Elspeth knew better than to push for more details. The past was a place Robert rarely ventured.

'I'm sorry,' she said after a moment. 'But you've built a good life here, Robert. And I'm glad you've found peace with it.'

He nodded, his fingers brushing the soft mane of a foal. 'Yes. It's been a long road, but this place—this farm—it's as close to home as I've ever had.'

Elspeth smiled, feeling the same. They had created something together here, in the peaceful hills of the countryside, surrounded by horses and the rhythm of their work. It wasn't perfect, but it was theirs.

Elspeth listened intently, her mind racing as Robert shared

his memories, the pieces of their past slowly coming together like a jigsaw puzzle they had never known how to complete.

'Aunt Kathleen never told us where we came from,' Robert began, his voice sad. 'We never knew where we were from. I remembered you, and I have clear memories of my father. I knew my grandmother when she came down to visit, and I used to ask her questions, but she never told us anything of home.'

Elspeth's heart ached as she recalled her own fragmented memories of the past. Robert continued, his voice holding the same quiet sadness that had been with her for years.

'It was after her last visit that Aunt Kathleen sent us away. I still remember her telling us that you and Father had been killed in a train crash. But she never told us where, and we never knew what happened to you.'

Elspeth felt the sting of those lost years. She had tried to make sense of it all, but the silence had always been deafening. Robert's voice softened as he spoke about their life after that, the orphanage in Brisbane, and how they had struggled to survive through the Depression.

'We didn't get much schooling. I went out to work, and when Edward was old enough, we lived in a boarding house in Brisbane. We both worked on the railways. It was strange, but for some reason, I thought that might help us find out what happened to both of you. But of course, it was all a lie. There was nothing.'

Elspeth nodded, the years of uncertainty and unanswered questions weighing heavily on both of them. Robert's story continued, his voice steady but laden with pain.

'When I decided to enlist, I had just turned nineteen. Edward was determined to go as well. He changed his name, falsified his date of birth, and pretended he was eighteen. The last time I saw him was on the ship bound for Borneo in 1945. I don't know where he ended up. When I came back, I looked. I searched high and low, but I never knew what name he took, so it was impossible to find him. It was impossible to find out what happened to him during the war. In the end, I gave up.'

Elspeth listened quietly, her heart heavy with this new knowledge of the past. But then Robert's expression changed, and Elspeth could see the glimmer of hope in his eyes.

'But how did you know to come here?' she asked, her voice tinged with curiosity.

Robert's brow furrowed as he considered her question. He took a deep breath before answering.

'It was strange. I was at a race meeting in Sydney about four months ago. I've always loved horses, and I've always wanted to be around them when I came back from the war. I was working at the stables at Rose Hill when a horse came in. I lit up when I saw the name,' he explained, his voice catching slightly. 'It was

"Babir" something.'

'Babir Son,' Elspeth said, blinking back tears.

'How did you know that?'

'Because we don't send many horses down to Sydney, but I remember him going down. He won the Rose Hill Cup.'

Robert nodded. 'Yes, that's the one. He was from *Strathallyn Station*. I hadn't heard that in all those years, but as soon as I heard it, I remembered. I packed up and grabbed a train to Brisbane. I went back to the orphanage to see if they could tell me more, but of course, there were no records. What was there was probably lies anyway.' He paused, staring past Elspeth. 'It took me a few days to travel to Bowen, and then I hitchhiked out here. And here I am.'

She smiled at him, still unable to believe her son had come home. For the first time in years, she felt at peace.

***

Robert, just like his grandfather, mother, and father, inherited a love for horses. He lived in the same house at Suttor River where he had been born, lived a full life, married, and had a child. When he passed away at eighty-five, he left behind one grandchild: Leanne Delaney.

He was never able to find his brother Edward or his grave. For all of his life, he believed Edward was buried in the jungles of Borneo.

Chapter 39

Alva Beach - Tuesday.
Bec

We left before dawn, the Stinger eating up the kilometres on the Bruce Highway. The early light painted the horizon in pale pinks and golds, and as we crossed the Johnson River, I was in awe of the wide, bare sands on both sides of the bridge. On the northern edge near the mangroves, the water gleamed like liquid glass in the soft light. The serene flow of the river contrasted with the tension that built in my chest as we headed towards the interview ahead. Was I taking too much on? But then I reassured myself that both Todd and Mark trusted that I could do it.

Todd drove this morning, his jaw set, while I watched the cane fields go past in a blur.

'This highway's a disgrace,' he muttered, swerving slightly to avoid a pothole that could swallow a wheel. 'Makes you wonder where all the funding goes.'

I nodded. 'Could use a bit of love, that's for sure. Guess it keeps us sharp, though—always scanning for the next crater.'

We lapsed into silence, both mentally preparing for the interview ahead. I went over the plan in my head: play it cool, let Todd start rough, then step in as the calm, reasonable one. Classic good cop, bad cop.

It had been arranged that Teddy Valentine, our suspect, would be brought in by the local police. He'd agreed to talk, though from what we'd heard, he wasn't exactly cooperative.

When we finally rolled into Alva Beach, the station was a modest building, its faded sign barely legible. Sergeant Walsh met us at the door, his weathered face set in a permanent scowl.

'He's waiting in the interview room,' Walsh said. 'Seemed pretty cocky. First thing he asked was if this was about the croc cull.'

Todd shot him a sharp look. 'Croc cull?'

Walsh sighed, leading us inside. 'Yeah, there's this group of cowboys around here who think it's fun to go out after dark in their four-wheelers, spotlighting and shooting crocs. Totally illegal, of course. We've never caught them in the act, but Valentine's been bragging about it down at the pub.'

'Charming,' I muttered.

'That's not all,' Walsh added. 'Word around the pub is Teddy's about to come into some money. Big money.'

Todd and I exchanged a glance. That little detail could be the piece we were looking for.

Inside the interview room, Teddy Valentine was sprawled in his chair, picking at his teeth with a matchstick. He was overweight, with a ruddy complexion and two gaudy gold chains around his wrist that clinked when he sat up.

The sergeant introduced us. 'This is Detective Whitfield and Detective Davenport.'

My ego shot sky high, and so did my confidence. Mark had instructed me not to wear my uniform; I was in navy trousers and a white shirt.

Teddy barely glanced at us, his attention on the matchstick. 'Didn't shoot any crocs,' he said, his tone laced with defiance.

Todd leaned on the table, his voice low and firm. 'Why don't you tell us about this little "crocodile cull" you've been bragging about at the pub? We know you've been shooting them.'

Teddy sneered. 'Just a bit of fun, mate. Crocs are a bloody menace. We're doing the government a favour.'

Todd's eyes hardened. 'You're aware it's illegal, right? And that fines aren't exactly pocket change?'

I placed a hand lightly on Todd's arm. 'Detective Davenport, let's give Mr Valentine the benefit of the doubt. I'm sure he knows the law and wouldn't do anything to jeopardise his . . . reputation.'

Teddy gave me a once-over, his eyes lingering where they shouldn't. My skin crawled, but I kept my composure.

I waited a few seconds and then leaned in slightly. 'Teddy, let's forget about the crocodiles. I want to talk about Bowen

River. Leanne Delaney.'

'Who?' For a moment, I thought he was going to deny knowing her.

'Have you been to her place recently?'

'Don't know where she lives.'

'That's interesting. Your hat was on the hall stand.'

Some of the ruddiness left his complexion, and he sat up straighter. 'I forgot I went there once a while back.'

'What's a while back?'

'A month. Maybe two.'

'What's your relationship with her?'

He stared at me. 'We're cousins.

'And the kids call you Uncle Teddy?'

'Yeah. She said it was more respectful.'

'You go there a lot?'

'Not really.'

'So more than once.'

'Maybe. I forget.'

'How long have you known her?'

'What's it to you? I told you. We're cousins.'

'So, you've known her all your life.'

'Yeah. Look, her being missing has nothing to do with me.'

Bingo. We had him; we hadn't told him she was missing, and the media release wasn't going out until this afternoon.

Todd changed tack. 'You only moved to Alva a couple of months back. You were living up in the Kimberleys, I believe.'

'So?' Teddy's belligerence was growing as Todd pushed him.

'So, the police in Wyndham would probably be interested in knowing your whereabouts. There are a couple of outstanding warrants over there.' Todd stared at him, and I knew that we had managed to unsettle him.

'Bullshit,' he said. 'You're just trying to wind me up.'

'When's the last time you saw her?' I asked.

His smirk faltered for just a second, but he quickly recovered. 'Leanne? I already told you. A while. Why?'

Todd jumped in. 'What date exactly?'

Teddy shrugged. 'I told you before. A month. I was up there looking for work at the mine. I called in to see her—heard she was looking for someone to do some work on her property.'

I leaned forward. 'And where were you the week she disappeared? The tenth of March.'

His face darkened, and the bravado cracked. 'How the hell should I know? You think I keep a diary?'

Todd's tone sharpened. He leaned in, his gaze unwavering. 'How did you know Leanne was missing, Teddy?' he asked, his voice sharp.

Teddy's eyes darted to the side, and for a moment, he

seemed to struggle with the question. His fingers drummed nervously on the table, his cockiness slipping further.

'I heard about it from me mates,' he snapped, his voice rising in frustration. 'They were talking about it at the pub, and I didn't think much of it at the time. But I didn't touch her, alright?'

His face flushed red as he pushed back from the table, trying to maintain his composure, but his voice shook with unease. 'I'm done talking about this. I'm not saying anything more. I need a lawyer.'

'Okay, one more question. Give me the names of your mates who told you she disappeared. Oh, and tell us how they knew she was your cousin.'

His eyes shifted from side to side, and he shook his head. 'Lawyer.'

'Was it because you were bragging about all the money you were going to share from the sale of her property.'

'He is entitled to a lawyer, Detective Davenport,' I said.

Todd stayed silent for a moment, his eyes boring into Teddy, watching for any sign of a crack in his facade. It was clear the pressure was getting to him now.

'Where were you when she went missing?'

Teddy's eyes flicked between us, his irritation bubbling over. 'I was at home, alright? Ask anyone here! Any of me mates. And I'm done talking about this. I didn't have anything to do with her going missing.'

He swore under his breath, glaring at me as if I'd personally offended him.

We left him in the interview room while Todd and I debriefed with Walsh.

'He's lying,' Todd said, crossing his arms. Walsh grunted in agreement. 'We'll keep digging. In the meantime, I'll see if anyone can confirm his alibi.'

Todd didn't waste a second when we went back in. 'Before you call your lawyer, I want you to listen to me. You don't have to say anything.' He leaned in closer, his tone cold and measured. 'You're running out of options here. No one knows Leanne is missing. So, you obviously had something to do with it.'

Teddy's face tightened, his breath coming faster now. His bravado was gone, replaced by something more defensive. His eyes flicked from Todd to me, and for the first time, his confident exterior cracked. He swallowed hard, the muscles in his jaw twitching. For a moment, he didn't speak. Then, when he did, his voice came out as a shaky growl.

'I don't know where she is now!' he spat, his hands shaking slightly. 'I didn't do anything to her! She was talking about running off, going somewhere far away—maybe she just left.'

Todd's eyes narrowed as he pressed further. 'That's not what we're hearing, Teddy. We know you were around. So, stop lying.

Your ute was seen there by more than one person.'

The tension in the room was thick now, and I could feel the adrenaline kicking in. This was the moment. Teddy's resolve was cracking, and he knew it.

Todd leaned forward and glanced at the policeman standing behind Valentine.

'Teddy Valentine, I am arresting you on suspicion of your involvement in the disappearance of Leanne Delaney. You are not obliged to say anything unless you wish to do so. However, anything you do say may be used as evidence. You have the right to contact a lawyer, and we can provide you with access to one. If you do not want to contact a lawyer, you can waive this right, but you must do so voluntarily. You also have the right to remain silent during questioning. If you wish to answer questions, you may do so but understand that your responses may be used against you in court. If you wish to speak with a lawyer, let us know, and we will arrange for that to happen.'

Todd and I both leaned forward as Teddy's words spilled out, his voice thick with anger. Spittle flew from his mouth, his eyes wide and frantic.

'The silly bitch asked me to take her out to Suttor Causeway,' he yelled, his face flushed with fury. 'She had some bee in her bonnet about them putting more solar panels out there. She was a stupid fool.'

His hands shook, and his words were erratic as he tried to get out of the lies he'd told us. I did not doubt that he was lying now, too. My fear for Leanne's safety grew and lodged in my chest. The words tumbled out in a rush as if he couldn't keep them inside any longer.

'She wouldn't shut up about it, talking about how they were ruining the land and how we should be doing something about it. I didn't want anything to do with her stupid little crusade, but she wouldn't leave me alone, kept badgering me. So, I took her out there—thought it would be easier to just get it over with,' he continued, his voice thick with frustration.

Todd's expression remained calm, but his eyes were sharp, watching closely for any inconsistencies or cracks in Teddy's story. Each word Teddy said was a piece falling into place, but I wasn't about to let him off the hook just yet.

'So, what happened when you got there?' Todd asked, his voice low and controlled, pressing for more. Teddy's eyes darted around the room, his agitation growing as he began to realise that he had admitted to being out there with her.

Todd's voice dropped, his tone sharp, cutting through the tension. 'Did you hurt her?'

Teddy froze, his eyes locking with Todd's, a flicker of fear flashing across his face. For a split second, it looked like he might backtrack, but he swallowed hard, his breath coming in shallow gasps, and sweat beaded on his forehead. His jaw tightened as he opened his mouth, but no words came out at first.

Todd didn't break his gaze, his face stoic, waiting for the truth. And then, almost in a whisper, Teddy muttered, 'I didn't mean for it to go that far.'

My stomach churned as the implications of his words settled in the room. Todd and I exchanged a look, both of us knowing we were getting close to the truth.

Teddy's chest heaved as he continued, his words tumbling out like a man unravelling. 'She wouldn't stop. She kept yelling at me, saying I was part of the problem, part of the whole damn system. She was crazy. And then—' His voice cracked, and he looked down at his shaking hands.

'Then what, Teddy?' Todd pressed him, his voice low but unyielding.

Teddy's gaze darted around the room. He wouldn't look at either of us. 'I just wanted her to shut up and get back in the car.'

'Where were you? Why did you get out of the car?'

'She wanted to show me something near the river. I didn't mean, she was—' Teddy stammered, his words stumbling over each other. 'I mean, she was being a stupid fool. She always was. A do-gooder, always trying to save the world, thinking she could fix everything. Didn't care about all the money . . . wouldn't take their offer.' He spat the words hanging in the air with bitterness.

'And I'm entitled to half of it. I am.'

Todd's gaze never wavered, and his voice dropped lower, dangerous now. 'So, tell us what happened, Teddy. Where is she?'

The room fell silent for a long moment, only the hum of the air conditioner and the distant sound of traffic outside breaking the stillness. Teddy's eyes darted around the room, clearly on edge, and then he sighed, his shoulders slumping as if the truth was finally starting to take hold.

'We were out on the Old Bowen Downs Road. She was harping on about solar panels like it was all some big conspiracy. Like I said, I didn't want to go, but she insisted. In the end, I agreed to go out there with her. I'd show her how the big companies really work. Show her that people like her don't get a say in all that.'

'What were you going to show her exactly?' Bec asked. 'I don't know a lot about the solar farms. What would be out there to convince her she was wasting her time?'

He paused, his eyes shifting uneasily.

'Okay, I was trying to convince her to buy land out there. They'd offered her a big payout, and the silly bitch refused it. I was trying to show her it made sense.'

'Why would it make sense?' Todd interrupted. 'What did it matter to you?'

'I didn't want to hurt her, but she kept pushing me, kept talking, making me look like a fool. She wanted to talk about what's best for the community and all this garbage. I just snapped.' Teddy's breath caught in his throat as his hands shook. 'I didn't mean to . . . I didn't mean to go that far, but when she wouldn't shut up, I . . . I lost it.'

Todd leaned in closer, his voice as steady as steel. 'And after that, Teddy? Where is she?'

Teddy's face twisted in a grimace, a flicker of guilt flashing before he looked away. 'I don't know. I left her out there. She was . . . she was already gone when I left.' Teddy's voice grew strained as he continued, his words tumbling out in a rush. 'She got out of the car, said she wanted to show me something—some spot along the causeway, I dunno.' He shrugged, his eyes darting around the room. 'She tripped and fell down the bank. I didn't see exactly what happened, but I know she ended up in the river. I couldn't see her after that; she just disappeared under the water.' He paused, his breathing growing heavier, eyes darting around, not looking at either of us.

'I panicked,' he muttered, his tone low and ashamed. 'I didn't know what to do. So, I just . . . I just drove off. I didn't even stop to check. I couldn't. I didn't know if she was dead or alive, and I didn't care. I just wanted to get outta there.'

Todd's jaw tightened as he leaned forward, his voice cold.

'And you didn't report it? You didn't try to help her?'

Teddy shook his head, the guilt and fear obvious in his eyes, but the bravado was fading fast. 'What was I supposed to do, huh? She was already gone. And if I said anything, I'd be the one in the firing line. I panicked. I thought maybe nobody would find out.'

Todd didn't respond immediately. He was watching Teddy closely. He already knew the truth, but I knew he was lying, too. Enough.

'Where is she now, Teddy?' I said.

Teddy's eyes flickered, his voice wavering as he spoke. 'I don't know. I swear . . . I just drove home and left her there. You're gonna find her, right?' His words trailed off, not sounding as confident now. 'You can't blame me . . . she was the one who tripped, not me.'

Todd's voice cut through the tense silence, his tone firm and controlled. 'So you drove home to Alva Beach?'

'I did. I didn't want to get blamed for the accident.'

'And have you been back to Leanne's place in your ute?'

Teddy hesitated and then drew himself up straight in the chair. 'No, why would I?' Perspiration was rolling down his face and neck.

'I suggest that sometime a few days later you went back to her place, didn't you? What were you looking for? Something you could use to get the money she'd been offered for the place? Did you see her kids? Is that why they are so scared? What did you tell them?' Todd's voice grew louder. 'Then you took the number plates off your ute right around the time the sergeant and my colleague showed up at the house and were about to replace them with new ones. And then, when Senior Constable Whitfield arrived, you knocked her unconscious.'

Teddy's eyes widened in shock, and I could see the realisation hit him. He stared at Todd, then glanced at me.

'Detective Whitfield can identify you,' Todd said, his voice unwavering. 'Now, tell us where we can find Leanne Delaney and what really happened.'

The air felt thick, the tension crackling between us. Teddy looked as though he might try to protest, but Todd didn't give him the chance. He gestured for me to leave, a clear signal.

I stood up and moved towards the door, my heart racing. I knew what Todd wanted. He wanted me to call Mark. Let him know where to search for Leanne.

As I stepped out into the hallway, I quickly grabbed my phone and dialled Mark's number. My mind raced, thoughts swirling as I tried to calm my breathing. I had to keep it together. This was the moment we'd been waiting for.

'Mark,' I said as soon as he picked up. 'We need to get a team out to the Old Bowen Downs Road. Just before the causeway that's collapsed. Teddy just admitted to leaving her out there in the river.' I quickly explained what had ensued, the words coming out in a rush.

'On our way,' Mark replied, his voice steady. 'We'll be there soon.'

I ended the call, my heart pounding. This was it. The breakthrough we needed. But what Teddy had just confessed lingered in my mind. What else had he done? How far would he go to cover his tracks? How much of it was the truth?

I couldn't afford to think too much about that. Not now. I had to focus on Leanne. We were so close to finding her.

As Todd flicked the siren on and pushed the car through the early morning traffic, I sat beside him, my mind racing just as fast as the engine. The kilometres ticked by, but it felt like we were getting nowhere. What Teddy had said disturbed me. I couldn't shake the image of Leanne—her smile, her determination, her stubbornness—thinking about her out there with him. Falling? No. I couldn't believe it.

The thought of her body being out there—I couldn't finish the thought. Just the idea of it was enough to make my stomach turn and my chest tighten.

'Calm down. I can hear your mind churning from here,' Todd said, his voice breaking through my thoughts. He glanced over at me, concern in his expression.

I shook my head, more to myself than him. 'I feel sick,' I said, my voice trembling despite my effort to hold it steady. 'I know what we're going to find. Her body.'

My throat tightened, and I swallowed hard. The tears welled up before I could stop them, and I brushed them away furiously. I didn't have time for that.

Todd's hand lifted briefly from the wheel, and he took mine. The gesture was simple and I appreciated it more than I could say.

'We'll find her, Bec. We'll find out the truth, no matter what,' Todd said softly, his eyes briefly flicking back to the road. There was a quiet determination in his voice.

But I didn't know if I shared his certainty.

'What about them?' I asked, my voice barely a whisper. 'What happens to the kids if she's dead?'

Todd squeezed my hand tighter, his eyes softening as he focused on the road. 'We'll make sure they're okay, Bec. We'll make sure they're taken care of.'

I nodded, but the knot in my chest wouldn't loosen. Nothing would until we knew the truth. Until we found Leanne.

Chapter 40

Heidelberg Repatriation Hospital
Edward Valentine - March, 1946.

The sterile smell of the hospital ward clung to the air, and the sound of faint beeping filled the room, broken only by the soft murmur of voices in the hallway. Edward Valentine lay in a bed, his body battered and broken, though his mind was sharper than it had been in a long time. The war was over, but the memories of it haunted him. The images of the jungle, the constant tension, the loss of comrades—these were the ghosts that stayed with him. A friend from Brisbane had been on the hospital ship with him and told him that Robert's platoon had been ambushed and killed, unaware peace had been declared.

He shifted slightly, a soft wince escaping him as his injuries made themselves known. It had been months since the war ended, but the scars were far deeper than the physical ones. Yet, there was one thing that seemed to have rooted itself in his mind—a memory or perhaps a dream. A place, a farm, filled with horses—so vivid, so real, yet just out of reach.

A nurse walked in with a gentle smile. Geraldine. She had been his constant nurse since his arrival, always kind, always there, tending to his wounds, both physical and emotional. She had a way of calming him, of making him feel less lost, though he couldn't explain why.

'Another day, Private Valentine?' she asked softly.

Edward shifted in his bed, staring out of the window at the sun-dappled trees outside. 'It's funny,' he said slowly. 'I can't seem to shake the memory of a farm, a place with horses. It's so vivid—like it was real. I'm sure I couldn't remember being there, but when we went to the orphanage, I think my brother once told me we were born on a farm.'

Geraldine sat down beside him, her face softening with curiosity. 'What kind of place was it?' she asked.

Edward paused, trying to grasp the elusive fragments of the memory. 'There were horses, lots of them, and fields stretching out for miles. It felt peaceful like everything in the world was right in that moment. But when I try to think about it more, it slips away from me, like it never existed at all.'

Geraldine smiled faintly. 'Sometimes dreams feel more real than reality,' she said quietly. 'Perhaps you'll remember more one day. Where is your brother?'

'He was killed the week peace was declared.' Edward shook his head slowly, though he wasn't sure he believed that he would ever remember more. But something about her presence made him feel grounded like he wasn't entirely lost, even if he couldn't find the truth of his memory. Over the next few weeks, their conversations became longer, and more personal. They shared stories of their pasts and their hopes for the future, and slowly, a bond deepened between them.

Eventually, Edward was discharged from the hospital, but he couldn't shake the feeling of longing that seemed to be a part of him now. He kept returning to the memory of the farm with the horses. Even after the sterile white walls of the hospital had faded behind him, the memory was still there, nagging at the edges of his thoughts. He couldn't stop thinking about Geraldine either. There was something in the way she cared for him, something steady and constant that made him want to hold on to it.

He began visiting her at the hospital on her days off, and over time, their friendship blossomed into something more. The day he turned twenty-one, Edward asked her to marry him, and she accepted with a smile that told him she had been waiting for the same thing.

They settled in Melbourne, where Edward worked a variety of jobs, trying to build a life beyond the shadows of war. But no matter how hard he worked, the memory of the farm stayed with him, like a faded photograph tucked away in the back of his mind. The peace it promised was something he could never quite grasp.

Three years later, in a small hospital room, Edward stood by Geraldine's side as she gave birth to their son. It had been a difficult labour, but when they heard their son cry, all the pain seemed to melt away.

It was a bittersweet day for Edward. He wasn't sure how much longer he would be around, but in that moment, everything seemed bright. Geraldine cradled their newborn son, and Edward could see in his eyes the promise of a future, of a legacy.

'Thomas Edward,' Edward whispered, a smile crossing his face. 'Thomas was my father's name. That's one thing I do remember.'

Geraldine looked at him with tears in her eyes. 'He's perfect,' she said softly.

As their son grew, he became a reminder of everything Edward had longed for—a family, a future, and a sense of peace after years of turmoil. The only thing that stayed in his heart, the only regret, was the loss of his brother during the war, a wound that never fully healed.

Years passed, but the war left its mark on Edward in ways he couldn't escape. The humid jungles of Borneo had left him with more than just memories. At first, it was only a cough, persistent and deep, but soon it worsened. He was coughing up blood and struggling to breathe. Doctors misdiagnosed him at first, attributing his symptoms to the stresses of war, but when the diagnosis finally came—tuberculosis—it was almost too late. The infection had ravaged his lungs.

Edward remembered how, when he first returned to Australia, he had been eager to resume a "normal" life, refusing to admit the weakness in his body. He had survived the war, after all. But the disease was relentless, and soon, breathlessness became his constant companion.

Despite the toll the disease took on him, Edward fought to live. His thoughts often returned to that farm with the horses, the peace it had offered him, and the family he had built with Geraldine. Her kindness and her unwavering care became his anchor through it all.

As the years passed, his condition worsened, but Edward remained steadfast. He kept working when he could, focusing on building a life with Geraldine—a life that was quiet and stable, even if it wasn't the adventure-filled one he had once imagined.

Edward lived long enough to watch his son grow into a fine man, and just before the end of the nineteen seventies he had the blessing of meeting his grandson, also named Thomas Edward, but everyone called him Teddy. The boy's bright eyes and boundless energy gave Edward a renewed love for life. He couldn't always keep up with him, but when Teddy visited, Edward's face would light up with joy.

In 1970, complications from tuberculosis finally caught up

with Edward. He had endured more than most men, but it was his lungs that failed him in the end. He passed away quietly, surrounded by his family, in the home he had built with Geraldine.

Before his passing, Edward shared many stories with his grandson—stories about the farm with the horses, a place that felt so real yet so distant. Teddy would sit by him, asking about the farm and his grandfather's past. Edward would always end his stories the same way: 'It may not have been real, Teddy, but it's a dream I'll carry with me forever.'

Chapter 41

Old Bowen River Road - Tuesday
Bec

Todd flicked the siren on and pushed the car through the heavy highway traffic. I sat beside him, my mind racing ahead, wondering what we would find. Caravans and B-doubles slowed us at times, and the siren and the flashing lights of the Stinger got a workout. When we hit the small towns of Ayr and Home Hill, the traffic eased a little, and he pushed the speed up a notch.

The drive back to the turn-off to Bowen River seemed to take forever, but we got there in less than an hour. The tension grew as we hit the dirt road and roadworks just before Collinsville. Todd glanced across at me. 'I'll call dispatch.'

I nodded and leaned forward as he activated the radio with a voice command.

Todd flicked the radio on, his voice steady but urgent. 'Base, this is 10-32, over.'

The crackle of static came through before a voice responded.

'10-32, this is Base. Go ahead, over.'

'We're about forty clicks out from Suttor Causeway. Half an hour at most. Any updates on the search, over?'

There was a brief pause, and then the dispatcher's voice came through, calm but terse. 'Search teams are still out in the field. Nothing to report so far, over.'

Todd's jaw tightened, but his tone stayed professional. 'Copy that. Let the team know we're en route. We're about forty kilometres out, over.'

'Roger that. I'll pass the message along. Base out.'

Todd clicked off the radio, his hands gripping the wheel as he pushed the car faster.

I sat in silence for a few moments, unable to shake the sinking feeling in my gut. I glanced out the window as we passed Leanne's farm, the familiar sights of the landscape failing to comfort me now. Todd's eyes flicked to me briefly, but he didn't say anything. We both knew that we had to focus and not let ourselves get caught up in what we might find.

My mind raced through every piece of information we'd gathered over the past week. I sifted through what Teddy said, what Jean Purdue told me, the school, and the children themselves. Every piece of information that would help us, no that *might* help us pinpoint where Leanne could be.

Pinpoint!

I turned to Todd, gripping the edge of my seat. 'You said they'd triangulated her mobile, didn't you? Last week? And there was no signal?'

'That's right,' Todd replied, keeping his eyes on the road. 'Jean Purdue said that was strange. Leanne always kept her phone on her, especially when the kids were at school. She even sewed a special pocket into her apron at IGA, so it'd be handy.'

'And there was no sign of it at her house, which means she must've had it with her when he took her. It has to be out there. If Teddy had it, it would have come up wherever he was.' I stared out the window for a moment, the pieces clicking together. 'What number did we source her mobile from?'

Todd glanced at me briefly. 'Justin found the bill at her place. We took the number from that. Why?'

I reached for my phone. 'I'm going to call Jean. Something's not adding up.'

Jean answered on the second ring. 'Hello?'

'Jean, it's Bec Whitfield. Just a quick question—can you tell me what Leanne's mobile number is?'

There was a pause, and then she recited the number. I jotted it down in my notebook. 'You know it by heart?' I asked, surprised.

'No,' she said, her voice quiet. 'I read it off the board in the office. It's a new number. She's only had the phone for a week. That's the number I've been calling, trying to reach her.'

My heart skipped. 'A new phone,' I repeated so Todd would hear. 'Thanks, Jean. That's really helpful.'

'Is there any news?' she asked, her voice heavy with worry.

'Not yet,' I said gently. 'But we're following a lead. I'll let you know as soon as we find out anything. How are the kids holding up?'

Jean sighed. 'Unsettled. They're missing their mum, asking why she left them. It's been hard.'

'You're doing a great job, Jean,' I said softly. 'We'll talk soon.'

I ended the call and turned to Todd, my pulse quickening. 'We've had the wrong number this whole time. She's got a new phone.'

Todd's grip on the steering wheel tightened. 'If she's only had it for a week, it might not be in the system yet. That could explain why we couldn't track it.'

'And why he didn't leave it behind,' I added. 'It's on her. Wherever she is.'

Todd nodded. 'We'll find her.'

I called Mark straight back, and he was going to get them searching for the phone as soon as we disconnected.

'We're not far away, Mark,' Todd said. 'We'll be at the causeway in about ten minutes.'

The land past Leanne's farm was vast and flat, stretching out in every direction, the earth cracked and dry from the harsh sun. The sun was high in the sky, burning down on the barren landscape. A few clusters of trees dotted the sides of the road, their branches gnarled from years of harsh conditions. It was beautiful in its own way, but now, it felt eerie.

The silence in the car was almost suffocating, but I couldn't bring myself to speak. Todd's grip on the wheel tightened slightly, his eyes focused on the dirt road.

How close were we?

A few kilometres before the causeway we spotted four police cars parked along the road, with several officers walking along each side.

Mark hurried over as we got out of the car. 'Bec, Todd, got a location on the phone. It's within a hundred-metre radius. The three towers to the west, north, and south picked it up as the last location. We've only just moved to here. We're searching the sides of the roads first, and then we'll split up.'

'He said the river,' Todd said.

'Yeah, it's about five hundred metres that way.' Mark pointed across the road from where Todd had parked. 'You can't see it from here because of the bank that runs along from the causeway for—'

'Sergeant!' One of the officers was pointing to the ground.

My heart skipped a beat. The tension in my chest ratcheted up as I followed Mark and Todd to where the officer stood about two metres into the low scrub.

'The phone?' Mark asked.

'No, a shoe.' He pointed to the left, and we turned. A single sandal was sticking out from under a low bush.

'It's not been there long,' Todd said. The faintest trace of pink was covered by dust, and the heel was bent slightly as if it had been carelessly tossed away. My stomach turned.

'Leanne's?' I whispered, not even sure I wanted to know the answer.

The constable nodded grimly. 'It could be.'

We all stood there for a moment, staring at it, and then Mark pointed to a bare patch of dirt about a metre further into the bush. 'Look, there are scuff marks there.'

We walked over carefully, and sure enough, there were two distinct sets of prints in place: small bare footprints and prints of what looked like large work boots.

'We'll head down his way,' Todd instructed. 'Mark, can you divide the others into three groups? We'll spread out and work from here to the river.'

Within minutes, the search formation was in place, and we made our way into the bush toward the river.

Almost immediately, one of the officers in the line closest to Todd and me yelled out to us. 'I've found her phone!'

I turned quickly, my eyes locking onto the officer's outstretched arm as he held up the phone, smashed and broken.

My throat went dry.

Todd took a step forward, his voice quiet but firm. 'Where did you find it?'

'Just a few metres up from here at the top of the bank,' the officer replied, holding it carefully as if it might fall apart at any moment.

I couldn't breathe. The phone had been shattered, the screen cracked and warped beyond recognition, but it was still there. Leanne's phone. Her connection to the world, and now it was in pieces. It was hard to ignore what it meant.

Todd looked at me then, his gaze steady. He didn't say anything—he didn't need to. His eyes spoke what I already knew. Leanne had been here. She had been right here, at this spot.

And now, we needed to find her.

Chapter 42

Old Bowen River Road -Tuesday.
Bec

The search felt endless. Time stretched as we moved through the scrub and along the riverbank. An hour passed. Then two. Todd divided the team again, spreading us out to comb both directions along the river. Each step felt heavier than the last, the sun beating down relentlessly, the bush dry and unyielding.

My hope began to dwindle. Leanne had been missing for well over a week—too long in this heat, too long without help. If she were alive, surely she'd have made her way to the road, to the farm, to anywhere she could find someone. Tears stung my eyes, but I blinked them away, my breath catching as a low-hanging branch whipped across my face.

Todd appeared at my side, his voice calm but firm. 'Are you okay?'

I nodded, but he could see I wasn't. 'I'm fine,' I murmured, though my head felt light, and my mouth was dry as sandpaper.

Todd frowned. 'Take a breather. It's hot. I'll head back to the car and grab some water. We should've brought some with us.'

I wanted to protest, to keep going, but the dizziness made

me pause. 'Maybe you're right,' I admitted.

He pointed towards a flat rock beneath a weeping paperbark near the river's edge. 'Sit there. I'll be quick.'

Reluctantly, I sat, grateful for the cool stone beneath me. Todd jogged up the bank, disappearing over the top. I leaned back, letting my eyes close for a moment, listening to the rustle of water over the stones and the distant cawing of crows. The world narrowed to those sounds, grounding me until something else broke through—the faintest cry. A voice.

My eyes flew open, my pulse racing. I held my breath, listening intently. There it was again—a faint, broken cry for help.

I scrambled to my feet and ran along the bank, following the sound. My heart pounded as I rounded a bend, and there she was. Leanne. Half sitting, half lying on the ground beneath an overhanging rock, her lips cracked and dry, her face flushed with fever. Her glassy eyes flickered towards me, struggling to focus.

'Bec? Is that you?' she croaked, her voice barely a whisper. 'Am I dreaming? Am I dead?'

I dropped to my knees beside her, my throat tightening. 'No, Leanne. You're here. You're alive. We've been looking for you.'

Beside her lay a small pile of dark fruit, and some chewed water lily bulbs lay in the shade, evidence of her desperate attempt to survive. Relief and sadness mingled as I took her hand, careful not to overwhelm her.

'Stay with me, Leanne,' I said softly. 'Help is coming. We've got you.'

Her voice cracked, barely a whisper. 'It was Teddy.'

'Don't talk,' I interrupted gently, brushing a damp strand of hair from her forehead. 'Save your strength. I'm calling for help.'

I fumbled for my phone, my hands shaking as I pulled it from my pocket. A single bar of service flickered on the screen. I pressed Todd's number, my heart pounding, but the call wouldn't go through. Swallowing my frustration, I quickly typed a message: **I've found Leanne. She's alive. Near where you left me. Call an ambulance.**

The moment I hit send, I squeezed Leanne's hand. 'Help's on the way. Just hold on.'

She gave a weak nod, her eyelids fluttering closed. I stayed by her side, listening to her shallow breathing, the tension in my chest easing slightly now that I knew help was coming.

Minutes felt like hours, but soon, the crunch of boots on dry grass and the hum of voices grew louder. I looked up to see a crowd of officers descending the slope, Todd at the front, urgency in his expression. I met his eyes and blinked tears away.

'She's here,' I called out, my voice steady but thick with emotion. 'She's alive.'

Todd crouched beside us, his hand briefly brushing my shoulder before he focused on Leanne. 'Ambulance is on its way,' he said quietly. 'You did good, Bec. Really good.'

As the others moved in to assist, I leaned back for a moment, taking deep breaths.

Leanne was safe. She was going to make it.

Chapter 43

Bowen River Health Centre - Tuesday 5.00 p.m.
Bec

The late afternoon sun filtered through the blinds of the small health centre room, casting soft golden light across the bed where Leanne lay. She looked tired, her face pale, but there was a strength in her eyes that hadn't been there earlier. Her broken ankle was wrapped and elevated, and despite everything, she managed a small smile when Todd and I entered.

'Jonas and Mandy are on their way,' I said gently, stepping closer to the bed. 'Mark called Sheree. They'll be here soon.'

Leanne let out a trembling breath, her hands twisting in the blanket. 'That's all I've wanted. I need to see them. I need them to know I'm all right.'

Todd pulled up a chair, his expression unreadable as he sat beside her. 'They'll know, Leanne. You've been through hell, but you're here. And you're tougher than you think.'

Her voice cracked as she began recounting her week. 'Teddy tricked me, you know. He said he wanted to show me something by the river. I didn't want to go, but he wouldn't let me say no. When I tried to turn back, he pushed me—attacked me—and left me for dead. When he hit me on the head with his gun, I closed my eyes, and I held my breath. I knew he was watching me, and I didn't move.'

'What happened then?' Todd asked quietly.

My throat tightened as she described the fall.

'I was on the edge of the bank, and he put his boot under my back and pushed. I went over the side and landed in the river, but I must have gone under. I let the current take me a little way; when I came to, I didn't move or open my eyes; I thought he might be watching from the bank above me.'

'Bastard,' Todd muttered.

'I ended up in the water. I think that saved me. The cool water kept the swelling down in my ankle, and I had something to drink. After that, all I could think about was Jonas and Mandy. I couldn't let them grow up with no mother . . . left with him.'

Her voice broke, and tears streamed down her face. Instinctively, I leaned over and wrapped my arms around her, holding her tightly. 'You did it, Leanne. You kept going, and you made it back to them.'

Todd shifted in his seat, his jaw working as if holding back words. When I glanced at him, I saw the faint twitch of his muscle, the emotion he was trying to suppress. He caught my gaze and gave a slight nod, his silent way of saying. *You did well.*

Leanne wiped her face and managed a faint laugh. 'I crawled

out of the river and settled myself under the overhanging rock. I knew I could find food, and there was an abundance of water only metres from me. I found lily roots to dig up, and not far from there, I spotted a tree with Burdekin plums. They were green, though.' She pulled a face. 'Made me so sick, I thought my belly would never stop hurting. Worse than my ankle.'

We all laughed softly, a moment of welcome levity.

'I vowed I would survive. If it hadn't been for my broken ankle, I could have walked home.' Then her expression sobered, and her eyes darted between us. 'What happened to him? Teddy. Did he tell you he left me? Where is he now?'

Todd's voice was steady. 'He's in custody, Leanne. He'll be charged with attempted murder.'

Leanne stared at us for a moment, then covered her face with her hands. The tension in the room was palpable, but as Todd and I exchanged a glance, his faint smile reassured me. I returned it, the moment of shared understanding grounding us both.

Then, from the hallway came the sound of children's voices. Leanne's head shot up, her eyes filling with tears again, but this time they were tears of joy.

'Jonas! Mandy!' she called out, her voice trembling. The emotion in those two words brought tears to my eyes, too.

The door swung open, and two small figures rushed inside. Mandy reached her mother first, throwing herself into Leanne's arms. Jonas hung back for a second, his lower lip trembling, before he moved forward and buried his face in her shoulder.

'I'm here,' Leanne murmured, holding them close as fresh tears ran down her cheeks. 'I'm here, my darlings. Mummy's here.'

Todd touched my arm lightly, and we stepped out into the hallway, giving the family the privacy they needed. As we walked away, the sound of Leanne's soft reassurances and her children's voices followed us.

'Mummy, where did you go?' Mandy asked.

'Don't worry, Mum. I looked after Mandy.' Jonas's words ended with a sob.

'That's why we do this,' Todd said quietly, his gaze ahead, but his words stayed with me.

I nodded, my chest tight with emotion. 'Yeah. That's why.'

Chapter 44

Bowen River Police Station - Six weeks later

Bec

The afternoon sun cast warm light across the Bowen River police station's common room, where the team had gathered for my farewell. Plates of lamingtons, scones, and Tim Tams sat next to the jug of iced tea and a row of takeaway coffee cups. Aaron had gone to the café and brought back everyone's favourite orders, earning a round of gratitude.

Mark was still being teased about the lack of a decent coffee machine at the station. 'I'm just saying,' Todd quipped, holding up his cup like a toast, 'if we can afford this iced tea, surely we can spring for a coffee machine?'

Aaron leaned over to me with a conspiratorial grin. 'I've already put one through requisitions. Should be here in a week.'

I glanced around at the familiar faces, my chest tightening with a mix of gratitude and nostalgia. These people had been my colleagues, mentors, and, in some cases, friends. Todd stood near the corner, arms crossed as he listened to Mark's story about a particularly bizarre call-out, a faint smile tugging at his lips.

At the table, Leanne sat with her two children, Jonas and

Mandy, the three of them smiling and chatting with Jean and Sheree. Leanne's moon boot was gone, and although she moved carefully, she looked stronger and more like herself. Over the past few weeks, she and I had started to rebuild our friendship, and seeing her here with her kids, safe and healing filled me with quiet happiness.

When Mark finished his tale, he turned to me, raising his cup. 'To Bec Whitfield—soon-to-be Detective Whitfield of Mission Beach. We're going to miss you, mate, but we know you're going to do great things over there.'

A round of cheers followed, and I smiled, feeling a blush creep up my cheeks. 'Thanks, Mark. And thanks, everyone, for putting this together. I'm really going to miss Bowen River, but I'm excited about this new chapter.'

Todd caught my eye, and I felt a flicker of reassurance in his steady gaze. Knowing he'd still be close by, just an hour away, made leaving a little easier. Over the past two months, we'd developed a firm friendship built on mutual respect and the successful outcome of the case.

As I mingled with the team, thanking each of them, I spotted my parents near the door. It was still a little surreal to see them here. Dad, in his usual button-down shirt and weathered hat, looked slightly out of place among the uniforms. Mum stood beside him; her face soft with a proud smile.

'Well,' Dad said, clearing his throat as I approached. 'Detective Whitfield, eh? Who would've thought?'

'Thanks, Dad,' I said cautiously, waiting for the rest of it.

He scratched the back of his neck, his eyes fixed somewhere over my shoulder. 'You've done well, Bec. Real well. I'm . . . proud of you.' His voice was gruff, and his words came out like they'd been dragged over hot coals, but they hit me harder than I'd expected.

Mum beamed at him and then at me, her delight clear. 'And we've got news,' she said, her tone bright. 'We're moving to Tully to be closer to you! I've wanted to get away for years, and now I've finally talked your dad into it.'

I blinked in surprise, glancing at Dad, who grumbled, 'Your mother's been on about it long enough. Figured I'd give in while I'm still young enough to carry the boxes.'

Todd sidled up beside me, a plate of scones balanced precariously in one hand. 'Looks like you've managed to impress everyone, Whitfield. Even the old man.'

I smirked. 'Took his daughter to know how to crack him.'

Todd chuckled, his gaze sweeping the room. 'You'll be missed here. Mission Beach is lucky to have you.'

'I'll try to stay focused. Besides, I've got a feeling we'll be working together again soon.'

His smile widened slightly, and he raised his cup. 'Here's to that.'

As the afternoon tea wound down, I found myself sitting with Leanne and her children. Jonas and Mandy were finishing their snacks, laughing at something Jean said, while Leanne leaned towards me.

'Thank you, Bec,' she said softly, her voice steady but thick with emotion. 'For everything.'

I shook my head. 'You don't have to thank me, Leanne. You saved yourself out there. I'm just glad we found you in time.'

Leanne smiled, her hand brushing Jonas's head as he leaned against her. 'I wouldn't be here without you. And I'll never forget it.'

The sound of Mandy's laughter broke through the conversations, her giggle infectious as she leaned into her mother. Leanne glanced my way and mouthed, 'Thank you' again. I gave her a slight nod, my chest tight with emotion.

As Todd and I stepped outside into the warm evening air, the sound of children's laughter still faintly audible behind us, I glanced over at him. He looked at me, his expression soft but thoughtful, and smiled.

I smiled back, the bittersweet moment settling into a quiet sense of closure. For the first time in a long time, I felt ready for what came next. And with Todd stationed in the north, I knew this wasn't really goodbye. It was just the beginning of something new.

THE END

Did you enjoy Bec Whitfield's first mystery?

Book 2 will be out in 2025.

Stay posted for the release of Shadows on the Shore by subscribing to Annie's newsletter here: http://annieseaton.net

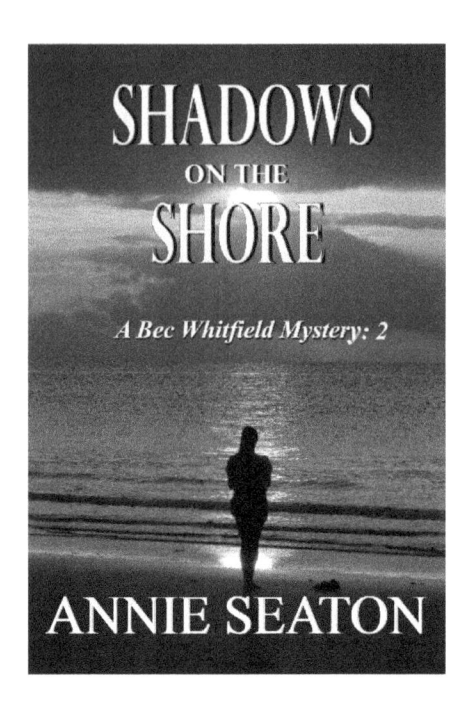

Shadows on the Shore

June 2025

When four backpackers vanish on Dunk Island, Detective Bec Whitfield is thrust into a chilling search mission. The island's natural beauty masks a dark reality, and as the days pass, the hunt grows desperate. Two bodies are discovered, but the others remain missing, and suspicions of foul play rise.

As Bec digs deeper, she uncovers a disturbing connection—each of the missing women had a relationship with a well-known resident of the small town. With the community in turmoil, the man becomes the target of relentless social media persecution;

his reputation is dragged through the mud as rumours swirl about his involvement in the disappearances.

The investigation grows increasingly complicated as Bec uncovers conflicting stories, personal motives, and dangerous secrets that threaten to tear apart the tight-knit coastal community. As the pressure mounts, Bec must navigate public outcry, a volatile investigation, and her own doubts to uncover the truth before the killer strikes again, leaving little time to focus on her growing relationship with Detective Davenport.

In Shadows on the Shore, a seemingly peaceful island paradise becomes the setting for a deadly game of secrets, vengeance, and the fragile line between truth and rumour.

Will Bec uncover the real killer before the community's relentless pursuit of justice leads to more bloodshed?

Acknowledgements

Bowen River is a small, remote locality in the far north of Queensland, situated on the banks of its namesake river. It is part of the broader Bowen Shire, known for its picturesque landscapes, agricultural history, and proximity to the Whitsunday Coast. A few years ago, Ian and I visited the Bowen River pub for lunch one day after I had spoken at Collinsville Library.

The area is rugged and scenic, with hilly terrain, dry plains, and the Bowen River cutting through it, providing a crucial water source for the region. The river is historically significant, playing a role in the development of local farming and the transport of goods in the past century as the area was settled.

These days, the landscape is dominated by solar farms, with expansive arrays of panels stretching across hectares, capturing the abundant sunlight. The pub is all that remains of Bowen River now.

Bowen River is the first book of the *Bec Whitfield Mystery series*, and I'm looking forward to researching the rest of the series in the north.

As always, I've been supported by many people in the writing of this book, and I would like to acknowledge them here.

To the many friends, I have made in the writing world over the past fourteen years who constantly support me on my journey. I often say I have found my "tribe", and I value the daily contact with like-minded people all over the world. Again, a special mention and thank you goes to my dear friend, critique partner and editor, Susanne Bellamy, and to my wonderful proofreaders: Roby Aiken, Kristen Woolgar and author Rhonda Forrest.

To my loyal readers, who contact me by mail and on social media to tell me they enjoy my stories.

If I had known when I began writing that I would gain such a loyal reader base, I wouldn't have believed it! Without readers, there would be no need for stories!

It would be impossible to write without support in your personal life:

To Ian, the love of my life and my partner in research, as we travel this magnificent country seeking stories each winter. I could not do this without you. My driver, my chef, my bringer of wine, my fisherman, and my husband of almost fifty years.

To our children and their partners and our grandchildren: thank you for your love and support.

Again, my love and appreciation go to my wonderful aunt, Maureen Smith, who not only supports me but supports so many Australian writers through years of reading, loving and sharing their stories. Sadly, Aunty Maureen can no longer read due to failing eyesight.

And to you, the reader: thank you for choosing this book. I hope when you read that you love it and talk about it, and that maybe you will want to visit this wonderful part of Australia. I would love to hear from you.

Drop me a line at annie@annieseaton.net

Reviews on Goodreads and eBook sites are always welcome and much appreciated!

eBook links:

https://www.annieseaton.net/books.html

Print Store:

All books are available in print at Annie's store:

https://annieseatonstore.ecwid.com/

Awards

2023: Winner of the long contemporary RUBY award for *Larapinta*

2023: finalist in the Australian Romance Readers Awards for *Kakadu Dawn,* the sixth and final book in the Porter Sisters series,

2018 and 2020: finalist for the NZ KORU Award

2017: Winner Best Established Author of the Year 2017 AUSROM

2017: Winner: Author of the Year 2014 AUSROM Best Established Author, Ausrom Readers' Choice

2016, 2017, 2018, 2019: Longlisted for the Sisters in Crime Davitt Awards

2016: Finalist in Book of the Year, Long Romance, RWA Ruby Awards for *Kakadu Sunset*

2015: Winner: Best Established Author of the Year AUSROM

www.ingramcontent.com/pod-product-compliance
Ingram Content Group UK Ltd.
Pitfield, Milton Keynes, MK11 3LW, UK
UKHW042100131224
452457UK00005B/395

9 781923 048607